How fitting that the Marquess of Templeston should die in the arms of his mistress. And how like his responsible son to make sure the terms of the will are carried out—no matter how outrageous. But he never imagines that one woman is living in a cottage on the grounds of his family's country estate. Even more shocking is her identity . . .

Kathryn Stafford abandoned Andrew at the altar and disappeared five years before. That she should emerge now, as his own father's lover—and with a bastard son—is a crushing blow to his pride . . . and to the longing that her betrayal couldn't quite destroy. But Kathryn has secrets Andrew doesn't know: secrets of her vanishing, of her devotion to the marquess, and of a scandalous past that could be her ultimate downfall—or prove her ultimate devotion to the only man she has ever really loved . . .

Turn the page for acclaim for Rebecca Hagan Lee . . .

A Hint of Heather

"Rebecca Hagan Lee captures the allure of Scotland through the eyes of her memorable characters. Her gift for describing a time and place enables her to enchant readers."
—*Romantic Times*

"*A Hint of Heather* gets stronger and more exciting as the pages turn. The sensuality . . . is steamy, the wit and humor bring smiles, the romance has you sighing, and the ending has you cheering." —*Under the Covers*

"A seductive Scottish historical . . . *A Hint of Heather* is going to be a big hit." —*The Romance Reader*

"For those who love Scottish romances . . . *A Hint of Heather* is likely to please. [It] features the sort of well-defined characters that enrich the world of the romance novel. A real treat." —*All About Romance*

"An entertaining Scottish romance . . . filled with action and intrigue." —*Painted Rock Reviews*

Gossamer

Once a
Mistress

Rebecca Hagan Lee

JOVE BOOKS, NEW YORK

This is a work of fiction. Names, characters, places, and incidents either
are the product of the author's imagination or are used fictitiously, and
any resemblance to actual persons, living or dead, business
establishments, events, or locales is entirely coincidental.

ONCE A MISTRESS

A Jove Book / published by arrangement with
the author

PRINTING HISTORY
Jove edition / September 2001

Visit our website at
www.penguinputnam.com

ISBN: 0-515-13168-7

A JOVE BOOK®
Jove Books are published by The Berkley Publishing Group,
a division of Penguin Putnam Inc.,
375 Hudson Street, New York, New York 10014.
JOVE and the "J" design
are trademarks belonging to Penguin Putnam Inc.

PRINTED IN THE UNITED STATES OF AMERICA

10 9 8 7 6 5 4 3 2 1

Books always belong to people. They bear the marks of the people who own them as well as the people who create and inspire them. This book bears the mark of my father, David Hagan.

Thank you, Daddy, for the generations of foxes and hounds. For the doves and the quail. For the pointers, setters, and spaniels and the life lessons learned in the woods.

From the little girl who followed you everywhere and spent countless hours in the front seat of a pickup truck listening to the stories of a generation of Southern gentlemen who have come and gone and whose kind will never come again.

With love.

Codicil to the Last Will and Testament of
George Ramsey, fifteenth Marquess of Templeston

My fondest wish is that I shall die a very old man beloved of my family and surrounded by children and grandchildren, but because one cannot always choose the time of one's Departure from the Living, I charge my legitimate son and heir, Andrew Ramsey, twenty-eighth Earl of Ramsey, Viscount Birmingham, and Baron Selby, on this the third day of August in the Year of Our Lord 1818, with the support and responsibility for my beloved mistresses and any living children born of their bodies in the nine months immediately following my death.

As discretion is the mark of a true gentleman, I shall not give name to the extraordinary ladies who have provided me with abiding care and comfort since the death of my beloved wife, but shall charge my legitimate son and heir with the duty of awarding to any lady who should present to him, his legitimate heir, or his representative a gold and diamond locket engraved with my seal, containing my likeness, stamped by my jeweler, and matching in every way the locket enclosed with this document, an annual sum not to exceed twenty thousand pounds to ensure the bed and board of the lady and any living children born of her body in the nine months immediately following my Departure from the Living.

The ladies who present such a locket have received it as

a promise from me that they shall not suffer ill for having offered me abiding care and comfort. Any offspring who presents such a locket shall have done so at their mother's bequest and shall be recognized as a child of the fifteenth Marquess of Templeston and shall be entitled to his or her mother's portion of my estate for themselves and their legitimate heirs in perpetuity according to my wishes as set forth in this, my last will and testament.

George Ramsey,

Fifteenth Marquess of Templeston

Prologue

Though the night was made for loving,
And the day returns too soon,
Yet we'll go no more a roving
By the light of the moon.

—GEORGE GORDON,
6TH LORD BYRON, 1788–1824

IRISH SEA
April 1819

"*George!*"

The fifteenth marquess of Templeston looked up and caught sight of the young woman clinging to the polished brass rail of his yacht, the *Lovely Lady*, as she struggled to make her way across the rolling and pitching deck. The storm seemed to have come out of nowhere.

One minute the sky was clear and blue and the next minute it was black and roiling. The clouds unleashed a fury of thunder and lightning and wind and rain, and a waterspout appeared off the port bow. The waves had risen and the yacht had been battered against them and dashed about like a leaf caught in a whirlwind.

He considered himself an expert sailor, but he was very much afraid that it would take more than one expert sailor to keep the *Lovely Lady* from crashing against the treacherous rocks lining this part of the Irish coast.

"Go back!" he shouted. "Go below where you'll be safe!"

"What about you?"

He couldn't hear her words, but he read her lips and knew what she was asking. "Go below. I'll be right behind you."

She shook her head as she let go of the railing and launched herself toward him. "Not without you."

He caught her, hugging her close against his chest, feeling her shiver as she came in contact with him. He was drenched; his clothing, soaked to the skin and freezing. He'd spent the last three-quarters of an hour in the icy wind and rain battling to lash the wheel into place long enough to go below and check on his young mistress. But the ever impetuous Mary Claire had tired of waiting and come looking for him. Now she was as cold and wet as he was and in greater danger of being swept overboard.

George kept a firm grip on her as he worked to untie the knot in the rope that held the wheel secure so he could lash both of them to it. The ship rolled and Mary Claire fell to her knees. He pulled her up.

"Tell me we're going to be all right," she begged, clinging to his coat and the ends of his cravat.

George looked up and saw the massive wave. He knew it would crest over them—knew that unless he succeeded in lashing them to the wheel in the next few seconds, they'd be swept away. He stared into Mary Claire's unwavering brown eyes. "I can't," he said honestly. "Because I don't know." He held her gaze. "I've never lied to you before and I'm not going to start now."

The wave was upon them. George gave up on the rope and wrapped both arms around Mary Claire. "I love you, my dear," he whispered as the wave swept them over the rail and into the raging sea.

It was true. He loved the beautiful young woman he held in his arms with all his heart. In truth, George Ramsey, fifteenth marquess of Templeston, loved every one of his mistresses with all his heart.

Chapter 1

*Nothing happens to any man that he is
not formed by nature to bear.*

—Marcus Aurelius, A.D. 120–180

LONDON
A fortnight later

"Are they quite certain it's my father?" Andrew Ramsey asked as he stood at the window
in the study of his Mayfair town house and stared out
at the darkened sky, watching as the spring downpour
flooded the streets.

"Local fishermen found the *Lovely Lady* abandoned
and drifting off the coast of Ireland. And when the bodies of a man and a young lady matching your father's
and his companion's description washed ashore several
miles down the coast, the magistrate went down to in-
vestigate. He knew George personally and he identified
his body." Drew's companion shook his head. "The
weather is usually so mild. I'm sure no one thought that
it would rain for so many days here or that there would
be a storm of that magnitude at sea."

"The magistrate could be mistaken." Drew turned to

face his father's longtime friend and solicitor, Martin Bell, and realized Martin was already wearing a black mourning band on his sleeve.

"I'm sorry, Drew, but there was no mistake. The man was wearing these." Martin reached into his jacket, withdrew a package, and handed it to Drew.

Drew unwrapped the brown oilskin paper to reveal a gold watch and fob on a chain and a signet ring. The air rushed out of his lungs and he sat down on the edge of his desk as his knees wobbled beneath him. "Christ, it's true."

Drew lifted the watch and opened the lid. He waited for the familiar sound of the minuet that played when the lid was opened and the quiet, efficient ticking, but the watch was silent. Its hands were permanently stopped at forty-three minutes past three. Drew stared at the inside of the cover and the exquisite miniature of his mother painted there before he carefully closed the lid and turned the watch over. The inscription on the back leaped out at him: *To my darling George, on the tenth anniversary of our wedding. With love from your adoring wife, Iris.* Drew swallowed hard, then placed the watch on the desk and regarded the ring engraved with the crest of the marquess of Templeston.

"What was he doing yachting off the coast of Ireland? He should have been here for the Season." Drew closed his fingers around the ring and clenched it tightly in his fist.

"He said the London Season bored him," Martin replied.

"Nevertheless he should have known better than to go sailing alone. That boat was too big for him to handle on his own."

Martin rubbed at the wrinkle lines in his forehead, took a deep breath, then slowly expelled it. "George was an excellent sailor and at any rate, he wasn't like other men. He was special. He lived each day to the fullest."

"I knew my father as well as anybody, Martin. And to George Ramsey, living each day to the fullest meant avoiding obligations and postponing any plans for the future."

"He didn't schedule every moment of his life," Martin admitted. "George was carefree. Spontaneous."

"Unlike me." Drew shot Martin a knowing glance.

"Unlike you," Martin agreed. "But that doesn't mean your father shirked his responsibilities. He was a very wealthy man and he understood his duty. He left you a very large estate." Bell studiously concentrated on wiping the lenses of his gold-rimmed spectacles with a snowy white handkerchief.

"Damn it, Martin, I don't care about the size of his estate or anything on it," Drew said. "I would rather have him alive."

"That goes without saying," Martin said softly. "But part of my responsibility as your father's solicitor is to inform you of the size of your inheritance along with the other details of his will." He stepped forward and took a sheaf of folded papers and a black armband out of his coat pocket and offered them to Drew.

Drew accepted the black armband but motioned for Martin to put the papers away. He'd known his father was going sailing, but Drew didn't know there had been an accident until the Irish authorities sent word that two bodies, identified as those of the marquess of Templeston and his lady friend, had washed ashore. Drew had learned of the tragedy yesterday afternoon and he still found it hard to believe that his father would never return.

He appreciated Martin's loyalty and dedication to his duty, but Drew wasn't ready for the finality of the reading of his father's last will and testament. "Don't bother," he said as he pinned the mourning band around the sleeve of his jacket. "I know, almost to the ha'penny, how much my father was worth."

Martin looked surprised and a little alarmed, as if he wondered whether Drew had suddenly become excessively greedy.

Drew hastened to allay Martin's unease. "I've been handling his investments for him for years. The older he got, the less he wanted to concern himself with mundane financial dealings. He was happy to let me handle things."

"He enjoyed all life had to offer."

"Especially opera singers thirty years his junior," Drew replied with an edge of bitterness. "Mary Claire." He leveled his gaze at Martin. "Her name was Mary Claire. Father mentioned that he planned to take her sailing on his new yacht. We were having dinner at the club several weeks ago and he told me he had to be backstage at the opera in time to present Mary Claire with her bouquet of flowers."

Martin nodded. "He didn't live a celibate life before he met your mother. Did you expect him to live one after she died?"

"Yes. No." Drew opened his fist and slipped the signet ring on the ring finger of his right hand. It looked and felt foreign there. He shoved his hands into the pockets of his jacket and paced the confines of his office. "No, I didn't expect him to be celibate. But I expected him to show better judgment. He was King's Bench."

"George Ramsey was a man first and a judge second," Martin defended his old friend.

"Yes, well, in this instance, he should have been a judge first." Drew swallowed the lump in his throat. "If he had shown a measure of the judgment in his private life that he was famous for in his public life, then maybe he'd still be alive."

"And maybe not," Martin pointed out. "There are no guarantees in life. If he hadn't gone sailing, George might have lived to a ripe old age, but we don't know. Perhaps this tragedy was meant to be."

"Why?" Drew demanded.

"I don't know why. Nobody knows why. It's God's will."

"It wasn't just God's will," Drew said. "It was Templeston's will. He shouldn't have taken a yacht that size out alone—especially in rough seas. He had a crew. Why didn't he use them? Because he was the marquess of Templeston. Because he wanted a private outing with his mistress. Because he thought he could defy nature and go against the odds."

"The locals said the weather was perfect for sailing when George left the shore."

Drew ignored Martin's defense of his father. "He was always seeking excitement and adventure, always leaving chaos in his wake."

Martin studied the younger man. "You sound angry."

Drew paused. "Not at him," he said finally. "Only at the senselessness of his death." He wasn't angry with his father for drowning. The marquess hadn't wanted to die any more than Drew had wanted him to. Drew didn't blame him for dying.

But he was deeply disappointed by his father's lack of forethought. Drew was disappointed because the marquess had shown a typical disregard for his safety and that of the young opera singer. And beyond leaving his estate and all his personal responsibilities for his only son and his oldest and dearest friend to sort out, George Ramsey, fifteenth marquess of Templeston, hadn't planned for the future.

And Drew could only suppose the young opera singer had left her financial affairs in disarray as well. He raked his fingers through his hair and turned to face Martin, who was carefully hooking the legs of his spectacles over his ears. "What about the young woman? What do we know about her other than her name and occupation?"

"Nothing," Martin told him. "The Irish authorities say no one has come forward to claim the body. I have Bow Street interviewing the ladies from the opera, but they've yet to come up with any information that might help us locate relatives."

Drew leveled a stern look at the older man. "Make funeral arrangements for her. She can be buried along with my father."

"Here in London?"

Drew shook his head. "No, at Swanslea."

"You're the new marquess and it's your decision to make, but burying a gentleman's lady friend on the family estate is a bit unorthodox. Are you quite certain you want to do it?" Martin was surprised by Drew's unexpectedly generous offer.

"Swanslea is our country seat. If we keep the funeral small and quiet and restrict the guests to family and close friends, I see no reason for anyone to object as long as she's buried along *with,* not *alongside,* the marquess—unless you've found a marriage certificate for the two of them among my father's papers." Drew paused, noting with irony that where the late marquess was concerned, hope sprang eternal in his heart. He hoped his father had bowed before the rules of convention one last time and secretly married the opera singer.

Martin shook his head. "No marriage certificate. But . . ."

Drew expelled the breath he hadn't realized he was

holding. "Well, Martin, that's that. We'll go ahead with it."

"Drew . . ."

"I think we should arrange a place for her nearby with a simple marker. Her name and the birth and death dates should be appropriate. Provided we can ascertain the date of her birth." Drew was willing to go against tradition and bury his father's mistress in the family plot, but he wouldn't have the young woman buried beside the marquess unless she had a legal right to be there.

He removed his timepiece from his waistcoat pocket, opened it, and glanced down at the face. Unlike his father's, Drew's watch was plain. There was no miniature, no inscription, and no minuet, only the relentless ticking of the hands urging him to go forward, to move on with the business of life. "We can go over the terms of my father's will when I return from Ireland." He smiled at Martin. "But I don't have time to do it now, Marty. I have to announce my father's death to the House of Lords and take my place as the new marquess of Templeston in less than an hour, and I need a moment to think about what I'm going to say to my father's friends and colleagues. How about it, old friend? Why don't we continue this sad family business some other time?"

"I'd like to, Drew, but before you make arrangements to hold the funeral at Swanslea Park there's something you should know. Something important." Martin reached out and touched his young friend on the sleeve.

"Well?" Drew frowned. "What is it?"

"There is a codicil to your father's will. He named several. There were more than one."

"More than one what?"

"Ladybirds." Martin cleared his throat. He couldn't bear to use the term *mistress*.

"On the yacht?" Drew asked, his mind racing frantically, wondering how many more mistresses he might have to have buried in the family cemetery.

"Oh, no," Martin reassured him. "On land."

Drew breathed a sigh of relief. "How many?"

"He mentioned five. In addition to the young opera singer, there's a milliner in Brighton. An actress in Paris. A seamstress in Edinburgh. And a young woman in Northamptonshire."

Drew frowned at his father's oldest friend, a nagging suspicion forming in his brain. "Where in Northamptonshire?"

"In the cottage on Swanslea Park."

"He kept a mistress at my mother's family home?"

"Your mother's been dead for fourteen years, Drew. And she left the estate to George. It was his to do with as he saw fit," Martin reminded the younger man.

"He saw fit to keep a mistress in residence at Swanslea Park?" Drew turned and grabbed his hat from a polished brass rack.

"There were extenuating circumstances."

"I don't care. And you may be assured that her days in the cottage are now numbered."

"Drew, you can't. George's will specifically states that as the new marquess, you are to provide for his ladybirds and become the legal guardian of any issue thereof."

"Oh, I'll provide for them. All of them. But I'll not provide the cottage at Swanslea Park."

"Drew, you don't understand—"

"Unfortunately, I'm afraid I understand all too well." He frowned. "I hate to ask you to handle her eviction, old friend, because I'd rather like having the satisfaction of doing it myself, but you'll have to go to Swanslea because I leave for Ireland immediately after making my address to the House of Lords."

Martin shook his head. "I can't go to Swanslea."

"I want her removed from Swanslea, Marty."

"I understand, Drew," Martin replied, "but it's my duty to see that your father's wishes are carried out the way he wanted and I cannot go to Swanslea and to Ireland."

"*I'm* going to Ireland, Martin. It's my duty."

"No, it's *my* duty," Martin said. "In accordance with your father's wishes, I'm to see to his return." He held up his hand when Drew would have argued. "It's the way George wanted it and I'm duty bound to carry out his wishes."

Drew jammed his hat onto his head and headed for the door. "Then, I'll be leaving for Swanslea Park directly following my address to the lords." He paused in the doorway and gave Martin a grim smile. "We can't have one mistress overseeing the burial of another. There will be no end to the gossip if I allow her to remain in residence on the estate."

"Drew, you can't evict her."

"Of course I can," Drew said. "I'm the new marquess of Templeston and Swanslea Park is my home. My father's mistress will simply have to find a new pigeon and another place to roost."

Chapter 2

Come forth in the light of things.
Let Nature be your teacher.

— WILLIAM WORDSWORTH,
1770–1850

SWANSLEA PARK
NORTHAMPTONSHIRE

"*Tallyho!*"
Wren Stafford heard the distinctive cry of the foxhunt and picked up her pace. Lengthening her strides, she hurried along the gamekeeper's path at the edge of the parkland surrounding the dowager cottage. The hunters were getting closer. The master of the hunt's horn had grown louder and the baying of the hounds more insistent. "Now you've done it, Margo," she muttered, dropping to her knees as she reached her latest subject's favorite hiding place. "They've picked up your scent."

Wren tugged her knapsack from around her neck and stretched out on the ground, reaching as far into the earthen den as she could. "You can't stay here. Your cozy little hole in the ground is too shallow. They'll send the terriers in to roust you out and then . . ." Wren

clamped her jaw shut and closed her eyes. The rest of
her statement didn't bear thinking of. "This isn't a game.
Come here, Margo. Please." The ground vibrated beneath her as she wriggled further into the den. She
touched the fox's whiskers with the tips of her fingers.
"I've got kippers in my haversack. Just for you. All you
have to do is come get them. . . ." A note of desperation
crept into her voice. The hunters were covering the parkland at an alarming rate. If Margo didn't come out soon,
there would be no way she could save her.

"Come on, Margo." Wren's voice cracked and she
swallowed hard—once, then twice more—before she
managed to continue. "Be a good girl, Margo. Come
on. . . ." She wiggled her fingers. "Smell the kippers. . . .
That's right." Wren nearly shouted with relief as the
young vixen licked her hand. Shoving herself out of the
opening of the den, Wren fumbled for the canvas flap
of her haversack, reached inside it, and found one of the
kippers, left over from breakfast, that she'd tucked into
a square of oiled cloth. She shuddered at the thought
that she was to blame for Margo's current situation.
When she was working, Wren normally stayed in the
cottage with her menagerie of subjects, but George had
asked her to stay in the main house while he was traveling and Wren had agreed. She'd left Margo sleeping
on the sofa in the sitting room when she'd finished work
last evening and had let her out when she'd returned to
the cottage this morning. The notion that the hunters
might be encroaching on Swanslea parkland hadn't occurred to Wren. Until she heard the horn.

The moment she'd heard the horn and the hounds, she
remembered Margo was outside exploring and had gone
in search of her. Wren owed the fact that she had the
kippers to sheer luck. She'd turned back to the kitchen
on her way out the door this morning and grabbed a few

leftovers as a treat for the fox, wrapping them in oilskin paper and shoving them in her canvas bag as she left the main house.

Wren unwrapped one of the kippers and sat back on her heels, fish in hand. She pulled the knapsack closer to her and opened the flap before offering the kipper to the fox. Margo sniffed the air, then darted forward to grab the treat. Wren took advantage of her opportunity. She dropped the fish onto the ground and grabbed hold of Margo as the fox devoured the treat. Keeping a firm grip on the blue leather collar hidden among the soft red fur on the scruff of Margo's neck, Wren carefully tucked the vixen inside the canvas bag and buttoned the flap. Looping the strap over her head, Wren pushed herself to her feet, held the bag close against her body, and took off at a run.

They weren't supposed to hunt here. The land surrounding Swanslea Park was prime hunting land but George had asked the master of the hunt to refrain from hunting on it while Wren was in residence. And the master of the hunt had honored the agreement for the three years she had lived in the dowager cottage. But George was dead and the news of his death had spread like wildfire across the county. Even though he'd only been dead a fortnight and she remained in residence, hunting on the fields and in the forests of Swanslea Park had resumed three days after the marquess of Templeston was reported drowned in Ireland.

And the hunting played havoc with her work. Besides endangering the life of one of her prized subjects, the hounds and the men and women riding to them upset her other subjects. Wren glanced back over her shoulder and caught sight of the lead hounds. She was in good health, but she knew she couldn't outrun them—especially not while carrying Margo. She would never make it to the safety of the cottage. But if she was lucky she could make it to the old English oak tree that grew at the end of the drive. Its branches were low enough for her to reach and would be easy to climb.

Drew rode up the drive to find the parkland surrounding Swanslea House in chaos. From the looks of it, the Trevingshire—the local hunt—was in full progress. A pack of fifty or so hounds surrounded the base of the ancient oak tree that grew at the end of the drive leading to the dowager cottage. Massive limbs spread out from the oak, dipping low enough in places to make for ideal climbing. As he watched, several of the dogs leaped onto the lowest branch, braced their paws against the trunk, looked up, and began baying. The hounds had obviously found their prey, the fox having run up the branches of the oak in a bid to escape them.

He hadn't visited his mother's family home in years, but Drew recalled his father mentioning several years ago that the course taken by the Trevingshire hunt was disrupting several projects he was working on at Swanslea and that he had asked the master of the hunt to refrain from crossing the parkland. Either the master of the hunt had refused to honor the marquess's request or he assumed the request had died with the man, because the hunt had returned to Swanslea Park.

His parents had ridden with the Trevingshire hunt and had allowed him to be blooded at the age of eleven, but Drew never cared for the sport. He enjoyed riding, but not to the hounds. He loved horses but could find no sport in tearing up the countryside in pursuit of a fox or in endangering the lives of the mounts and their riders while doing so. And he wasn't about to watch the hounds, which outnumbered the fox fifty to one, tear the animal apart on his property.

Foxes were nuisances, but Drew found the hunt crowd to be a bigger nuisance. He had little respect for the members of his class who apparently held his father in such low esteem that they disregarded his wishes and hunted on his land within days of his death. Swanslea House was a house of mourning and now that he had arrived to take up temporary residence, the Trevingshire hunt would have to move elsewhere.

Urging his horse forward, Drew hurried toward the hounds circling the huge oak tree. The field of riders had caught up to the pack and twenty or so horses galloped toward him at breakneck speed. Drew hoped to reach the big oak before the other riders and to intercept the master of the hunt, but he arrived moments too late. Several of the horsemen had gathered around the base of the tree and were looking up through the branches.

"Be still, Margo! Stop wiggling. Get down, you stupid hound! Go home! Leave us alone!" A woman's voice— low, husky-toned, and filled with exasperation—carried from the branches above. The sound of it sent a tingle of awareness through Drew's body.

"Jolly good show, eh?" one of the men commented, reaching over to prod his companion with the tip of his riding crop.

The other man laughingly agreed. "Best prize these hounds have cornered in ages."

"Call them off," the voice from above ordered. "Take your hounds and go. You're trespassing."

The first man chuckled. "We could say the same thing about you."

"I live here," she said. "And I happen to know that the marquess refused to allow hunting on Swanslea Park."

"Well," drawled the first man, "you happen to be mistaken. As you can see, we're surrounded by horses and hounds and riders all in their pinks and that means that not only is the hunt allowed on Swanslea Park, but that it's definitely in progress. Of course, that's just our opinion."

His companion chuckled. "Besides, the marquess of Templeston is dead."

"The old one is," Drew said, maneuvering his horse close enough to the others to be heard above the baying of the hounds. "The new one is not."

The men turned in unison and one of them recognized him. "I say—Ramsey!" He stared at Drew and noticed his mourning band. "I mean Templeston. I'm Harris. Remember? Dormand and I"—he nodded toward his companion—"were at Eton and Cambridge with you and your friend St. Jacque. How is St. Jacque? Is he still in Town? Haven't seen him in ages. Not since Nappy was sent into exile."

"Julian was wounded at Waterloo," Drew replied.

"I remember now," Harris said. "I heard you earned a medal of some sort saving him. Have to show it to us sometime. St. Jacque was always a lucky fellow."

"His luck ran out," Drew corrected. "He didn't recover from his wounds."

"Don't remember hearing about that," Harris told him. "Or reading it in the paper."

"Why should you remember?" Drew asked, an edge of bitter cynicism coloring his words. "The war's been over a long time. St. Jacque has had the misfortune to take an inordinate amount of time to die. The fact that he's wasted away from wounds suffered in battle isn't the sort of thing a once strong, proud, and handsome young soldier wants his friends and schoolmates from the ton to read about in the morning paper. His death isn't going to be quick or glorious. It's ugly and painful and it's already taken four years."

"Not like your father, eh?" Dormand chimed in. "Now, that's the way to go. On a yacht in a storm and with one of your wenches for companionship."

An audible gasp drifted down from the oak leaves above.

Dormand grinned, continuing to make light of the situation. "And speaking of your father's wenches, we seem to have treed one."

"What do you think, old man?" Harris pointed at the branches above them. "We were after the fox's brush, but we'll take what brush we can get, eh?"

Drew looked up. Several leafy boughs obscured his view of her face and her upper torso, but he was treated to a fine view of her rounded derriere and her long, slim legs.

She was properly dressed in colors of deep mourning but her skirt had twisted beneath her, exposing her legs to her knees and revealing the row of delicate black lace along the hem of her dyed petticoat. The sight of those shapely limbs, encased in almost sheer black silk stockings, dangling above his head was incredibly provocative. A row of tiny red flowers on trailing green vines encircled her ankles and the design of blood-red flowers and lush green foliage painted on the black silk aroused and intrigued him.

It had been a while since he'd had the opportunity to observe such magnificent limbs at such close quarters, and never dangling from the branch of an oak tree above him, but unlike the dolts beside him, Drew recognized quality when he saw it. The woman these blighters had treed was not a servant. Over the years many a serving girl had offered him the opportunity to catch sight of her undergarments and none of those undergarments had ever been made of silk, trimmed in lace, or adorned with exquisitely detailed hand-painted flowers.

He sucked in a breath. If the rest of her looks matched the perfection of her legs, his father had definitely earned his reputation as a connoisseur of beautiful women. And that was unfortunate. Because the victim of the Trevingshire hunt could be none other than his father's Northamptonshire mistress. And Drew had come to Swanslea Park for the express purpose of evicting her.

"I think it's time you called off your dogs and let the *lady*"—Drew emphasized the word ever so slightly—"down from her perch. It's also time you showed some respect for the dead." He glared at the master of the hunt, who had joined the group of riders beneath the sheltering branches of the oak tree. "The fifteenth marquess of Templeston is no longer with us, but his order against hunting on Swanslea Park still stands."

There were protests from the rest of the field as the master of the hunt gathered the pack from around the tree.

"What about the fox?" someone asked.

"What fox?" Drew demanded.

"The one up that tree." The master of the hunt returned Drew's glare. "These are some of the finest hounds in all of England. If they say there's a fox up that tree, there's a fox up that tree."

"I see a woman up a tree," Drew answered. "But I fail to see any sign of a fox."

"Actually, there are both." The voice, low and husky in tone, carried from above his head once again.

"What?" Drew looked up through the branches. "Where?"

"In my knapsack."

"You have a fox in your knapsack?" He knew he

sounded like an idiot, repeating back to her what she said, but Drew couldn't seem to help it. His father's mistress was chock-full of surprises.

"I couldn't let *them* get her." Her tone of voice was full of contempt for the field of hunters. "She's tame. I've had her since she was a kit."

Drew faced the master of the hunt. "You heard the lady. You'll have to find some other poor fox to hunt. This one is a pet."

"You can't keep a fox as a pet," one of the riders protested. "They're vermin."

"I can keep anything I want as a pet," Drew said. "Including vermin. As long as I don't allow it to stray off my land. And the fact that Swanslea Park has a tame fox on the premises is undoubtedly the reason my father refused to allow hunting on it. Now that you've been made aware of the animal's presence, I'll thank you, *ladies and gentlemen*,"—he stressed the courtesy titles— "to respect the late marquess's wishes and refrain from hunting across this particular fox's dominion. You may conduct your slaughter elsewhere. Now, I'll bid you all good day." He nodded toward the master of the hunt. "And good riddance," he added sotto voce when the field withdrew.

"You can come down now. Your fox is safe." He waited until the last of the hunters was out of earshot before he spoke.

High above his head, Wren hesitated.

Drew dismounted from his horse and leaned against the trunk of the tree, tapping his toe impatiently. "Do you require assistance? Shall I climb up after you? Are you stuck?"

She checked her knapsack one last time to make certain Margo couldn't escape, then left the security of the tree's branches and dropped to the ground beside him. "No, it's just that I'm . . ."

Drew faced her and the air left his lungs in a rush. "Kathryn."

Chapter 3

*D*rew *took an involuntary step toward her be-*
fore he could stop himself. She was every bit as
lovely as he remembered and the mere sight of her, after
all these years, was enough to twist his gut into knots
and send his senses reeling. Realizing that she still had
the power to inflict pain, Drew stepped back far enough
to gain some distance and, he hoped, some perspective.

Wren lifted her face and met his gaze. "Hello, Drew."

Hello, Drew. Whatever perspective he'd hoped to gain
by distancing himself from her was shattered. Those two
simple words, spoken in her rich, husky voice, sent a
rush of conflicting emotions coursing through him.
Once, long ago, he'd dreamed of meeting her again.
He'd carried the memory of her face and the sound of
her voice with him as he slogged through the mud and
gore in Belgium. He'd dreamed of seeing her standing
before him, dreamed of having her open her arms to him
and murmur his name in the voice that had always reminded him of warm, expensive brandy. He had lain

awake on his cot, staring up at the ceiling of his tent, memorizing each feature of her exquisite face, trying to blot out the agonized cries of the wounded and the dying with mental images of her. And now Drew realized his memories had been faulty. They hadn't begun to do Kathryn justice. Kathryn. For him she had always been Kathryn. Never Wren. Drew despised the pet name her father had given her and had never understood how a man renowned for his observation could compare his only child to a dull, common wren instead of seeing her for the beauty she was. God help him, but she was even lovelier than he remembered. He had forgotten that a man could get lost in her extraordinary gray-green eyes. Forgotten that *he* had almost gotten lost in them—once. He would have to remember not to repeat that painful mistake.

Drew tightened his fist around his horse's rein and shoved his memories aside. "You're the last person I expected to find at Swanslea. Tell me, *Miss Markinson,* to what do I owe the honor?"

"Stafford," Wren informed him.

"What?"

"My name is Stafford. I married."

"Did you indeed?" A muscle began to tick along his jaw as Drew lifted one elegant eyebrow in query. "When?"

Wren met his gaze without flinching. "Four years ago."

Drew whistled in mocking admiration. "He must be quite a fellow to have gotten you to appear in church at the appointed place and time in order to exchange your vows. Apparently you thought enough of him not to embarrass him in front of his family and friends and the whole of London society. I don't suppose you kept *him* waiting all morning."

"Our wedding wasn't like that," she began. "It wasn't like—"

"Ours?" he cut in. "Then, tell me, Kathryn, how was it?"

Wren frowned. "Small. Private." She caught herself before she uttered the word *intimate*. She searched Drew's face, looking for the tiniest bit of understanding. "We thought it best to keep it quiet and private. After all, I'd just . . ."

"Left one bridegroom standing at the altar?"

"Drew, I . . ."

"So, where's the fellow who got Kathryn Markinson to the altar? Where is this paragon of a husband?" He glanced around. "I must congratulate the man."

His sarcasm cut like a knife. She had expected him to be hurt and angry, but she hadn't expected him to be bitter. The Andrew Ramsey she had known and loved was incapable of bitterness. Wren lifted her chin a notch and ruthlessly blinked away the tears that filled her eyes. "He died. Three years ago."

"Leaving you the grieving widow."

The contemptuous look in his eyes and the cynicism of his words were almost more than Wren could bear. She would have turned tail and run from the look on his face and the sneer in his voice, but the oak tree at her back prevented a cowardly retreat. The oak tree and the fact that he had called her Kathryn.

He had called her Kathryn. Just as he had the first time she'd met him. For him, she had always been Kathryn—Kathryn the Enchantress—never Wren. Wrens were dull and plain and common, he'd said, but Kathryn was an enchantress because she'd bewitched his heart and his head until all he could think about was her.

But no enchantment lasted forever and hers had apparently worn off shortly after she'd failed to appear at their wedding. Wren understood his anger, but that didn't keep it from hurting. It didn't keep her from wanting to escape. But she was cornered, just as Margo had been, and there was nothing to do for the moment except stay and fight back. Bracing herself for another attack, Wren pressed her shoulders against the bark of the oak tree and tightened her grip on her knapsack. Margo grunted in protest and Wren immediately loosened her hold, patting the canvas, soothing the restless fox while seeking comfort and solace for herself in the reassuring rhythm of Margo's steady heartbeat. "Yes," Wren answered, "I *was* a grieving widow."

"For how long?" he demanded.

"What?" Blood pounded in her ears and Wren had to fight to keep her knees from buckling.

"How long did you grieve, Kathryn?" Drew snorted in contempt. "You couldn't have known your husband very long before you married him. You were engaged to me. And I seem to recall that you spent nearly every waking moment of the months of that engagement in my company. So forgive me if I seem a little skeptical but how long did you grieve? I want to know." He leaned closer to her. "How long, Kathryn? How many days or weeks or months did you grieve for your husband before you threw off the yoke of widowhood and climbed into my father's bed?"

The sound startled them both. Wren looked down at her hand as if she'd never seen it before. She didn't remember raising her arm or slapping him, but her palm stung and his left cheek bore the mark of her hand—a handprint that was just beginning to turn a bright shade of red. "How could you? How could you think—" She clamped a hand over her mouth to stop the flow of words.

Drew pressed his palm against his cheek. "What else

should I think?" he countered. "You're living in his house. On the estate he gained control of when he married my mother. We've always considered Swanslea to be our family home. And the fact that my father installed you in a house that belonged to my mother is very significant. It means that you held a much higher status than his other mistresses."

"It means that George was a generous man who offered a close family friend a place to live," Wren informed him.

"You ceased to be a close family friend when you left me standing at the altar."

Wren didn't know if she could penetrate his implacable expression or tap the reservoir of compassion she knew he held within him. She wasn't even sure she deserved to after slapping his face for the insult he'd given to her and to his father, but she felt compelled to try. "Perhaps I didn't become a close family friend *until* I left you standing at the altar," she replied, cryptically. "At any rate, I had no place to go and no one to turn to for help after my husband died."

"What a pity." Drew clucked his tongue in mock sympathy. "Especially since you discarded someone who would have been much more than a 'close family friend.' Someone who would have seen to your every need in life." He stared down at her. "What happened to your father? Where was he? Why didn't he offer you a home?"

Wren sighed. "He did. My father was living in the dowager cottage pursuing his nature studies. George was his benefactor."

"What happened to his post at Queen's College?"

"Papa left his post to come here because there was no place for me to live at Queen's. George offered us both a home at Swanslea. When Papa died, George asked me to stay on and finish Papa's work. In effect, he became my guardian and my benefactor."

Drew arched another eyebrow at that. "So you lived with him."

Wren sighed. "George occupied a suite of rooms in the main house when he visited, but he never really lived here. He came for the Christmas season and he left before Lent. You had to have known that he didn't stay anywhere for any length of time after your mother died," she said. "And as I said before, I live in the dowager cottage."

"That's a minor distinction when you consider my father's reputation and the fact that you're within shouting distance of the main house."

"A fat lot of good that does me!" Wren glared at him. "I'm within shouting distance of the main house and the entire Trevingshire hunt rides onto the grounds after my fox and winds up treeing me." She shrugged her shoulders. "Did you see any of the staff? Did you see anyone rush to my aid?"

"*I* rushed to your aid."

He looked so wounded, and so much like the Andrew she had known before, that Wren's heart began to race. Her breathing grew shallow and she stumbled over her words. "I—I know you did. And I thank you. I thank you for defending Margo and for saving her life. There's no way I can repay you for that, but—"

"There are several ways you can repay me," he interrupted. "And the first one is to answer my question."

"I can't answer your question," Wren told him. "I can't offer you further explanation for why George felt compelled to offer me a home here."

Drew's implacable expression reappeared and the light that had warmed his eyes moments before vanished. "Can't or won't?"

"Can't." She met his gaze, silently asking him to understand. "But it's something he wanted to do."

"I'm certain of that." He raked his gaze over her body.

Hot color flushed her face. Wren forced herself to remain impassive as she endured yet another of his insulting insinuations. "I have morning chores to attend to and Margo has reached the end of her endurance."

She leaned forward and opened the flap of her knapsack. A small red fox wearing a blue leather collar poked her head through the canvas opening, then leaped gracefully out of the bag and trotted down the white gravel path toward the dowager cottage. Wren squared her shoulders and looked up at Drew. "If you don't mind, I'll follow Margo's example and remove myself from your august presence."

Drew stepped aside to allow her to pass. "I don't mind at all," he said. "In truth, we appear to be in perfect accord." He smiled an ugly smile. "Because I came to Swanslea for the express purpose of seeing that you permanently remove yourself from the estate—before my father's funeral."

Wren stopped in her tracks, whirling around to face him so suddenly that her black muslin skirts wrapped around her legs, exposing her ankles and the delicate red flowers painted on the silk stockings encasing them. "I don't believe I heard you correctly."

"You heard me correctly." Drew smiled once again. "I'm here to evict you."

"You can't!"

"Oh, but I can."

"George would never . . ."

"My father is gone," Drew reminded her. "I'm the marquess of Templeston now and Swanslea is my home. I see no reason for it to come equipped with a mistress not of my choosing."

Tears welled in Kathryn's big gray eyes once again, although she made a big show of trying to blink them away. She was unsuccessful. Hot liquid spilled over her bottom lashes and left identical tracks across her cheeks. Drew watched as they trailed down her face and dripped off her chin. He hardened his heart against the sight. He had known that she would eventually resort to tears. What woman didn't? Tears were the female's eternal weapon against the male. Unfortunately for Kathryn, the sight of her tears no longer affected him.

"You chose me once," she said softly.

"That was a long time ago," he reminded her. "And I chose you to be my wife, not my mistress." He paused. "But you chose someone else. So I suggest, madam, that you begin packing. My father's body is on its way home from Ireland and I want you off the premises before he lies in state."

"No." She stood her ground.

"You're in no position to defy me, Kathryn."

"I can and I will defy you in this, Drew. You may be the marquess of Templeston and you may have more money and power than I do. But my obligation to your father didn't end with his death, and nothing on earth could induce me to miss George Ramsey's funeral. You don't have that right. You may be George's eldest son, but I have a responsibility to make certain that . . ." Wren stopped, taken aback by the look of stunned disbelief on Drew's face. He seemed unable to comprehend the fact that she would and could defy him. She took a deep breath, then looked him in the eye and drove the point home. "You have no authority over me."

She didn't give him the opportunity to reply, but simply turned to follow Margo down to the dowager cottage.

Chapter 4

'Tis a stinger.
—THOMAS MIDDLETON,
1580–1627

Wren opened the cottage door and breathed a heartfelt sigh of relief. Margo preceded her over the threshold, barking a greeting to the other inhabitants of the cottage as she entered. The welcoming chirps and squeaks, the sounds of tiny feet scurrying across the floors of their houses, and the familiar odors of paints and charcoal gave Wren a feeling of calm after the chaos brought about by the unexpected appearance of the Trevingshire hunt and of the new marquess of Templeston.

But Wren's sense of peace and calm was cut short when Drew flung open the cottage door and stepped inside. "We aren't finished. What did you mean about—what in the name of bloody hell is all this?"

The sparsely furnished room, with its cream-colored walls and morning sunlight pouring through the tall, uncovered windows, caught Drew off guard. When he'd last been inside the dowager cottage—some seven or eight years ago—his paternal grandmother had lived

there. The salon windows had been covered with burgundy velvet drapes and the walls covered with huge
needlepoint tapestries and priceless oil paintings in gilt
frames. The place had been stiflingly dark and stuffy,
the rooms packed with massive mahogany furniture
from the Tudor period, most of which had made up his
grandmother's dowry. Drew had been fond of his grandmother but he'd hated visiting her in the dowager cottage, which smelled of dust and mold and decay. He had
spent most of his time coaxing her outside and into the
garden.

It looked as if Kathryn had brought the garden inside.
The cottage radiated sunshine and life. The only characteristic it shared with the room he remembered was
the clutter. But this time the room was cluttered with
easels and canvases, with jars of brushes soaking in
cleaner, with pots of ink and palettes of paints and boxes
of charcoal. And nature. His grandmother's salon had
smelled of old age and death, while the salon's current
incarnation resonated with the smell of life—of ferns
and greenery growing in huge pots of moist earth and
of the assortment of small animals that had obviously
found a home here. A small owl snoozed on a wooden
perch, a red squirrel chattered in what looked to be a
straw bonnet on the top shelf of a bookcase that ran the
length of the wall—a bookcase Drew hadn't known existed because his grandmother had kept it hidden behind
a hideous tapestry rendition of the plagues visited upon
the Egyptians. A tiny hedgehog was curled atop a cushion near a jar of paintbrushes on a wooden table and the
fox called Margo had retreated to a rug beneath a Queen
Anne table. The only disconcerting notes in the whole
room were the frames of mounted butterflies, moths, and
small birds and the stuffed otter that was perched atop
a log near the fireplace.

"My home," Kathryn answered. "And my studio. These are my subjects." She spoke like a queen and looked like one, too, as she waved an arm to encompass the animals. "I'm completing the work my father started: *Flora and Fauna Native to Britain*."

Drew walked over to the nearest easel and stared at a watercolor study of the owl. The painting was clearly a work of art depicting features so exacting and detailed that Drew was compelled to touch it to make certain it was paper and not the living, breathing model asleep on his perch. "Your father's?"

Wren shook her head.

He stared at her in wonder. He knew her father's work. Dozens of Sir Wesley Markinson's drawings and paintings adorned the walls of the marquess's London town house. Kathryn's father had been a most respected naturalist and a fine artist, but Drew hadn't realized Kathryn shared his incredible gift. "I never knew you had such talent."

"Neither did I," she told him. "Until Papa's health began to fail." She recognized the look of skepticism on Drew's face and shrugged. "Oh, I knew I had a flair for watercolors. But many girls do. Watercolors are part of a gentlewoman's education—like needlework, the piano, and flower arranging. It's something we're taught from an early age. It doesn't make one an artist."

Drew nodded toward the easel. "That does."

Wren smiled. "Desperation is a great teacher."

"How so?"

"My father fell ill. When I came to live with him, his hand had already begun to shake so much he couldn't control his paintbrush or the pen he used for his ink drawings, and his eyesight was failing. But he had accepted a commission from the British Museum for watercolor depictions of wildlife in their natural habitats for the museum exhibits. And he had sworn to complete his life's work and he wouldn't hear of abandoning it. So he did everything twice. All of the color plates and many of the anatomical drawings he'd made for the book had to be re-created on canvas for the museum. Papa called it his personal Noah's Ark. I became his hand and his eyes and he taught me everything he knew about the study of nature and the painting of it."

"Including how to do that?" Drew pointed toward the otter mounted on the log and the butterflies and birds pinned and glued to wooden display panels in glass cases. "Was that part of your training?"

Wren gave a delicate shudder. "No. The live animals are ones your father's gamekeeper, Mr. Isley, brought to me as orphans." She paused. "I used the mounted specimens of lepidoptera and the *Fringilla coelebs,* of course, but I didn't dispatch them. I'm afraid they're part of the collection I inherited from Bertrand."

"Bertrand?" The name was too familiar. "Stafford?"

Wren nodded. "Yes, Bertrand Stafford. My husband."

"Your *husband*?" Drew was incredulous. "You married Bertrand Stafford? God's nightshirt, Kathryn, Bertrand Stafford must have been a hundred years old!"

"He was sixty-seven." Wren felt compelled to defend the man she'd married.

"I would have sworn he was over ninety."

"He wasn't."

"He looked it." Drew was reeling from the knowledge that Kathryn Markinson had left him at the altar in order to marry one of her father's colleagues—and not just any colleague, but a thin, pasty-faced, rheumy-eyed, wrinkled, stoop-shouldered man old enough to be her grandfather. And one who just happened to be the most famous professor of animal and insect anatomy in England. "What in God's name possessed you to throw me over for Bertrand Stafford?"

"I didn't throw you over." She blinked back a fresh surge of hot tears.

"Oh?" Drew lifted his eyebrow in sarcastic query. "What would you call it? I was waiting at the altar of St. Paul's at ten o'clock in the morning on the day of our wedding. Where were you? Pinning butterflies to a board with Bertrand? Studying otter anatomy? Because you couldn't have been interested in studying male anatomy. Not with Bertrand Stafford. Not when you could have studied it with me. So what were you doing while I was waiting at the altar, Kathryn? What was important enough to make our wedding day slip your mind?"

"Leave my mama alone!"

Chapter 5

Every man hath a good angel and a bad angel
attending on him in particular, all his life long.

—ROBERT BURTON, 1577–1640

$\mathscr{D}$*rew hadn't realized he was shouting until* the high-pitched and irate little voice demanded that he stop. He turned toward the door in time to watch a towheaded little hellion race across the studio and launch himself at his legs.

"Mama?" Drew looked from Kathryn to the boy and felt a daggerlike pang in the region of his heart. "You're a mother? You've had a child?"

Wren recoiled from the accusatory expression in his eyes.

"Don't you yell at my mama!"

"What the devil? Ouch! He bit me!" Drew shifted his weight from one leg to the other and roared his outrage at Kathryn. "Don't just stand there! If you're his mother, exercise some control over him!"

"That's enough, Kit. Let go." Wren reached down and gently pried the little boy from around Drew's legs. She lifted the child into her arms, anchored him on her hip, and looked him squarely in the eye. "What did I tell you about biting?"

"That only bad little boys do it."

"And are you a bad little boy?"

Kit shook his head. "No."

"Then, no more biting." Wren pinned him with her look. "Do you understand?"

"Yes, ma'am." He punctuated his reply with a solemn nod.

"Show me what a good brave boy you are and tell Drew you're sorry for biting him."

"No."

"Kit . . ." She spoke his name in a firm motherly tone that left no doubt about her displeasure.

"I'm not sorry." Kit reached up and touched Wren's damp cheeks before pointing a finger at Drew. "He was bad. He hurt my mama."

"No, sweetheart," Wren said softly. "He's not a bad man and he didn't hurt me. He made me sad. That's all."

"Master Kit!" A rather plump young woman, who looked to be a few years older than Kathryn, leaned against the doorframe huffing and puffing as she struggled to catch her breath. She looked up and saw Wren and began apologizing. "Oh, madam, I'm so sorry. The young master and I were traversing the garden when we heard the shouting." She pressed a hand against the bodice of her plain brown dress. "I tried to catch him, but he slipped through the hedge and came running to your rescue. I apologize for allowing him to escape my supervision, but I was unable to squeeze through the hedge. I had to go the long way around. . . ."

"It's all right, Ally." Wren turned to the governess. "I've got him and no harm's been done."

"It's all right? No harm's been done?" Drew remarked. "What about the teeth marks on my leg? That little scamp bit me."

"Miss Allerton, may I make Lord Andrew Ramsey, sixteenth marquess of Templeston, known to you? Lord Templeston, meet Miss Harriet Allerton, younger daughter of Viscount Rushfield, and Kit's esteemed governess." Wren successfully diverted Drew's attention away from Kit by making the necessary introductions.

Politeness demanded that Drew acknowledge them. "Miss Allerton." He took her hand in his, smiled slowly, and bowed. "A pleasure to meet you."

"Likewise, sir." Miss Allerton was careful to keep her face impassive and her voice devoid of emotion in a manner fitting to her current station in life.

"I apologize for being the cause of your young charge's escape." Drew spoke to Miss Allerton, but his apology was meant for Kathryn. "I didn't realize I was shouting."

Wren met his steady gaze. "Apology accepted."

She turned to the governess and dismissed her. "Thank you, Ally. I'll return Kit to the nursery in time for his luncheon." She waited until Miss Allerton left the room before turning her attention back to Kit. "It's your turn," she told him. "Apologize to your brother for biting him."

"Brother?" They reacted in unison. Drew sucked in a sharp breath as Kit looked up at him and repeated the unfamiliar word, trying it on for size.

"That's right." Wren focused her attention on Drew. "Lord Andrew Ramsey, sixteenth marquess of Templeston, meet your brother, Master Christopher George Ramsey." She ruffled Kit's baby-soft curls. "Affectionately known to one and all as Kit."

Drew would have liked nothing more than to dispute

Kathryn's claim and deny the relationship, but there was no denying the obvious fact that he and young Kit shared a blood bond. Looking at the little boy was like looking in a mirror and seeing himself at that age. Kit was definitely a Ramsey and that meant that George had to be the boy's father. He was the only man in the world who could be—except Drew himself.

And Drew knew without a doubt that he hadn't fathered Kathryn Markinson's son. Unless . . . The momentary thought gave him pause. He shook his head. He'd known a few women intimately since his return from Europe and was fairly certain that none of them had made him a father without his knowledge. The courtesans among his acquaintance tended to be quite avaricious and Drew didn't think that any of them would have missed the opportunity to present him with a bastard bill. Or to present his father with his bastard and demand payment in return.

As far as Drew was concerned, the only issue in question regarding Kit's parentage was the identity of his mother. Drew stared at Kathryn, daring her to confirm his suspicions. "Then he's . . ."

She met his challenge by lifting her chin and looking him squarely in the eye. "Your heir."

"God's nightshirt, Kathryn! This isn't the time for word games. You know very well what I'm asking. I'm not a fool. Nor am I blind. I can bloody well see the family resemblance. And I'm perfectly willing to accept that he's the new heir *presumptive* to the title, as well as my ward. I don't doubt that we're related." Drew leaned closer. "I do, however, harbor some doubt as to whether he's my half-brother or my son."

"He's your brother," Wren told him. "George was his father."

"How can you be certain?" Drew demanded.

"I am Kit's mother."

Drew stared at the child and felt a physical pain in the place where his heart had once been. *He should have been mine.* Kit continued to scowl at him from the safety of his mother's arms. Drew was tempted to scowl back at him, but he looked to Kathryn instead, silently begging her to take back her words, to convince him that it was a lie. Because while he'd been doing his bit to defeat Napoleon, Kathryn had married Bertrand Stafford. And in the months following the victory at Waterloo, while he kept vigil over his closest friend, desperately trying to nurse his boyhood companion back to health, Kathryn had buried her elderly husband and become the mistress at Swanslea. And sometime since the time of Drew's return to England with Julian St. Jacque, Kathryn had given birth to Christopher George Ramsey.

He continued to look at her and Wren recognized the doubt in his eyes.

"You're perfectly willing to believe I was George's mistress," Wren said. "Why don't you believe that Kit is my son?"

Because up until the time I saw Kit and heard him call you his mother, I thought I might have been mistaken about you. Because I wanted you to convince me that you weren't one of my father's mistresses. Because even though I know it's true and even though I know you gave yourself to him, I can't bear the thought of you lying naked in my father's arms. Because you should have lain naked in my arms. Because I should have been Kit's father. Drew touched the left side of his face. The mark of her hand had disappeared, but the memory of it resonated loudly. "Perhaps because you reacted so strongly to my suggestion that you were my father's mistress."

"I reacted to your deliberate cruelty and crudity,"

Wren informed him. "I reacted to your vulgar turn of phrase. I've never had any difficulty accepting the idea that George wanted another child or that he wanted me to be that child's mother." She studied Drew's face, waiting for him to erupt in anger once again, but his emotional outburst had ended as abruptly as it had begun.

This time the expression on his handsome face gave nothing away. He appeared to be calm and collected, the epitome of a jaded English lord, mightily bored by the topic of conversation. Wren wondered how long it had taken him to perfect that look, how many hours he had stood before his mirror and practiced it. She envied him that look despite the fact that her heart ached because he'd turned it on her.

"Then I don't suppose you had any difficulty taking a fifty-four-year-old man as your lover." His attack was swift and sudden and all the more painful because he uttered the harsh indictment without so much as a flicker of emotion.

"Why should I?" Wren retaliated in kind, struggling to conceal her true feelings as successfully as he concealed his. "I had no difficulty accepting a husband who was much older than that. Besides, George retained his youthful figure, extraordinary vigor, and incredible good looks. He was gentle and patient and—"

"Wealthy and titled?" Drew suggested.

And an older version of you. Wren caught herself before she blurted out the words. "Kind," she quickly amended. "I was going to say that he was gentle and patient and kind."

Drew snorted in disbelief. His father had had many attributes, but patience and gentleness hadn't been among them. "Are we talking about the same man?" he asked. "Because I never thought of my father as any of those things."

"Perhaps that's because you knew him differently," Wren said. "You knew him as your parent, as a judge, and as a peer of the realm. I knew him—"

"In the biblical sense."

Wren responded to the sneer in his voice. "Tell me, Drew, what bothers you more? The fact that your father gave me a home and a son? Or the fact that he gave me a home and a son after I jilted you?"

Drew shrugged his shoulders. "The fact that he gave you a home at Swanslea."

"I thought—" Wren stopped and shook her head. "I thought—" She looked up at him and blinked away the tears that threatened to fall. "But I was obviously wrong," she said. "You're nothing like your father."

Drew shrugged his shoulders once again. "I wouldn't say that," he replied. "I may not share his other qualities, but I am wealthy and titled."

"I'm sorry you've become so cynical, Drew."

"Then I'm sure you won't object to removing yourself from my property as soon as possible."

Wren set Kit on the ground and took him by the hand. "Not at all," she said. "If you'll be kind enough to arrange for someone to help, I can have Kit's and Miss Allerton's belongings packed and moved into the cottage by morning." She had no idea how she was going to fit Kit and Miss Allerton into the cottage—especially since a great deal of the space was taken up with her work and her menagerie, but Wren was determined not to let those details prevent her from moving Kit and Miss Allerton off Drew's property and onto her own.

"I'll arrange for someone to assist with your packing and provide transportation for *you* first thing in the morning," Drew told her. "But my ward and heir presumptive will remain at Swanslea Park with me."

Wren recoiled as if he'd struck her. His words sent a shaft of cold fear straight through to her heart. "You can't separate me from my son."

"I assure you that it's well within my power," he told her.

"The fact that you'd even entertain such an idea is despicable."

"You may think I'm despicable," Drew agreed. "But the fact that I'm the marquess of Templeston also makes me your son's legal guardian. You'd do well to keep that in mind, Kathryn."

"The fact that you're his older brother makes you my son's legal guardian," Wren corrected him. "But according to the terms of your father's will, becoming Kit's legal guardian doesn't give you the right to evict me from Swanslea or anyplace else or to remove him from my care, unless you've become tired of being the marquess and fancy being disinherited."

Drew couldn't believe his ears. "What do you know about my father's will?"

"More than you, apparently. I know George made special provisions for Kit and me. George not only told me about them, he read them to me as he recorded them and he made certain I understood them." Wren met his gaze. "There's a copy of his will in the safe in George's study. I'm sure you know the combination. The provisions in it are quite clear and quite legal. And you'd do well to keep that in mind as you read it, *And*rew." She leaned down to whisper something in Kit's ear, then led him past Drew and into the cottage's kitchen.

Chapter 6

*It is indeed a desirable thing to be well-descended,
but the glory belongs to our ancestors.*

—PLUTARCH, A.D. 46–120

Every word of what Kathryn had told him was
true. Drew carefully folded his father's last will
and testament and returned it to its kidskin envelope.
He'd often accused his father of being irresponsible,
only to find that George Ramsey, fifteenth marquess of
Templeston, had been more than responsible regarding
Kit and the woman named in the will as the boy's
mother—one Kathryn Markinson Stafford. The provisions he'd made for the care and welfare of his
illegitimate son and for his mistress showed a remarkable depth of feeling and admirable forethought.

According to the late marquess's will, the vast majority of the wealth and properties attached to the title
of marquess and the properties and holdings attached to
the lesser titles of earl of Ramsey, Viscount Birmingham, and Baron Selby, would be inherited by the sixteenth marquess and would, in time, pass duly on to the
seventeenth marquess in perpetuity.

Swanslea Park was the exception. The gardens, the

tenants' houses, and the acreage under pasture that made up the estate belonged solely to Drew but the main house was to be held in trust for the legitimate heirs or issue of Andrew Ramsey or the legitimate heirs or issue of Kathryn Markinson Stafford. The house was to be held in joint trust by Andrew Ramsey and Kathryn Markinson Stafford until the time that legitimate heirs or issue of Andrew Ramsey or Kathryn Markinson Stafford reached the age of majority. Should there be no living legitimate heirs or issue of Andrew Ramsey or Kathryn Stafford, the main house, gardens, tenants' houses, and the acreage under pasture would, upon their deaths, become the property of the Trevingshire hunt.

The dowager cottage and parkland surrounding Swanslea had been deeded to Kathryn for her sole use for as long as she lived, after which it would become a part of the estate held in trust for the legitimate heirs or issue of Andrew Ramsey or Kathryn Markinson Stafford. In addition, the marquess of Templeston would provide ten thousand pounds per annum for the maintenance of the jointly held property and the dowager cottage. The will was over two years old and although George had recognized Kit as his son and designated him as heir presumptive to the hereditary titles, he had precluded Kit from the possibility of inheriting Swanslea Park.

Martin had mentioned a codicil to the will but it wasn't included with the copy of the will in the safe in his father's study.

Drew raked his fingers through his hair and frowned. His father had provided generous annual allowances for Kit and Kathryn, as well as for his other mistresses and any children they might bear in the nine months immediately following his death. How Drew was expected to recognize his father's mistresses or offspring was beyond his ken. He could only hope that his father had supplied a list along with the codicil to his will.

The will named Drew sole legal guardian for any and all of his father's children except Kit. Drew's guardianship of Kit was to be shared with Kathryn. He could not remove Kit from Kathryn's home or care or travel with him unless she consented or accompanied them. He couldn't hire or fire any nannies, governesses, or tutors without Kathryn's consent, nor could he elect to send Kit to boarding school without her consent. And he could not arrange a betrothal or marriage for Kit unless Kathryn approved and gave him leave to do so.

Kit was Drew's heir and his legal responsibility, but he was Kathryn's son and George had gone out of his way to make certain that Drew would have no recourse where Kit was concerned, except to consult Kathryn.

The same was true for Kathryn. So long as Kit was his legal heir, Kathryn was bound by law to allow Drew access to him. She could not prevent him from spending time with the boy. She could hire and fire his nannies, governesses, or tutors without Drew's consent, but she could not pack Kit off to boarding school without Drew's approval. She had right of consent in all matters except those pertaining to the hereditary titles or finance. In those matters, Drew had the final say. If Kathryn died before Kit reached his majority, Drew would become sole guardian. If Drew died before Kit reached his majority, Kit's guardianship would be shared between Kathryn and George's trusted solicitor, Martin Bell, or Martin's designate.

Drew exhaled. An hour ago, he'd been blissfully unaware of his half-brother's existence, but Kit had suddenly become his heir and Drew was responsible for his care and well-being. And along with Kit came Kathryn. An hour ago, he would have sworn that he'd put Kathryn behind him years ago, but it seemed there was unfinished business between them and Drew was afraid there would be no escaping it. For now, Kit and Kathryn were part and parcel of the same package.

Drew pushed himself out of his father's massive leather chair and walked around the desk and across the room to the opened wall safe. Shoving the will back into the safe, Drew pushed the inner door closed and quickly spun the dial. He bit back a smile as he slid the small portrait that concealed the safe into place. The subject of the Holbein portrait was the second earl of Munnerlyn's favorite horse. Since Holbein tended to paint ladies who strongly resembled horses, Drew appreciated the irony. Apparently his maternal ancestor had appreciated it as well, because he'd been the one to offer the famous court painter a very large commission to paint the genuine article.

"Ring around a-rosy, pocketful of posies, ashes, ashes. We all fall down!"

High-pitched squeals of delight drifted up from the garden below, penetrating the quiet gloom of the study. Drew walked over to the window overlooking the garden, unlatched it with all the care of a midnight housebreaker, then leaned silently against the casement.

Kathryn and Kit lay on the grass near the maze. Kit squealed with glee and began turning somersaults across the lawn. "Watch me, Mama."

"I'm watching, my darling."

Drew smiled as Kathryn clapped her hands and praised Kit for his efforts as he rolled across a patch of lawn into the hedge forming the wall of the maze.

"Your turn, Mama," Kit ordered.

Kathryn shook her head.

"I'll show you," Kit promised before he leaned forward and put his head on the ground and rolled himself over.

She shook her head once again.

"Please?"

Kathryn glanced over her shoulder and back at the house. Drew stepped away from the window to keep from being seen, waited until she seemed satisfied that no one was watching, then quietly moved back into place.

"All right," she said. "Shall we do it together?"

Kit nodded.

Kathryn had gathered her skirts in one hand and knotted them.

She wouldn't. Drew caught another glimpse of the flowers and vines painted on her black silk stockings and his heart thudded in his chest. *She would.* He grinned as Kathryn followed Kit's lead, bending at the knees, placing her head on the ground, and rolling forward, over onto her back. Again and again. Until she lay tangled in the hedge, her skirts hiked high upon her thighs, the black garters plainly visible.

Kit clapped his hands together in delight, then pushed himself to his feet and ran to her. He tugged at Kathryn's hand, attempting to pull her out of the hedge and onto her feet, giggling as she resisted his efforts. "Please, Mama, swing me."

Kathryn pretended to think it over, but quickly gave in. She pushed her skirts back down over her legs, then stood up and grasped Kit beneath the arms. She held him close and whirled him around, swinging him into the air and around in a circle until dizziness forced her to stop.

She dropped to her knees and enfolded the little boy in her arms. "Oh, Kit," she said, "I love you so."

"I love you, too, Mama." He returned her embrace by wrapping his arms around her neck and squeezing her tightly.

Drew winced in empathy as the little boy tangled his fingers in the soft wispy tendrils of hair at the nape of Kathryn's neck and hugged her with a good deal more force and enthusiasm than was necessary. He watched Kathryn reach up and gently loosen Kit's grip enough to regain her breath.

But Kit didn't want to let go. "More," he demanded.

Kathryn shook her head. "Impossible." She smiled down at him. "For you've already made me quite breathless and dizzy."

Once again her words struck Drew with the force of a blow.

"More," he'd demanded, begging for more of her intoxicating kisses.

"Impossible," she'd answered with a shake of her head. "For you've already made me quite breathless and dizzy."

Drew squeezed his eyes closed in an effort to blot out the memory of that moonlit night in the duchess of Richmond's formal gardens. But it was an exercise in futility. He'd spent too many days and nights trying to remember every moment spent in her company to forget the most important one. He'd asked Kathryn to marry him in those gardens. He opened his eyes to find Kathryn gazing up at the open window.

Inexorably drawn by the sound of their laughter, Drew had tried to remain silent and observe without being observed, but the edge of the curtain flapping in the breeze had given him away. He stared down at her—brown eyes met gray-green—and Drew found the answer to his unspoken question in her eyes.

She remembered.

He remembered.

That sure knowledge nearly took her breath away. Wren put a hand to her hair and self-consciously tried to smooth it into place as she feasted upon the sight of Andrew Ramsey. He stood framed in the window of his father's study, the morning sun glinting off the silver strands in his dark hair. Wren stared up at the window, unable to look away. He was still the handsomest man she'd ever seen, but he had changed.

He was four years older than when she'd last seen him and those four years had left their mark. Then, his hair had been a rich coffee brown. Today it was more silver than brown.

She'd met Andrew, earl of Ramsey, during her London Season. The war had ended, the Treaty of Paris was in progress, and Napoleon was safely exiled on the island of Elba. Seven and twenty years of age at the time, Drew had just gone on half pay from his position as an officer in the War Office. Attached to Lieutenant Colonel Grant's staff, Drew had been charged with the task of deciphering French codes and recruiting men to relay those codes to Wellington. Although he'd spent the better part of four years immersed in the deadly business of war, he'd seemed unaffected by it. He had looked much younger than his years, somehow managing to retain an air of innocence and idealism and the arrogant assurance of his privileged youth.

But that was no longer the case. At one and thirty, his innocence and idealism and the arrogance of privileged youth were gone. The assurance remained, but it was assurance born of the knowledge that he was a survivor. He had faced war and deprivation and lived through it. Perhaps even lived to regret it. The years of hardship were reflected in the lines on his face. A web of fine creases framed the outer corners of his eyes and longer, deeper frown lines marked his forehead and bracketed his mouth. Waterloo had left scars. On his body and on his heart. The Drew she had loved was gone, but the jaded, angry, cynical, and bitter man who currently inhabited his body was every bit as attractive as the one she remembered and twice as intriguing.

Wren sighed. She had carried her memories of Drew Ramsey pressed like fragile blossoms in her heart for years. And while she dreamt of seeing him again, of meeting him and falling into his arms again, a tiny part of her had prayed that her dreams would never come true. A tiny part of her prayed that she had been a passing fancy for Drew and that once he got over his anger at having been left waiting at the altar, he would count himself lucky to have escaped the shackles. A part of her still hoped he'd feel that way. She didn't want to think that Drew Ramsey had wasted any precious time carrying a torch for her. Because the girl he had found so enchanting was gone.

At two and twenty, she'd been young and innocent and starry-eyed. Brought up to go from her father's keeping into the keeping of a respectable husband, she had been sheltered and inexperienced. Aunt Edwina had prepared her for her debut, teaching her the rules of society.

Wren had learned the lessons she'd needed to know in order to make her debut into society. She learned to run a household and to patronize the most fashionable dressmakers, milliners, and jewelers, and dutifully returned every morning call and invitation she received. She memorized the myriad array of titles and the names and faces that went with them. She learned how to curtsey and who to curtsey to and she'd been presented at Court.

She'd fallen in love with London the moment she arrived, but nothing London had to offer compared to her first meeting with grown-up Drew.

Because their fathers had been such close friends, Wren had known Drew all of her life. But they had only spent time in each other's company a dozen or so times during the course of their childhoods. The marquess of Templeston and Sir Wesley Markinson were friends, but their families didn't move in the same circles. As the only son of a wealthy peer, Drew had gone to Eton and on to Cambridge while she was schooled at home.

When she met him again during her London Season, she'd taken one look at him and tumbled madly, irrevocably, in love. Tall, dark, and handsome, he was the image of every fairy-tale prince she'd ever dreamed about. He'd asked her to dance and Wren had been so nervous she could barely keep from stumbling over her own feet. But he hadn't seemed to mind. He'd delighted in her conversation and by the evening's end, Drew had seemed as captivated by her as she was by him. He'd called for her the next morning and nearly every day after that. As if by magic, Wren had stepped into the fairy tale she had always dreamed of living. She became the perfect evening accessory—an enchanting innocent, who sparkled with wit and humor as she decorated Drew's sleeve, blissfully hanging on to his every word, relying upon his judgment and his greater knowledge of the world.

She hadn't realized how blissful ignorance was until long after life had begun to teach her that there would be no fairy-tale happily-ever-after ending for her. It was a lesson she'd learned quite well. In the four years since she'd last seen Drew, she'd become a wife, a mother, a widow, an orphan, and a grieving mistress in rapid succession. With the exception of Kit, her life since Drew had become one long endless and intimate acquaintance with loss.

She barely remembered the girl she'd been, but her precious memories of Drew had been achingly real and inviolate. So real and inviolate that she hadn't noticed the change in him when he'd appeared seemingly out of nowhere to rescue her from the hounds. He had looked the way she remembered—until now.

Now she recognized the signs of his suffering. Drew was also intimately acquainted with loss. He had come to Swanslea to bury his father. Kit's father. She glanced over at the little boy. Kit was too young to understand the magnitude of his loss. But Drew understood and was deeply affected by it.

Wren blinked back tears. The Andrew Ramsey she remembered had been more boy than man. But this Drew was fully-grown. She remembered him as completely virtuous—a hero without flaws—but the man before her was a hero with more than his share of wounds and flaws. The man she remembered existed only in her dreams. This man was very much alive and the idea that she might willingly discard her precious memories, after holding on to them for so long, for an older, angrier, living, breathing remnant of the man she'd loved frightened her.

She wouldn't lie to herself. Drew was a danger to her hard-won peace of mind and to Kit. She had fallen in love with him once before. Could she risk doing so again? Now that she had Kit to think about and his future to protect? Wren shook her head. Nothing was worth risking Kit. Not even his half-brother.

And protecting Kit meant staying as far away as possible from Drew.

She glanced up at the window. The curtain was still blowing on the breeze, but the window was empty. Her peace of mind was restored.

Drew was gone.

Chapter 7

The only certainty is that nothing is certain.
—PLINY THE ELDER, C. A.D. 23–79

*W*ren spent the afternoon sketching wildlife in the wooded parkland, concentrating on her work in an effort to keep from thinking about Drew. As always, work proved to be the remedy she needed. She'd barely thought of Drew at all and she had managed to complete several detailed drawings—two studies of the varieties of wood anemone found on the parkland and a spectacular preliminary sketch of a kestrel in flight. Still congratulating herself on her success, Wren returned to the dowager cottage and opened the front door.

Unfortunately the man she'd spent the afternoon working to forget was comfortably seated on the sofa in the main salon.

"We missed you at tea."

Wren propped her lapboard against the wall beside the front door and deposited her sketches on the closest worktable. "We?"

"Miss Allerton and I."

"You took tea with the governess?"

He raised an eyebrow at her. "I wouldn't have taken you for a snob. Miss Allerton may be down on her luck, but she is the daughter of a viscount."

"I'm not a snob," Wren replied. "I share the tea table with Ally regularly. I know very well that she outranks me in society. The fact that she's the daughter of a viscount in addition to being an excellent teacher was my primary reason for hiring her. I was simply taken aback by the notion of you being civil long enough to share tea with anyone—much less a gentle soul like Miss Allerton."

"I knew her late brother," he told her. "We fought together in Belgium. Miss Allerton asked me for news of Town and I was happy to oblige. It seems we have mutual acquaintances there."

"I'm sure she enjoyed your company," Wren responded politely, despite the fact that her tone of voice said otherwise.

Drew shrugged his shoulders. "There was no reason she shouldn't. Many people find my company quite entertaining. And as shocking as it may seem to you, I managed to be completely civil." He paused for effect, then added, "Of course, your conspicuous absence was most likely responsible for that slip in my behavior."

"I had work to do."

Drew shifted his weight, sliding to the end of the sofa closest to her in order to look at her work. "Those are quite good," he said.

His compliment took her by surprise. Twice he'd told her he was impressed by her paintings. Wren looked at him with softness in her eyes. "Thank you."

"But then, you always were talented. I simply didn't realize *how* talented or that your talents included *art*."

That hateful, knowing sneer was back in his voice, and she'd set herself up for the attack, allowing him to disarm her with a compliment before stabbing her and drawing blood. Wren sighed. "Get off my sofa. You're trespassing."

"Can't be." He stretched his arms high above his head and yawned. "I own the place."

"You own the land," she corrected him. "And if you had bothered to read your father's will, you'd know that he left the cottage to me."

"As a matter of fact, I did read my father's will." Drew stood up and began to walk around the room. "And you're absolutely right. He did leave the cottage to you. But he left the land to me and since the cottage sits on my land, I think it's safe to say I can't be trespassing."

"That's nonsense," Wren told him. "And you know it. You wouldn't dream of entering one of your tenants' cottages without asking permission, yet you think nothing of invading my home."

"Why not?" he asked. "You invaded mine."

"I was invited," she retorted. "You were not."

Drew walked over to her and leaned so close that his breath stirred her hair. "No," he whispered. "I wasn't invited. Not once during the three years that you've lived here did my father invite me to Swanslea Park. Why was that, I wonder?"

"You were in France," she answered.

"I returned from France three years ago. My father knew that. We often dined together and shared conversation and brandy at our club."

"George said you had obligations that kept you in London."

"When?" Drew demanded. "When did he tell you of the obligations that kept me in Town? And how dare he make you privy to the details of my life without allowing me to be privy to the details of his? I have a half-brother

I knew nothing about," he continued. "One who knows nothing about me. I can't have been the main topic of conversation at the tea table." He stared at her, noting the way her dark lashes framed her red-rimmed eyes and fanned her cheekbones each time she blinked. "But then, I don't suppose it would be good form to mention one's mistress's former love at the drawing room tea table. Especially if that former love happens to be one's eldest son."

He taunted her with deliberate cruelty, yet Wren recognized the hurt in his voice.

"It wasn't the way you imagine it, Drew."

"How was it?"

"We didn't take tea in the drawing room. When my father was alive I had tea with him here in the cottage every afternoon. When George was in residence, he'd often join us." She smiled, remembering. "After my father died, George's visits became fewer and farther apart. They dwindled to one or two a year—a few days at Christmas and occasionally on Lady's Day. After a while, I started to take my tea in the nursery with Miss Allerton and Kit." Wren closed her eyes.

"You must have been lonely."

She opened her eyes and turned her face to look at him, anticipating his attack. But if he was mocking her, his expression didn't show it. She waited a moment before answering. "I was."

"He wasn't."

Wren raised her eyebrow in silent query.

"He had another mistress."

"I heard," Wren answered flatly. "Your friend Dormand said she drowned with him."

"Yes, she did."

"I'm sorry."

"For whom?"

"For George. For his—his friend—and for her family." Kathryn looked up at him and there were tears shimmering in her eyes. "For you, for me, for Kit."

"For me?" He tried to sound outraged, but he simply sounded amazed. Amazed that she would admit to feeling sorry for him after everything he'd said and done since he'd discovered her perched in the boughs of that old oak tree.

"I know how it feels to lose a father, Drew. I know how it feels to lose a special friend. And I know how it feels to lose the person you love most of all." She stared at him, the expression on her face hauntingly familiar. He'd seen it a thousand times in his dreams.

Drew swallowed hard, then cleared his throat. "There were others."

"Not for me," she said in a whisper barely louder than a breath.

"For him."

She looked surprised.

He had the strangest urge to enfold her in his arms and protect her from the hurt he was inflicting. "The young woman on the yacht wasn't my father's only other mistress. There are several others. In England and on the Continent." He kept his gaze focused on her, studying the nuances of her expression. "You must have known about them. You read his will."

"I didn't read George's will."

"You knew what was in it. You knew about the land and the cottage."

"I knew about the cottage and the land because George *gave* my father the cottage when we came to live here. I inherited it from him."

"There's no—" Drew began.

"It's all been duly recorded," Wren interrupted him. "I have the deed to the cottage. George presented it to

Papa and Papa gave it to me. I was afraid you might challenge my right to it once you became the marquess, but George assured me I had no reason to worry. He promised he'd make certain you understood his wishes by mentioning the bequest in his will. He said he used my married name because he knew you wouldn't object to Mrs. Bertrand Stafford inheriting the cottage. Apparently, he was mistaken."

Drew made a little face at that. "No, he was right. I wouldn't have objected to Mrs. Bertrand Stafford inheriting the cottage or the acreage surrounding it. I would have recognized the name, of course, and remembered my father's patronage of Stafford's nature studies, but I wouldn't have had any reason or desire to intrude on her privacy."

"Unless she happened to be mother to your father's son," Wren said.

Her comment stung. Drew didn't bother to reply. He turned and paced the length of the room and back, stopping once to watch as the squirrel crawled out of its straw bonnet and began nibbling on an offering of seeds, dried berries, and nuts in a small silver sweets dish. "What else did he tell you?"

"He told me he'd recognized Kit as his son and made special provisions for his welfare. He told me that you would be Kit's legal guardian, but he promised me that as Kit's mother, I would have final say in his care and education until he reached the age of majority and that no one would be able to change that. He told me Martin—"

"You know Martin? You know my father's solicitor?"

"Of course," Wren answered. "He came here often when my father was alive. He handled the sale of the cottage and drew up my father's will. George assured me that Martin would take care of everything, that you would never have any reason to interfere with my life and that I would never have to see you or speak to you unless I chose to do so. He didn't mention anything about mistresses."

"Then you didn't realize that he charged me with the legal and financial responsibility for all of his mistresses and any issue from those relations." Drew smiled. "You see, Kathryn, I've not only inherited the title and Swanslea Park and Kit, but, in a manner of speaking, I've also inherited you."

Chapter 8

There is only one step from the sublime to the ridiculous.
—NAPOLEON BONAPARTE, 1769–1821

*W*ren gasped. *"You can't inherit me!"*

"I already have." Drew shook his head. "Christ, but I underestimated him! He had a brilliant legal mind." He smiled at the realization that his father had humored him for years. "Every time I accused him of paying too much attention to his amorous affairs and not enough attention to his business ones, he would smile and tell me that he didn't need to worry about business affairs because I spent more than my fair share of time taking responsibility for them."

"But why? George knew . . ."

"He knew I wouldn't shirk my duty," Drew concluded. "He knew I'd do as he asked. In fact, he counted on it. He could have sponsored your father's work and provided him with a house in any county in England and I wouldn't have noticed. He could have made a bequest to Mrs. Bertrand Stafford—even named her son as his own and arranged for Martin or any other solicitor to administer your income, handle any concerns that arose, and serve as an intermediary between us, and I would not have noticed or cared. Kit's existence doesn't threaten or undermine my position as marquess. Younger sons, legitimate or otherwise, don't inherit. But my father made certain I'd notice and care."

"How?"

"By requesting that *I* take responsibility for his mistresses and his offspring, by installing you in the one place he knew I'd object to, and by naming *you* in his will."

"But you didn't know that I married Bertrand."

"It didn't matter. Father didn't name Mrs. Bertrand Stafford in his will. He named *Kathryn Markinson Stafford* in his will."

"He what?"

"He named you knowing bloody well that I'd claim you and Kit because there was no way in Hades I could possibly mistake you for anyone else."

Wren stared in disbelief. The man she thought was her dearest friend had betrayed her. "He left me as chattel so you could assume responsibility for me."

"And for Kit," Drew reminded her. "You're a mistress, Kathryn. And even if you weren't, you're a woman with no father, brother, husband, or lover to protect or provide for you."

"I don't need anyone to provide for me," Wren retorted. "I'm providing for myself and for Kit by completing the work my father was paid handsomely to produce."

"That money won't last forever."

"It will last long enough for me to finish this work and secure a commission for the next."

"Who paid your father to produce *Flora and Fauna Native to Britain*?" Drew asked.

Wren hesitated for the merest second before she re-

plied. "The founder of the Royal Society for the Preservation of Flora and Fauna Native to Britain."

"Who is . . . ?"

"Was," she answered honestly if reluctantly. "George
Ramsey, marquess of Templeston."

Drew pinned her with his gaze. "My point exactly."

Wren looked him in the eye. "George may have sponsored this particular work, but I'm sure that once the
book is published, I'll be able to garner more commissions."

"Your father could have," Drew said. "But you
haven't the formal education or the renown your father
or your late husband had. And if you publish your father's work under his name rather than your own, who
will know you completed it? Who's going to commission you, Kathryn?"

She glared at him. He knew the answer to that as well
as she did and Wren would rather have bitten out her
tongue than say the answer aloud.

"Well?" he prodded.

"It doesn't matter," she announced. "I'll simply publish my next work myself."

"With what? Your father was a life peer. His title and
his income died with him. And if you had inherited anything of real value from your late husband, you wouldn't
have come to live with your father. You can't afford to
publish your next work."

"I'm not destitute, Drew." Wren lifted her chin a bit
higher and straightened her back. "When Aunt Edwina
died last fall, she left me a small income and a cottage
in the Lake District. It isn't much, but it's enough to get
by on. And"—she looked him in the eye—"I have talent. I'll secure commissions."

"You have tremendous talent," Drew agreed. "But talent isn't enough. You're going to need help."

"I'll manage without it."

"You don't have to manage without it," Drew said. "I'll be happy to finance the publication of your next work."

Wren eyed him shrewdly. "In return for what?"

"Your signature on a legal document relinquishing all rights to the cottage and to Kit."

Wren sat down on the nearest chair, her knees suddenly unable to support her weight. "No."

"The official notice of my father's death will appear in tomorrow's papers. Tear up the deed to the cottage and sign over your guardianship of Kit and I'll gladly finance any project you name, and if you don't want to go to your aunt's Lake District cottage, I'll set you up in a house anywhere you choose as long as it's somewhere far away from here."

Wren shot to her feet so fast she nearly bumped his chin with the top of her head. Drew retreated a step, shifting his weight to his heels to avoid the painful collision. "You can have the cottage. You can have anything you want—except Kit. I won't relinquish my rights to him. I'm his mother. I love him."

"Then I'm afraid we're stuck with one another."

"You didn't know Kit existed until a few hours ago. All you have to do is go back to London." She stared up into his brown eyes. "Go home, Drew. Go back to London and forget you ever saw us."

"I'd like nothing better. But the fact remains that my father named me as guardian to Kit and to you and I don't intend to abdicate my responsibility." Drew frowned. A trio of waxy green holly leaves from the hedgerow was tangled in the strands of her dark blond hair. He reached over to pluck it out.

Kathryn flinched.

Drew quickly pulled the leaves from her hair and let

them fall to the floor. "I can't go back to London and forget about you."

"Why not?" she demanded. "You've forgotten me for the past four years."

Wren couldn't believe she'd spoken the words aloud. But she had and there was no way to pretend he hadn't heard them or understood what they meant. And there was no way she could take them back. Wren turned her back on him, afraid for him to see the tears that brimmed in her eyes. Afraid he'd mistake them for weakness or longing or regret. Or something more.

"You think I forgot you?" Drew moved close enough that the buttons of his waistcoat brushed the back of her dress and he whispered the words so that his warm breath caressed her ear and tickled the hair on her neck.

She stiffened and began to tremble uncontrollably.

Drew exhaled his frustration. "Would that I could." He murmured the heartfelt words in a voice so low he couldn't be sure she heard them, then put his hands on her shoulders and gently turned her to face him.

Wren's eyes widened as he dipped his head toward hers and her pulse quickened in anticipation. She moistened her lips with the tip of her tongue and lowered her lashes.

Drew's kiss was hot and hungry, filled with anger and almost punishing. It began as something he couldn't keep himself from doing and quickly turned into something more. Liquid fire rushed to all parts of Drew's body as he covered Kathryn's lips with his own and felt her sway against him. He pulled her closer as he deepened his kiss, tangling his hands in her soft hair, before running them down her body. The thin muslin layers of her gown concealed little as he cupped her firm breast in one hand before continuing his exploration down her ribs, past her waist, over her hipbone, and around the curve of her derriere, pulling her up against his groin. He groaned in a mixture of need and agony.

Wren was overwhelmed by her response to his sudden kiss. She gripped his broad shoulders and parted her lips to allow his silken tongue to slip through to sample the warm recesses of her mouth. Surrounded by his arms, his mouth, his hard masculine body, and the taste and touch and smell of him, Wren melted against him. She reveled in the hot taste of his kiss and the faint, half-forgotten aroma of the exotic spices left by his shaving soap. Wren breathed in his scent and nuzzled closer to its source.

Drew groaned again.

Wren pulled her mouth away from his. She was weak in the knees and definitely in danger of losing herself in his embrace. She tilted her head back to allow him access as Drew brushed his lips against her closed eyelids, across her cheeks, and down her neck. He nipped at her earlobe, then darted his tongue into the pink shell of her ear. Wren gasped in reaction. She tightened her grip, hanging on to his shoulders for dear life, as Drew pressed hot, wet kisses behind her ear on the spot where her pulse hammered to keep pace with her raging emotions.

"Bloody hell!" Drew tore himself away and put some distance between them before their kissing got too far out of hand.

Looking thoroughly well kissed, and surprised by his abrupt retreat, Kathryn swayed on her feet as he released her. She stared up at him and Drew found the look in her gray-green eyes strangely disconcerting. She appeared confused and puzzled by his withdrawal and he was struck by the fact that she tasted the way he remembered—warm and passionate and impossibly innocent and pure.

She touched her fingers to her lips. "I don't understand. . . ."

"What don't you understand?" His voice was gruff, his words much harsher than he intended. "That I came here to evict one of my father's mistresses in order to avoid the scandal of having one mistress preside over the funeral of another, only to find that my father's mistress was the only woman I'd ever asked to be my wife? Or that I suddenly find myself once again stupidly ensnared in the web of her attraction?" He gave a snort of laughter. "How could you understand? I don't understand any of this madness myself."

Wren ruthlessly suppressed the tiny surge of hope Drew's kiss and his words gave her and concentrated instead on the purpose of his visit to Swanslea. "You're burying George's—lady friend—here at Swanslea Park with him?"

"What would you have me do with her? Consign her to a pauper's grave in Ireland?" Drew raked his hand through his hair in a gesture of frustration.

"But your mother is—"

"My mother is dead," Drew said. "She can't object to my showing a little Christian charity to the unfortunate young woman who shared my father's final moments. Besides"—he paused—"I don't see that I have a choice. She died with him. She probably died because she was with him. We know nothing about her except her given name and no one has come forward to claim her body. He left me to see to the care of his surviving mistresses." Drew gave Wren a pointed look. "Would you have me do less for the one who perished with him?"

"No."

"I've already sent Martin to Ireland to bring the bodies home to Swanslea Park. It shouldn't take more than a fortnight for them to get here. I plan to notify the rector and have the funerals as soon as they arrive. She'll be buried in the family plot." He glanced at Wren. "I think it's what he would have wanted."

Wren nodded. "Your guests will begin arriving for your father's funeral once the official notice is published. Mr. Isley can take care of the animals and Miss Allerton will remain with Kit." She looked up at Drew. "I don't like leaving him, but George was Kit's father. Kit should stand with you at the funeral."

"What about you?"

"I'll remove myself from the cottage and from Swanslea Park until the funerals are over and your guests depart." She bit her bottom lip and stared down at the toes of her black kid slippers to keep from meeting Drew's eyes. "We can decide the rest after."

"You told me this morning that nothing on earth could induce you to miss George Ramsey's funeral," Drew reminded her.

"That was before I knew you were burying George's lady friend with him."

Drew felt his disappointment as the knot in his stomach tightened painfully. Somehow he'd expected better of Kathryn. He'd wanted her to prove him right. "Finding out he had another mistress lessened your resolve?"

"No," Wren said softly. "Finding out that you were trying to do the right thing did. I didn't realize you were trying to avoid the scandal of having one mistress at the burial of another." She lifted her face and met his gaze. "I've caused you enough scandal and embarrassment to last a lifetime, Drew. And supplied the *ton* with all of the *on-dits* and speculation I intend to provide. You don't have to worry about me causing any more scandal."

The aching knot in the pit of his stomach grew larger. She hadn't disappointed him after all. He'd disappointed

himself. He'd done what he'd come to do. He'd succeeded in removing Kathryn from Swanslea Park, but
there was no satisfaction in the victory. His empty life
flashed before his eyes and suddenly, perversely, Drew
wanted—needed—her to stay. "What about Kit? If he
stands with me at the funeral, the *ton* will speculate
about him. Have you considered that? Have you thought
of how I should account for him?"

"Should anyone inquire you may tell them that Kit is
Bertrand Stafford's son," Wren replied.

"Do you think anyone will believe it? Especially since
Kit bears no resemblance whatsoever to old Bertrand
and bears an uncanny likeness to me?"

"Then tell the truth. Tell them he's your brother."

"And have the wags in the *ton* call him illegitimate?
Have them brand him a bastard? Have you taken leave
of your senses?"

"He *is* illegitimate," Wren protested.

Drew raised an eyebrow. "Is that how you want your
son to be known?"

Wren sighed. "Of course it's not how I want Kit to
be known—especially among those vicious gossip-
mongers who call themselves society. But it's too late
to do anything about it now."

"You could stand with us at the funeral."

"And do what?" Wren was stunned.

"Protect Kit."

Wren expelled her breath in a rush of hot air and
anger. "I've protected Kit from the first moment I held
him in my arms."

He appeared completely calm and unflappable. "Then
you should have no difficulty continuing the practice by
telling anyone who's bold enough or rude enough to
inquire that he's mine."

She couldn't have heard him correctly. "You mean your heir."

"No." Drew shook his head. "I mean my son."

"They were there when I didn't . . . when you waited for me at the altar. London society knows we didn't get married."

"You should know better than anyone that you don't have to be married to make a child," he reminded her.

"Even so, Drew, they can count. We aren't—we never . . . He's not your son."

"He should have been," Drew replied fiercely, finally giving voice to the idea that had eaten him alive since he'd first set eyes on Kit. "And as far as the *ton* is concerned, we were, we did, and he is."

"They'll think I married Bertrand just to give my son a name."

"Didn't you?" Drew moved closer, crowding her. "My father saw fit to leave you to me and I intend to claim you along with the rest of my inheritance."

"You're mad!" Wren's heart thudded against her ribs. Drew had come to Swanslea Park to evict her and suddenly announced his intent to claim her.

"Quite possibly," he answered, staring into her eyes.

"You want me to—"

"I want you." Drew cut her off.

"But, Drew . . ."

"I know." He nodded in agreement to her protest. "It makes no sense. There's no reason to it. I cut you out of my mind and my heart a long time ago. I thought we were done with one another. But it appears that I was wrong." Drew stared into her big gray-green eyes. "The kiss we just shared proves we've some business left to finish." He reached out and gently brushed her cheekbone with his knuckles.

His touch seemed to turn her bones to jelly and Wren fought to control her trembling. "No."

He traced the outline of her lips with the tip of his finger. "You're not unaffected by me, Kathryn." He touched her bottom lip with the pad of his thumb, then ran it across the seam of her lips. "There is something powerful between us. There always was. Why not explore it further?"

She stared up at him, her heart in her eyes. "I can't."

"Why not?" He graced her with his most devastating smile. "You've done it before. Why not do it with me?"

Wren blinked at the burst of raw pain that shot through her body as his words sliced through her, leaving dozens of bleeding wounds in their wake. She jerked away from his touch and stepped back, out of reach. "I've spent the past four years praying that God would forgive me for what I did to you."

"Then your prayers are about to be answered."

"I prayed to God, not to you."

"But I'm the one you wronged," he said. "You should have prayed for my pardon as well as God's."

"I did pray for it," she admitted. "And I hoped that someday you would grant it. But I will not share your bed in order to earn it." Wren pinned him with her gaze.

"Fair enough," he said. "Because, although I'm willing to try, I can't guarantee I'll be able to forgive and forget the past simply because you'll be sharing my bed."

"Too much has happened between us—"

"Not enough has happened between us," he said. "I've seen men—too many young men—die in battle. I've heard the whispered prayers and the regrets of the wounded and the dying. I know how rare it is to get a second chance in life and I mean to make the best of this one. You *will* be sharing my bed, Kathryn. Make no mistake about that. It's simply a matter of time."

"You would take your father's leavings?"

"I'll not go to my grave regretting the fact that I never made love to you." He fixed his gaze on her perfectly formed lips. "If that means taking my father's and Bertrand Stafford's leavings, then so be it. Suffice it to say that I want you in my bed. How you come to be there is of little consequence."

"I thought you had a heart," she said, "but I was wrong."

"Then we should make a fitting pair," Drew retorted. "Because I've thought the same of you." With that, the new marquess of Templeston walked toward the door. He reached for the cut-glass doorknob and paused long enough to turn back and look at her. "I'm not a doting old man you can twist around your finger, Kathryn. I won't change my mind or bend to your will. Once, long ago, I wanted you to be my wife. Now, I simply want what you gave my father."

Wren glared at him.

Drew managed a smile. "You have a fortnight to get used to the idea."

Chapter 9

All the world's a stage,
And all the men and women merely players;
They have their exits and their entrances;
And one man in his time plays many parts.

—WILLIAM SHAKESPEARE, 1564–1616

A fortnight. Wren carefully closed the door to the nursery and quietly made her way along the gallery, down the stairs to the entry hall, past the massive dining room, through the kitchens to the back door. Drew had issued an ultimatum and given her a fortnight—the length of time it would take for his father's body to arrive home from Ireland—to get used to the idea of becoming his mistress.

Wren grabbed her black stole from the hook by the door where she'd left it when she'd entered the main house. She wrapped the wool stole around her shoulders as added warmth against the chill of the evening and walked down the white gravel path that led from the mansion through the gardens to the dowager cottage. Drew had been full of ultimatums today.

A footman, dressed in black mourning garments, had delivered a note to the cottage shortly after Drew had left it. The black-bordered note, penned in Drew's distinctive hand, informed her that the sixteenth marquess of Templeston would be keeping country hours while in residence at Swanslea. Breakfast and dinner would be served at the accustomed time. She was expected to join him at the table for both. The supper she'd shared with Kit and Ally in the nursery this evening had marked the end of their simple quiet meals for a while.

Wren had apologized to Ally for the change in their evening routine as they'd bathed Kit and gotten him ready for bed. Ally was disappointed, but not surprised. She understood. Household routines invariably changed whenever the master of the house arrived. It had been so with her father and with the last marquess of Templeston and so it would be with the new one.

Wren kicked a pebble across the path. She'd assured Ally that their routine would have to be altered for a few days to accommodate the new marquess. But the change in routine was temporary. It would last only until the funeral guests arrived. Perhaps as long as a fortnight. *The fortnight she was supposed to spend getting used to being Drew Ramsey's paramour.*

Drew, it seemed, had no intention of sleeping or eating alone. He'd granted her one last evening alone with Kit and Ally, but from now until the first of his guests arrived, Drew expected her to take her meals alongside him at the massive table in the formal dining room.

Wren followed the gravel trail past the carefully trimmed rows of boxwoods bordering the beds of kitchen and medicinal herbs and around the displays of topiary and statues. The moon had risen, illuminating a stone bench in the center of a square of green lawn surrounded on all sides by a profusion of early blooming roses. Wren sank down on the bench and breathed in the heady aroma of the roses. The bench was wet with dew and the moisture soaked through the thin fabric of her gown and undergarments. But it didn't matter. No one would see the damp circle on the back of her dress in the dark and her thin silk pantalets and stockings would dry before morning. No one would know that she'd sat on a wet bench in the rose garden during the dark of night contemplating her future.

There had been dozens of times over the last four years when she had dreamed of sharing her bed and breaking her morning fast with Drew, but she'd always dreamed of being his wife. Not his mistress. And now, Drew had given her a fortnight to get used to the idea of having her heart's desire. If she would only agree to sacrifice her self-respect and her romantic dreams of being his wife.

Wren frowned. She had secreted her girlish, innocent dreams away and kept them well guarded from the harsh reality of her life when she'd married a man old enough to be her father. She'd been fond of Bertrand and had spent most of her life thinking of him as a kind, elderly uncle. When her world crumbled around her head, Bertrand had come to her rescue, offering her his name and his protection. Wren had married him with a profound sense of gratitude.

And Bertrand had understood. He had married her knowing her heart was otherwise engaged. He hadn't minded and had willingly accepted whatever affection she offered. Despite having been a lifelong bachelor, Bertrand liked having a young bride to show off to his friends and colleagues and had found married life quite satisfying.

Wren wished she could say the same. But marriage to Bertrand had held no surprises for her. It was exactly what she'd expected it to be. She'd been surrounded from dawn to dusk by elderly scholars, stacks of dusty Greek and Latin tomes, and scores of preserved biological specimens. Her marriage hadn't been demanding, but it hadn't been exciting or satisfying either—especially for a young woman who had been held in Drew Ramsey's arms and who had shared his passionate kisses.

Wren sighed. Her desire to be a good wife to her elderly husband had led her to become his secretary, his sometime research assistant, and his housekeeper. When Bertrand fell ill ten months after they married, she'd spent endless days and nights at his bedside, nursing him. She had lost everything when Bertrand died. The house they'd shared had been provided to supplement Bertrand's modest income at the museum and Wren had been forced to vacate to make room for the scholar hired to replace him at the new term. Wren glanced down at her black skirts. She'd forsaken her bright colors when her elderly husband died. She'd donned her first set of mourning clothes and moved into the dowager cottage at Swanslea with her father. Three years later she was still living in the cottage at Swanslea and still wearing mourning.

Merciful heavens, but she was heartily sick of black! So sick of it that during the past year, she'd begun using her clothing as a secret canvas, painting fanciful designs on her undergarments. She spent hours decorating her black silk pantalets and her black silk stockings and those decorations had become a series of greatly embellished studies of exotic flora and fauna.

Wren lifted her skirts a few inches. Twin circlets of bright green vines and crimson star-shaped blossoms wrapped themselves around her ankles. She flexed her feet and smiled at her secret handiwork. These miniature works of art were private indulgences, little bits of color used to relieve the seemingly endless yards of black fabric.

Wren stood up suddenly, lifted her arms to the sky,

and began twirling around the lawn. Soft laughter bub-
bled to the surface as she repeated the intricate dance
steps she'd learned long ago, moving in time to music
only she could hear. Wren stepped up onto the bench
and executed a graceful pirouette. She wondered, suddenly, what Drew would think if he knew she had spent
her evening dancing in the moonlight like a pagan
queen.

She paused in midturn. Thoughts of Drew always
brought back memories she thought she'd forgotten. But
there it was. Another unforgettable memory. Wren
smiled. The last time she'd danced, she had danced with
Drew. At the duchess of Kerry's ball. She breathed
deeply, remembering the way she'd felt when he'd held
her in his arms and led her around the ballroom, how it
felt to smile up at him and see an answering smile reflected in the depths of his deep brown eyes. And she
remembered how bereft she'd felt when the ball ended
and she had been forced to bid Drew good night and
accompany her aunt home.

The pain in the region of her heart caught her unawares. She dropped down onto the bench and pulled her
knees to her chest, gasping for breath. Her shoulders
shook from the force of her sobs as Wren laid her face
against her knee and allowed the hot tears to come. It
hurt so much to remember. It hurt so much to know that
there had been a time when she would have given anything to see the smile in his eyes. A time when she
would have given anything to be held in his arms again.
A time when she would have given anything to feel that
cherished again. So why was she balking at the idea of
becoming his mistress now? *Because she was very much
afraid that she wouldn't feel as cherished as his mistress
as she had felt as his wife-to-be. Because it wouldn't be
the same.* Drew wanted her again. Not because he loved

her, but because his injured pride demanded satisfaction.

She knew what Drew wanted, but what about her? What did she want? The answer to her questions came instantly. Love. And security. She wanted Drew to look at her with love in his eyes, to offer her sanctuary in his arms and in his heart once more. Wren tried to scoff at her foolish ideals. She wanted the impossible. She'd lost his love when she'd broken faith with him; and now she wanted the one thing she knew he couldn't give her.

Why wasn't she more willing to bargain? She had something he wanted—something other than Kit and the cottage. Why couldn't she give up on her romantic dreams? Why couldn't she allow him to take what he wanted? It would be so much easier than fighting him. And anything was better than living in fear. Wren frowned. She wasn't a virgin. Procreation wasn't a mystery any longer. She knew how it felt to have a man inside her, how it felt to conceive a child. She knew what to expect. She understood how it would be between them. So why didn't she go to him and get it over with? *Because she knew that whatever happiness she would feel at sharing his bed would be overshadowed by the knowledge that she'd sacrificed the last of her innocence in order to share it.*

Wren let go of her knees and began mopping the tears on her face with the hem of her dress. She should know by now that crying never did her any good. It made her feel worse than before and left her with a headache, a sore throat, red swollen eyes, and a stuffy nose.

She dried her eyes and raised her head. She caught a whiff of a tantalizing aroma and saw a tiny pinpoint of orange light across the garden. She couldn't see him, but she knew he was there in the pavilion atop the hill in the center of the maze. His cigar had given him away.

Wren peered into the darkness for a long moment. She

wondered if he'd seen her, wondered why he hadn't made his presence known. Or had he? She stood up and stared at the darkened pavilion. The tiny orange glow had disappeared. Wren squared her shoulders and took a deep breath. The faint aroma lingered. She exhaled softly, then turned and retreated to the cottage, feeling more confused than ever before.

Calling himself ten kinds of a fool, Drew quickly lowered his arm and hid the glowing tip of his cigar with his hand. She'd seen the orange light and knew he was there in the dark watching her. Drew exhaled a stream of smoke. He'd been witness to her exuberant dance and to her display of grief and Kathryn wouldn't thank him for spying on her during her most private moments. Nor would she forgive him.

He heard her soft sigh and listened as the sound of her footsteps—the soft tread of leather against gravel—faded from his hearing. Drew wanted to follow her. He wanted to see her safely to her cottage door and once she reached the door, he wanted to see her safely to bed.

But Drew stayed in the pavilion long past time for her to reach the cottage. He stayed where he was, tamping down his need, fighting the urge to go to her and beg for what he wanted, beg for what he needed and for what he'd waited so many years to recover. He crushed out his cigar and stretched his legs out in front of him, crossing and uncrossing his ankles, adjusting his position in a futile attempt to allow more room for the burgeoning arousal pressing against the front of his snug trousers. He stayed in the pavilion until the damp and the chill forced him to return to the house. He entered his father's study and helped himself to a large brandy before sinking down in the chair before the fireplace.

He must have lost his mind. There was no other explanation for his abrupt about-face. He had kissed her and the years of pain and torment had fallen away as if they had never existed. He forgot everything except the feel of Kathryn's lips against his own—the feel of her body pressed against his. Drew shoved his fingers through his hair, struggling to come to terms with the rapid turn of events.

Kathryn was right. He'd finally lost his mind. Hadn't he told her he saw no reason for Swanslea Park to come equipped with a mistress not of his choosing? Hadn't he told her he wanted her to permanently remove herself from Swanslea? So why was he begging her to deck herself out in black crepe and veil and stand up with him at his father's funeral? Why was he demanding that she get used to the idea of becoming his mistress?

Because he wanted her. Drew exhaled as he admitted the truth. It was as simple and as complex as that. He wanted her. He had wanted her before their aborted wedding and he'd wanted her after it. He'd been rocked by the need to make Kathryn Markinson his the first time he'd met her and the years since hadn't changed that. He still wanted her.

The fact that she'd been his father's mistress should be abhorrent to him. Hell, it was abhorrent to him—so abhorrent it made his gut clench. Drew wished it had never happened. But if Kathryn hadn't become his father's mistress, Kit would not have been born. And after meeting Kit—after meeting his half-brother—how could he wish he'd never been born? The knowledge that she mourned his father's death as much as he did should deter him. But it didn't. His need for Kathryn transcended pride and nobility. Drew had fought a battle with his better judgment and lost to that most powerful of adversaries—lust.

Mourning or not. Swathed in black crepe or not. He wanted Kathryn in his bed. And he intended to have her there. It seemed that where Kathryn was concerned, he had no conscience.

Drew frowned down at the empty brandy snifter in his hand. He had given her a fortnight to become accustomed to the idea. He'd allotted that space of time in which to court her. Drew pushed himself up from the depths of the comfortable leather chair, crossed over to the sideboard, and poured himself another brandy. He could already hear the snickering of the *ton*. There would be no end to the gossip once they discovered that he'd resumed a relationship with the woman who'd made him a laughingstock four years earlier. And he dreaded hearing what St. Jacque would have to say.

He set his glass of brandy down on the lamp stand and untied his cravat and unbuttoned his shirt collar. He sank onto his chair, stretched out his legs, and studied the blue-orange flames consuming the coal in the fire grate and reflecting off the highly polished leather of his black Hessians. While his other acquaintances in the *ton* would gossip behind his back, speculate as to his mental faculties, and snicker at his gullibility, his best friend would call him a flaming idiot to his face.

And he couldn't say he'd blame him. Drew snorted in self-contempt. Julian wouldn't hesitate to speak the truth as he saw it or bother couching his disapproval in politeness. The friendship they'd struck up as children had flourished through school days and the university, survived the excesses of youth and more than a fair share of courtships and love affairs, and been melded into an unbreakable bond by the death and destruction of war.

He lifted the globe of brandy and inhaled the aroma,

swirling the liquor in the glass before taking a bracing swallow. His bond of friendship with Julian was constant and true, enduring triumph and tragedy and death. Too much death. First his mother and the brother or sister she'd carried, then the scores of soldiers he and Julian had commanded, and now his father's untimely death.

Drew sighed. Soon there would be another death. Although he couldn't envision a life without him, Drew doubted Julian would last the summer. The field surgeon had removed much of the grapeshot after Waterloo, but neither he nor the subsequent surgeons Drew had found to attend Julian had been able to remove all of the iron balls or repair all of the damage they had wrought. Several of the wounds failed to heal and Julian was slowly succumbing to them.

The bond of friendship between them would survive even Julian's death. Drew swallowed another mouthful of brandy and raked his fingers through his hair. It had survived everything else—including his courtship of and aborted wedding to Kathryn. When Kathryn failed to show up for their wedding, Julian had urged him to forget her. But he didn't want to forget her. He wanted her. And he wanted to know why she'd decided she didn't want him. When she refused to see him, Drew sent Julian in his stead. But Julian fared no better. Kathryn refused to see either of them.

A week passed and with his wedding canceled and his plans for the future abruptly altered, Drew joined Wellington in his campaign against Napoleon. St. Jacque bought a commission and followed him. He'd spent most of the campaign of the Hundred Days avowing that Drew was lucky to have escaped leg shackling himself to Sir Wesley Markinson's heartless spawn of a daughter.

After Waterloo, Drew had devoted his energy and his considerable resources to helping Julian recover from his injuries, studiously avoiding the mention of anything that might upset him. Including Kathryn. He had carried his memories of her into battle, but Drew hadn't spoken her name aloud in over four years. He managed a wry smile, imagining Julian's inevitable reaction to the news that, in the space of a single day, he had allowed himself to fall under Kathryn's spell once again.

There was no doubt about it. Andrew Ramsey, sixteenth marquess of Templeston, was a first-rate fool. A first-rate fool with an almost overwhelming need to turn back the clock. To return to the brief interlude following the Congress of Vienna, before the Hundred Days, when Napoleon had been safely confined on Elba and Drew had met and courted Kathryn. He wanted to go back to the time when life had held such promise. Before Kathryn had left him waiting at the altar, before the scandal and gossip. Before he'd run away to Belgium to kill his heartache along with Napoleon's soldiers. Before his father had mysteriously assumed the role of Kathryn's benefactor and lover.

There was a part of him that had always wondered what would happen if he chanced to meet Kathryn Markinson again. And now he knew. Drew downed the rest of his drink and blew out the lamps. He sat in the dark, stared at the soft glow of the coals, and remembered.

He had kissed her.

And time stood still.

The question that had plagued him for the past four years had been answered. Now he was left to wonder if she'd take him up on his ultimatum and how he was going to manage to face her across the breakfast table in the morning.

Chapter 10

*Whene'er I look into your eyes
Then all my grief and sorrow flies,
And when I kiss your mouth, oh then
I am made well and strong again.*

—HEINRICH HEINE, 1797–1856

The staff was already hard at work, cooking and cleaning the house from top to bottom in preparation for the funerals. They had stopped the clocks, covered the mirrors, and begun draping the windows in mourning cloth by the time Drew appeared for breakfast. He sidestepped to avoid a collision with a maid carrying an enormous bolt of black crepe as he entered the breakfast room.

Ignoring the mahogany sideboard and the mingling aromas of the breakfast foods it held, Drew walked to the Palladian windows and drew the heavy velvet drapes closed, effectively shutting out the morning sun. Once the room was sufficiently dark, he sat down at the table and poured himself a cup of coffee from the silver pot.

A freshly ironed newspaper lay folded at the head of the table. Drew glanced at the headlines and noticed that it was over a week old. He picked it up anyway and began reading the news he'd read before he left London.

"Good morning, milord."

Drew looked up to find Newberry, the butler, standing at his side.

"I've taken the liberty of preparing a plate for you." Newberry had removed a plate from the rack on the sideboard and dished up a spoonful of scrambled eggs and two slices of dry toast. He set the plate in front of Drew.

Drew waved it away. "I'll wait for Mrs. Stafford. Will you send someone upstairs to inform her that I'm awaiting her arrival in the breakfast room?"

"Mrs. Stafford has already broken her fast, milord."

"She was to join me for the morning meal."

"Mrs. Stafford is an early riser, milord. She waited as long as she could for you to appear and when you didn't she had breakfast in the nursery with Master Kit and the governess, then returned to the cottage to begin work."

"Then I'll see her there." Drew finished his coffee and pushed his cup and saucer aside, leaving his breakfast untouched.

"There's no need for you to rush, milord," Newberry volunteered. "Miss Wren isn't at the cottage this morning. She's sketching in the woodland."

"Do you know where?" Drew asked.

"No, milord, but she asked me to order the pony cart for Miss Allerton and Master Kit and to send a basket luncheon with them to the copse of trees by the stream near the mill at the nooning."

"Have you ordered the pony cart for Master Kit and his governess yet?"

"No, milord."

"Good," Drew pronounced. "Because there will be a change in plans. I'll take the luncheon basket to Mrs. Stafford." He closed his eyes for a moment and gritted his teeth against the pain in his head.

"Master Kit will be very disappointed."

"I'll make it up to him later," Drew promised. "If I live that long," he added beneath his breath.

"Very good, milord." The butler studied him closely. "Enjoy your breakfast."

"Thank you, Newberry, but I'm not dining this morning."

"I see." Newberry nodded. "Will there be anything else, milord?"

Drew started to shake his head, then thought better of it. He winced as he replied, "Not at the moment."

"As you wish, milord." Newberry bowed to Drew, then quietly backed away from the table and out of the room. He returned a few minutes later carrying a pewter mug on a small tray. Removing Drew's empty cup and saucer, the butler replaced them with the pewter mug.

"What's that?" Drew asked, without looking up from the paper.

"A posset for what ails you, milord." Newberry set the tray aside, then stepped to the windows and opened the drapes.

"No!" His objection was instantaneous and necessarily muffled as Drew lifted the paper higher in a futile attempt to shield his face from the painful sunlight. But it was too late. A shaft of morning sunlight pierced his eyes and sank deep into the sensitive area of his brain.

"Beg pardon, milord." Newberry returned to the table and carefully plucked the newspaper from Drew's hands and pushed the pewter mug in front of him. "But you'll feel better if you drink your posset."

Drew lifted the mug and sniffed at the steaming brew. "What's in it?"

Newberry ignored his question. "It's best if you drink it straight down, milord."

Drew took a tentative sip and nearly gagged. "I can't

drink this." He would have set the drink aside, but Newberry intervened.

"Allow me, milord." The butler leaned forward, pinched Drew's nostrils closed with one hand, and tilted the bottom of the mug up with the other, so that the young marquess was forced to swallow the contents or drown. "There now, milord." Newberry placed the pewter tankard on the tray. "You'll be feeling as right as rain in no time."

"I wouldn't be too sure of that." Drew's stomach was threatening revolt at any moment and he sounded exactly like a petulant child.

Newberry almost smiled. "Trust me, milord."

"Why should I?"

"Your father did," Newberry replied. "And my posset never failed to set him to rights."

"My father drank that devil's brew?" Drew was surprised. His father had enjoyed the usual wine with dinner, after-dinner port, and brandy and cigars on occasion, but Drew had never known him to drink to excess.

"Nearly every morning for two years after the marchioness died. And it never failed him." Newberry pinned Drew with a penetrating look. "He couldn't sleep alone. So he closeted himself in his study and drank himself into a stupor every night. When he relocated to London in order to return to the bench, I went with him and taught the cook and my counterpart, Mr. Chappell, how to make the posset."

"I had no idea."

"Of course not," Newberry said. "A man in your father's position could never allow a muzzy head to interfere with his work or impair his judgment."

Drew was thoughtful. "How long have you been here, Newberry?"

"A quarter of a century next spring, sir," Newberry answered proudly.

"After a quarter of a century in his service, you must have had my father's measure."

"I like to think so," Newberry said.

"What kind of man was he?"

Newberry raised an eyebrow at that. "Milord?"

Drew couldn't help but smile. "I know what kind of father he was," he said, "but I've no idea what kind of man he was. What kind of employer he was. I'm afraid that I saw him from a child's point of view—even after I reached my majority."

"He was a good man," Newberry said. "A wise and moral man who was loyal to his family and friends and the memory of his beloved wife."

"A wise, moral man with several mistresses," Drew said. "How many did he present to the staff at Swanslea Park?"

"None, milord."

"None except Mrs. Stafford."

Newberry shook his head.

"Then how do we explain Master Kit?"

"What is there to explain? He's Lord Templeston's son," Newberry replied.

"What about Mrs. Stafford? What was she to my father?"

Newberry knew what Drew was asking and he didn't hesitate to answer. "She's Master Kit's mother. Lord Templeston offered the marchioness's suite to Miss Wren after Master Kit came along, but she refused to accept his hospitality. She remained in the cottage with Master Kit. When Lord Templeston insisted that Master Kit be installed in the nursery, Miss Wren slept in the nursery with the boy until Miss Allerton came to live with us. After Miss Allerton arrived, Miss Wren moved back to the cottage. She didn't usurp your mother's place as mistress of this house or of your father's heart." Newberry looked him in the eye. "When the marchioness died, Lord Templeston moved out of the master bedchamber. He refurbished the master chamber and the one connected to it for you and your bride. It remained unoccupied until you arrived last night." The fact that Newberry called Kathryn by her pet name did not escape Drew's attention. "Miss Wren's manner has always been beyond reproach. She's quite a lady." Newberry's voice was full of admiration.

"She was once," Drew said softly. *She was my lady once.*

"Your father was a splendid judge of character, sir," Newberry said. "And up until this moment, I believed you shared that gift."

The lunch basket was loaded in the pony cart and his horse saddled and tied to the back by the time Drew exited the house. He climbed onto the seat, took hold of the reins, and urged the pony down the drive. His headache had disappeared by midmorning but Newberry's censure lingered. It had been over twenty years since the butler had given him a scolding, but Drew felt Newberry's censure as keenly as he had as a young lad caught filching sweets from the kitchen.

Drew clucked to the pony, then flicked the reins and headed the cart in the direction of the mill. Newberry hadn't begun to doubt that he'd inherited his father's ability to judge character until today. Drew snorted. He'd begun doubting it the day Kathryn Markinson left him waiting at the altar. Up until that day, he'd been very secure in the knowledge that he was an excellent judge of character. His position in the War Office had proven it and his choice of friends echoed it time and again. Men trusted him with their lives and Drew had never doubted that their trust was warranted—until his wedding day.

He hadn't doubted it since. Newberry might choose to believe otherwise, but Drew's experience with Kathryn had taught him that he'd misjudged her the first time. Fortunately he'd learned enough from his mistake to know better than to repeat it. Drew knew he could be a miserable judge of character where women were concerned. It should be quite apparent to Newberry or to anyone else who cared to look at his past that if he'd inherited his father's famous judgment, he wouldn't have fallen in love with Kathryn Markinson in the first place. He wouldn't have been left standing at the altar on his wedding day and he wouldn't be about to make a fool of himself all over again.

He topped the last rolling hill and caught sight of Kathryn sitting on a blanket with a thick sketchbook opened on her lap. She looked up from her work and waved when she heard the rumble of the pony cart, but the welcoming smile died on her lips when she recognized Drew.

"What are you doing here?" Kathryn closed her sketchbook and laid it aside, but made no effort to stand up.

"I brought lunch." Drew pulled the cart to a stop a few feet away from where Kathryn sat, then turned and lifted the picnic basket from the back of the cart.

"Miss Allerton and Kit were supposed to bring lunch," she said.

"There was a change in plans," he said. "I decided to come in their stead." Drew jumped down from the cart and walked around to the back of it. He untied his horse and left him free to graze, then walked over to the blanket and set the basket down beside Kathryn.

"I'd rather have lunch with Kit and Ally."

"I thought as much," he admitted. "But I came in their stead nonetheless."

She glared at him. "Made that decision on your own, did you, milord?"

He ignored her sarcastic comment and focused his attention on the suffering that had prompted it. She looked terrible. Her face was pale and drawn; her red-rimmed eyes were swollen and underscored by deep purple shadows. Her nose was a bright, shiny, unbecoming shade of red. She'd spent the night crying and it showed. Drew felt a pang of guilt in knowing that he was responsible, at least in part, for her tears but he couldn't allow his feelings of guilt to become the chink in his armor against her. He couldn't allow Kathryn to slip past his guard. He couldn't give her the opportunity to lay siege to his heart and his soul a second time because he knew he wouldn't survive another disappointment.

"Kit and Ally were looking forward to this outing," she continued. "It was probably the last one we'd get to share until after the funeral and you spoiled it. I imagine they were every bit as disappointed with your decision as I am."

"I'll make it up to them."

"Really? How?"

"I promised Kit I would teach him to ride."

"That's impossible," Wren told him. "There's nothing in the stable for him to ride. That's the only pony we have." She pointed to the black Dales pony hitched to the cart. "And he isn't broken to the saddle."

"I know what I have in my stables, Kathryn." Drew knelt on the blanket.

"Then you made Kit a promise you can't keep."

He closed his eyes, ground his teeth together in frustration, and mentally counted to ten. "*I* always keep my promises." He opened his eyes and looked at her, his message crystal clear. "I've already sent the head groom into the village to secure a selection of suitable ponies so Kit can choose the one he likes best."

"What about Miss Allerton?" Wren knew she was being unreasonably waspish, but she couldn't seem to help it. She hated having him see her when she wasn't at her best. She hated seeing the look of scorn on Drew's face and disgust in his eyes. She hated knowing that he could manipulate her future and that he felt completely justified in doing so. But more than any of that, Wren hated knowing that he didn't love her anymore.

Keeping a safe distance from Drew when he was being nasty, making threats and accusations, and issuing ultimatums was hard enough, but keeping a safe distance from him when he was in a generous, conciliatory mood was almost impossible. "Are you going to buy her a pony, too?"

Drew bit his lower lip to keep from laughing aloud at her spate of ill temper. "Jealous?"

"Of course not!"

"Then it shouldn't bother you to learn that, in a manner of speaking, I did promise to buy Miss Allerton a pony."

Wren was speechless.

"At one time, her father maintained one of the finest stables in England. Unfortunately, Lord Rushfield has a weakness for the dice and he was forced to sell his holdings and his stables in order to discharge his gaming debts." Drew glanced at Kathryn as he reached for the picnic basket. "You should have seen Miss Allerton's face when I mentioned taking Kit riding. She was as excited as he was. Then she told me that Kit hadn't begun his lessons yet."

She tried to ignore the note of criticism in his tone of voice and failed. "I see."

"I doubt it," he replied. "Or you'd realize that Miss Allerton has missed being able to ride. I offered her the use of the stables and invited her to share my morning rides."

"Is that all you invited her to share?" The ugly retort escaped before Wren could stop it.

Drew laughed. "Tell me, Kathryn, are you this ill tempered every morning or might I hope that this is a rare occurrence?"

"I didn't sleep well."

"Didn't the fresh air of the garden agree with you?"

"You should know," she retorted. "You were there."

"I suppose you sensed my presence."

"Nothing so mysterious, sir," she told him. "I smelled you."

Drew raised an eyebrow at that. "Indeed?"

"You smoke a very distinctive cigar."

"And you have a very good nose, madam." Drew tenderly traced the length of her reddened nose with his index finger.

Wren shrugged off his touch and attempted to shrug him off as well. "I appreciate the sacrifice you made in bribing my son and his governess in order to bring my luncheon to me, sir. I know you're a very busy man with places to go and ponies to purchase, so please, don't let me detain you any longer."

"I didn't bring *your* luncheon, Kathryn." Drew reached for the basket, then opened the lid and began unpacking the crystal, china, and the cutlery. "I brought *our* luncheon." He smiled at her. "Didn't you get my message? I thought you understood that from now on, we're keeping each other company during mealtimes."

"You sent a message informing me that my company was requested at breakfast and at dinner," she corrected. "You didn't say anything about lunch."

"You missed breakfast," he said. "I thought you might appreciate an opportunity to make up for the oversight."

"It wasn't an oversight, Drew. I didn't miss breakfast. You did. I waited over an hour for you to appear."

"I know." His honesty was disarming. "I apologize for keeping you waiting at breakfast. I overslept. You see, I stayed in the garden and finished my cigar after you left. Then I returned to the house and spent the rest of a long night in a leather chair in my father's study staring into the fire while I drained a bottle of very fine French brandy. I didn't sleep until dawn."

Wren looked at him, a tiny smile playing at the corner of her mouth. "At least one of us managed to get some sleep." She reached up and self-consciously smoothed several stray strands of hair back into place. "I must look a fright."

Drew shook his head. "Not to me."

He emptied the picnic basket, uncorked a bottle of wine, and spread the food out on the blanket. He loaded his plate with a half of a roasted game hen, a wedge of cheese, a slice of freshly baked bread, and a ripe, juicy pear.

The warmth in his eyes and the tenderness in his voice were enough to take her breath away. Wren picked up the other plate to cover her embarrassment and was dismayed to find her face reflected in the shiny surface. She frowned at the image. "You flatter me."

Drew reached for her plate, filled it to match his own, and poured each of them a glass of wine. "Flattery was never one of my vices," he said. "You should know that."

Wren took her plate and balanced it on her lap. "Interesting that you consider the ability to flatter another person a vice. Most people would consider it a virtue."

"Insincerity is never a virtue," he said. "And, as I said, not one of my particular vices."

"Until yesterday, I had no idea you had vices." She nibbled at a piece of chicken and followed it with a sip of wine.

"Everyone has vices, Kathryn. I don't gamble or drink to excess the way some of my acquaintances do, but I admit to a weakness for fine horseflesh, expensive cigars, and expensive brandy. And although I'm not a spendthrift by nature, I've found that since returning from war, I indulge a need for creature comforts. For coal fires whenever I want them, fine linens, soft mattresses; well-fitted clothing and the best leather boots money can buy." He stretched out his legs and flexed his ankles, showing off his black leather Hessians.

She was silent for a moment. "I suppose it's strange that I don't recall any vices. I only remember your virtues."

Drew downed his glass of wine in one gulp and poured himself another. "That's because I was always on my best behavior around you."

"So was I." She looked at him. "After all we shared, it seems strange to think that we never really knew one another at all. How is it that we thought we could marry and live our entire lives on our best behavior?"

"We were in love."

His quiet pronouncement ripped at her heart.

"Or rather, I was in love with you." Drew met her stare. "And believed you felt the same for me."

"I did."

"Then how is it that we lost each other?"

Wren bowed her head. "I would have waited longer,"

she whispered. "For you at breakfast this morning. But the staff began stopping clocks and draping the house and suddenly I couldn't stay there any longer. I had to get away. If only for a little while."

"I know," Drew answered. "So did I."

"I can't believe he's dead."

"Neither can I."

Wren looked up at him. "It doesn't seem possible that I'll never see him again."

Drew stared into her eyes. "I can almost believe you loved my father as much as I did."

"Perhaps even more."

Drew frowned.

"How could I not love him? He gave me a son."

"Why didn't he marry you and make that son legitimate?"

"He couldn't."

"Of course he could," Drew protested.

"He never stopped loving your mother," Wren told him. "He made a promise to her, on her deathbed." She managed a smile. "Like you, George always kept his promises."

"What did he promise?"

"He promised no one would ever take her place. He promised her that he would never marry and make another woman marchioness of Templeston or allow any other child to take precedence over hers."

Drew sucked in a breath. "Christ!" He raked his fingers through his hair. "He told you that?"

Wren shook her head. "As far as I know, he only told one other person."

"Then how did you know about it?"

"He told my father." Wren deliberated for a moment before adding, "It was his way of apologizing to Papa for not offering to marry me."

"He should have married you."

"It wasn't necessary," she said. "I never wanted to be his marchioness." She managed a smile. *I only wanted to be your countess.*

"But you and Kit . . ."

"Have become a part of your life," she reminded him. "Whether we like it or not."

Drew looked her in the eye. "To life," he said, raising his wineglass and clinking it against hers. "Here's hoping we learn to make the best of it."

Wren met his gaze and accepted the toast. It seemed they'd suddenly stumbled upon common ground once again.

Chapter 11

*No passion so effectually robs the mind of all
its powers of acting and reasoning as fear.*

—EDMUND BURKE, 1729–1797

Wren awoke with a start. She opened her
eyes and discovered that she was lying on her
side on the blanket with her face pillowed against a
firmly muscled thigh fashionably covered in buff-
colored breeches. She stared down the length of the gentleman's leg and noted the glossy black leather Hessian
boot gloving his well-molded calf and his foot. Her heart
thudded in her chest and her blood roared in her ears as
she struggled to sit up.

"Easy, Kathryn. Stay where you are. It's all right."
His voice was warm and familiar and as soothing as the
touch of his hand on her hair.

She relaxed, rolled onto her back, and smiled. Looking up at him seemed the most natural thing in the world.
"What happened?"

Drew leaned forward and returned her smile. Feeling
an almost overwhelming urge to kiss her, he bent close
enough to feel the whisper of her breath against his
mouth. He paused, waiting for some sign that she

wanted him to continue. But she didn't seem to notice his desire, so Drew sat back and answered her question with words instead of kisses. "You were tired. You fell asleep."

"How long?" Her throat was dry and scratchy and her voice sounded foreign to her ears.

He looked up to gauge the position of the sun. "An hour or so."

Still too languid to move, Wren covered her eyes with her forearm and groaned. "I can't imagine what came over me."

He shifted his weight and stretched his arms over his head. "I'd like to think you enjoyed my company," he said wryly. "But it was probably the wine." He yawned. "See? There's no need to be embarrassed. We shared a meal, a bottle of wine, and a sleepless night. It's perfectly natural for you to need a nap. I was tempted to curl up beside you and take one myself."

"Why didn't you?" She surprised herself with the question and he surprised her even more with his answer.

"Who would have watched over you and kept you safe from roving packs of foxhounds and their owners?"

"Margo's not here," she said. "I'm safe from all foxhounds and their owners."

"I wouldn't say that." His voice was low and husky, filled with meaning. "Margo may be a huge temptation for the hounds to resist, but I guarantee that finding you here like this—seeing you like this"—Drew slid his hand down her skirts, smoothing them over her knees and calves, covering the soft purple blooms and the delicately rendered butterflies peeking from among the tangle of pale green vines winding their way up her black silk stockings—"would be an even bigger temptation for the hunters."

He frowned. Those stockings of hers were a world of temptation in themselves. He'd accidentally revealed them when her skirts had become twisted around her legs when she turned in her sleep. He had grabbed hold of them and tugged the fabric loose, intending only to untangle her but managing to expose the enticing length of her legs and hidden artwork in the process.

The timbre of his voice and the expression on his face alarmed her. She stiffened instantly.

So did he. But for an entirely different reason.

"This was a mistake." Wren scrambled off his lap and onto her knees. She haphazardly gathered her pens and charcoal and began shoving them into her knapsack. Drew had behaved in a gentlemanly fashion by watching over her and making certain that her black muslin skirts kept her decently covered, but that didn't change the fact that she had been sleeping on a blanket miles away from the main house oblivious to the world around her. "I didn't think about the hunters. I didn't realize. . . ." She glanced around. "I've always felt safe here, but now . . ." If Drew hadn't been there she would have been alone and helpless, completely vulnerable to anything or *anyone* who happened along.

She reached for her sketchbook, but Drew intercepted her, covering her hand with his own. "There's no reason for you to be alarmed. You weren't alone. You were safe here with me."

Wren shivered in reaction. He'd protected her from trespassers. But he had made no secret of the fact that he wanted her for himself. Who was going to keep her safe from him? Who was going to keep Drew Ramsey from taking what he wanted?

Drew let out an exasperated sigh. When she looked at him like that with her penetrating gray-green eyes he almost believed she could see right into his soul. "You were asleep," he began. "I didn't see the harm. . . ." But he *had* seen the designs painted on her stockings and those images haunted him. Drew couldn't stop thinking about the exquisitely detailed features of the tiny blue-eyed wood nymph he'd glimpsed winking at him from behind a purple blossom decorating the inner portion of her right thigh, just below her garter. The images she painted on her stockings were a complete contrast to the precise, scientific color plates of the plants and animals she painted to illustrate *Flora and Fauna Native to Britain* or the canvas watercolors the British Museum had commissioned for its displays. The paintings destined for public display were true-to-life representations of nature, painstakingly re-created in exacting detail. Her private artwork was a lush, exuberant foray into the realm of fantasy, where wood nymphs and water sprites, fairy children and pixies and elves cavorted in flower gardens turned tropical jungles. "All right! I admit it. I apologize. It wasn't the gentlemanly thing to do, but I took advantage of the opportunity—"

Kathryn wrenched her hand out of his grasp and scurried to the edge of the blanket as far away from him as possible. She stared at him with eyes as round as saucers. Drew wanted to check to see if he'd suddenly sprouted two horns and a pointed tail to go along with his other male appendage. He recognized that look of stark fear. He'd seen it on the faces of scores of men and boys on the battlefield, but never in peacetime and never on the face of a woman.

He knew what she intended, almost before she did. He came up on his knees and reached for the hem of her skirt. He caught hold of her foot instead and her half-boot came off in his hand.

In the blink of an eye, her demeanor changed from one of stark fear to one of deadly determination. She abandoned the idea of fleeing and turned to fight. Drew recognized the battlefield reaction. She'd decided to kill or be killed. Her demand, when it came, was cold and unemotional and all the more threatening because of it. "Kindly give me back my shoe."

She wasn't armed, but Drew was careful to move slowly as he got to his feet and handed her the boot.

Wren snatched it out of his hand. "What have you done?"

"Nothing," he answered softly.

"Then why did you apologize?"

"I apologized for not being more of a gentleman."

"How much of a gentleman weren't you?"

"I looked," he said. "At your artwork."

She blinked at his explanation, recovered slightly, then skewered him with her big gray-green stare. The expression in her eyes contained a message more powerful than anything she could have said. It told him she'd been expecting an admission far worse than the one he'd given her.

"You looked at my sketchbook? While I slept?"

He shook his head. "I looked at your other artwork." He winced when he realized she still didn't understand, but he refused to lie. "The flora and fauna painted on your stockings."

She opened her mouth to speak, but nothing came out.

Drew expelled a sigh of relief. Not because he'd rendered her speechless, but because she no longer looked terrified or ready to kill and she no longer looked at him as if he were a monster. He took that as a good sign and decided a little levity was in order. "I particularly liked the wood nymph winking from behind the purple flower." He glanced up to gauge her reaction. "I believe it's on your right thigh, just below your garter."

He grunted in pain as her half-boot bounced off his

chest. "For God's sake, Kathryn! All I did was look!"

"How could you!"

"Your skirts were twisted around your legs almost up to your waist," he said. "I'd have to have been blind not to notice."

"A gentleman would have made sure I was decently covered."

"I did."

"After I woke up," she accused. "After you looked your fill!"

"Any gentleman who could make sure you were decently covered without looking would have to be blind, a fool, or a eunuch. And I don't happen to be any of those things." He bent to retrieve her shoe and handed it back to her. She flinched when he brushed her fingers, but Drew reached for her hand again anyway. Her hand was ice cold. Drew caressed the back of it with his thumb. "I know you may think otherwise, but your trust in me hasn't been misplaced."

Wren snorted in contempt, but she didn't pull her hand out of his.

"I looked at your legs while you slept," Drew said. "Where's the harm in that?" He continued to soothe the flesh on the back of her left hand with his thumb as he tilted her chin up with the index finger of his other hand so that he might look her in the eye. "I looked, but I didn't touch."

"You did it while I slept." Her voice trembled with emotion and Drew was afraid her words would give way to tears at any moment. "You allowed me no say in the matter."

"Would you have lifted your skirts and shown me your stockings if I'd asked?"

"Of course not!"

Drew shrugged. "That's why I didn't ask."

"That doesn't excuse you."

"Maybe not," he agreed. "But it doesn't make me a monster either. I looked at your legs. And while your legs are incredibly lovely, I *was* able to contain myself. The sight of your legs, or any other woman's, no matter how lovely, isn't enough to provoke me into tossing your skirts over your head and forcing my unwanted attentions on you."

Drew knew he'd said the wrong thing the moment he heard her involuntary gasp. He watched her eyes widen as she jerked her hand out of his grasp and backed away. Now he understood why she'd reacted so strongly. *He* hadn't attempted to toss her skirts over her head and force himself on her but someone else had.

Think, he told himself, *think.*

"Kathryn." Drew spoke in the soft, tender tones used to calm frightened horses and children. *Stafford had been an old man, but it was possible. Why else would Kathryn have left him standing at the altar and married Stafford weeks later?* "Did Bertrand Stafford force himself on you? Is that why you married him?"

Kathryn shook her head. "Bertrand never . . . He would never . . ."

"But someone did." It wasn't a question.

She didn't answer. She didn't have to. He knew the answer. She'd already told him.

Drew's palms grew sweaty and he began to shake. His heart seemed to plummet to the pit of his stomach and his gorge rose in his throat. "Kathryn . . ."

Her gray-green eyes were filled with compassion. "It's in the past," she said. "Don't ever speak of it again. If not for my sake, then for Kit's and your own."

Wren dropped her shoe onto the ground and stepped into it, then quickly gathered the lunch basket, her drawing supplies, and her blanket and loaded them onto the cart. She climbed onto the seat of the pony cart, gathered the reins, and turned the pony for home, leaving Drew to collect his horse and follow.

Chapter 12

Things are not always what they seem.

—PLATO, C. 427–347 B.C.

The fact that he didn't mention the subject again didn't mean that he had decided to forget about it. Drew stood at the window of the library overlooking the front lawn watching as his head groom and a stockman from the village led a string of ponies up the drive. It only meant that he'd decided to let it rest while he pursued a different course of action. Christ, but it hurt to think that the reason Kathryn hadn't shown up at the church on their wedding day was because someone had assaulted her prior to it. And it wounded, almost beyond bearing, to know that she hadn't trusted him enough to tell him about it. If not Bertrand Stafford, then who? Who could have done such a thing? Who was Kathryn protecting? A stranger? Someone of their acquaintance? Her father? His?

Drew suddenly began to shake. He gripped the window casing and sank to the floor on his knees. *His father.* There could be no other explanation. Kathryn was protecting someone. Who better than the father of her child? He released his grip on the window casing and raked his hand over his head in a show of agitation. It made sense. Everything made sense. Too much sense. His father's unstinting patronage of Wesley Markinson, the gift of the dowager cottage, the unusual terms of his father's will.

But to force his son's fiancée? Had George Ramsey been capable of that? Tears burned in Drew's eyes. He loved his father. And despite his grumblings about his father's irresponsibility, he admired him. After his mother's death, Drew had born witness to his father's apparent preference for young women, but he hadn't noticed any inappropriate interest in Kathryn. His father had wholeheartedly approved of his choice of a bride and had seemed genuinely fond of Kathryn. It was inconceivable to Drew that he could have. . . . But something had happened. Something terrible that had altered the course of his and Kathryn's lives.

Someone had to know something about it. Drew exhaled. And who better than Martin, the man who had been privy to all of his father's secrets? Drew would have the opportunity to gain the answers to his questions when his father's solicitor returned from Ireland. Martin may not have knowledge of all of them, but he knew enough about his father's other liaisons and the private business he'd conducted with Wesley Markinson and Bertrand Stafford to provide Drew with a few answers. It was simply a matter of time before he could begin to unravel the ugly tangle of events in Kathryn's past.

Kathryn. Drew closed his eyes and inhaled deeply, pinching the bridge of his nose between his thumb and his index finger to forestall the headache he felt coming on. She'd ridden off without a backward glance. And she hadn't stopped until she reached the stables.

Drew expelled the long breath. He'd only been at

Swanslea Park a day and he'd already made a mess of things. He had expected to find one of his father's mistresses living on the estate, but he hadn't expected her to be Kathryn Markinson.

And having Kathryn Markinson in residence had his stomach tied in knots. Her presence made him feel as if his every footstep was mired in quicksand. She had provided more questions than answers. But answers were what he required. And he'd have them—somehow. He'd have to make amends—somehow. But first, he had to keep the promise he'd made to his brother.

He turned as the door to the library opened and Newberry stepped over the threshold. "Is everything all right, milord?"

"Yes, of course," Drew replied. "Why?"

Newberry discreetly cleared his throat. "I thought you might require assistance, milord?"

Becoming aware of his butler's discerning gaze, Drew realized that he was still kneeling on the floor in front of the window. He pushed himself to his feet and wiped his eyes with the back of his hand. "I'm fine now, Newberry. But thank you."

"You're welcome, milord." He gave Drew a moment longer to compose himself before announcing his reason for disturbing him. "Riley has returned from the village with the selection of ponies you requested. He requires your presence in the stables."

"Very well."

"I beg your pardon, milord, but I wasn't entirely certain I heard Riley correctly." Newberry gave a dramatic pause. "He did say ponies, milord?"

"He did." Drew glanced at Newberry. "I've a surprise for Master Kit."

"Indeed, milord."

"Yes, indeed," Drew confirmed. "Every boy should

have a pony of his own choosing to ride, Newberry. Hence the selection of suitable mounts. I wanted Master Kit to have a choice. Will you please ask Miss Allerton to bring Master Kit downstairs? I'd like them to accompany me to the stables." He paused. "And send someone to the cottage to ask Mrs. Stafford to join us at the paddocks and tell her that she might want to bring her sketchbook."

"As you wish, milord."

Drew pulled on his coat and a pair of leather gloves. "I'll await Miss Allerton and Master Kit here."

Newberry sketched a hasty bow and left to do Drew's bidding.

Harriet Allerton and Kit entered the library a quarter of an hour later. "Good afternoon, milord. You asked to see us?"

"Yes, I did." Drew looked up as Miss Allerton, with Kit in hand, entered the library.

He couldn't help but smile at the mutinous expression on the little boy's face as the governess gently nudged a reluctant Kit forward with the words, "Say hello to his lordship, Kit."

Kit looked down at his feet and mumbled a greeting.

"Thank you for coming," Drew said. "I have a surprise for Kit."

Kit apparently understood the meaning of the word *surprise,* for he looked up at Drew and grinned.

Drew reached out to ruffle Kit's hair, but caught himself as his young brother ducked behind Miss Allerton's skirts. "And I'd like you both to accompany me."

"Milord, I don't think . . ."

Drew recognized the note of concern in the governess's voice. "Only as far as the stables."

"The stables, milord?" Miss Allerton repeated.

"I've asked Mrs. Stafford to join us there," he added

as incentive. "If you recall, I made a promise to Kit this morning and I always keep my promises."

"But, milord, you promised to teach Master Kit how to ride," Miss Allerton said. "And I'm afraid that Swanslea Park lacks a mount suitable for a child of his tender years."

"I'm almost four," Kit interrupted his governess to protest her comment about his tender years.

Drew grinned down at Kit. "And a boy your age ought to know how to ride."

"But, milord . . ."

"It's all right, Miss Allerton." Drew held up his hand to forestall the governess's worried protest. "I sent my head groom into the village earlier this morning to secure a few p-o-n-i-e-s, so Kit will have a selection from which to choose."

"A selection, milord?" Harriet Allerton's eyes lit up, her voice fairly vibrated with excitement, and she forgot her dignity long enough to bounce up and down on the balls of her feet.

Drew laughed. "Yes."

"How many?" she asked.

"I counted seven of all shapes and sizes as they came up the drive," he told her.

Miss Allerton glanced down at the way her young charge was dressed—in short trousers that buttoned at the knees, knitted stockings, and leather buckle shoes. "I suppose his attire is suitable for a trip to the stables and an inspection of the p-o-n-i-e-s." Like Drew, she spelled out the word to keep from spoiling the surprise. "But he'll need a proper pair of boots, trousers, and a jacket and gloves once he begins lessons."

Drew nodded in agreement. "I'll send for my tailor and boot maker. He can make up several sets of riding clothes as well as mourning garments. But Kit is dressed

well enough for an afternoon excursion to the stables."
He motioned for Miss Allerton and Kit to precede him
out of the library. "Shall we?"

She was shaking by the time she reached the
cottage. Shaking with nerves and fear and desire and
longing and a hundred other emotions she couldn't
name. She feared the power he held over her—legally
and emotionally—but that didn't change the fact that
Drew was the only man she'd ever loved and would
most likely retain that status for the rest of her life. He'd
come so close to guessing her secret that she'd ordered
him never to mention the topic again and had driven off
in a blind panic, leaving him behind.

She sighed. Now all she wanted to do was lay her
burden down by revealing the secrets of the past and
telling him the truth. And if she knew that he would
believe her, she'd do it. In a heartbeat. But she didn't
know and until she could be sure, her secret must remain
her own.

Wren sat on a wooden stool in front of an easel in
the dowager cottage, where she'd spent the better part
of an hour or so fighting to keep her attention on the
detail of the anatomy and wing markings of the English
peppered moth, part of the *Noctuidae lepidoptera* she
was painting. Unfortunately she was having little success. The Pandora's box of secrets locked inside her had
been cracked open and now it couldn't be completely
closed; the secrets it held were quietly seeping out, and,
once they did, her life and the lives of the people she
loved would never be the same. Afraid to risk days of
work on the slip of the paintbrush or a thoughtless mix
of colors, Wren rinsed her paintbrush in the water basin,

blotted it dry, and placed it upside down in the jar on her worktable. If only Drew hadn't come to Swanslea Park. If only George hadn't died and made it impossible for her to keep Drew out of her life . . . If only she didn't love him so much . . .

As she always did when painting was difficult, Wren reached for the hedgehog lying curled atop a velvet cushion fashioned from an old cloak and began to stroke the soft fur on her chin and belly. The hedgehog, whom Wren had named Erin, short for *Erinaceus eropaeus,* the scientific name given to the genus of small insectivorous mammals to which the hedgehog belonged, began to purr. It wasn't as loud as a cat's purr, but it was recognizable. Wren cuddled the hedgehog and listened to the sound of it purring as she gazed out the window past the thick hedge of *Ilex aquifolium,* or English holly, to where the chimney tops of Swanslea Park were visible in the distance. *He* was there. And nothing she had done since she'd returned from their unexpected picnic could make her stop thinking about him. Her painting hadn't done it; nor, clearly, was the mental game she was employing, of using the scientific classification names of the flora and fauna of Britain instead of the more common ones each time she came in contact with them. Even the agouti hair surrounding Erin's quills reminded her of the salt-and-pepper color of Drew's hair. Nothing had made her forget the look in his eyes when he'd leaned forward as if to kiss her or the exchange of conversation that had followed.

She knew she'd behaved badly. By suspecting, even accusing, him of taking liberties while she slept, by throwing her boot at him, and by driving off and leaving him behind. She'd been unfair to Drew and had overreacted, but she hadn't been able to prevent it.

She didn't give her trust easily. But she had given it

to him. She had trusted him and he'd betrayed that trust by peeking at her stockings while she slept. It wasn't a gentlemanly thing to do, but it wasn't a terrible transgression either. He had looked, but he hadn't touched, and Wren knew that had Drew been less of a gentleman, she might have suffered far worse.

Unless . . . Wren paused. It was entirely possible that she had found her reaction to his admission of guilt more frightening than his betrayal of her trust. She liked his kisses. She more than liked his kisses. And once, long ago, she'd thrilled to and craved his forbidden touches. Even now, after all these years, she could still remember the warmth of his hand as he caressed her breast through the thin muslin of her evening gown, the feel of his thumb teasing her nipple, and the intimate pressure of his body pressed against hers.

Unfortunately, for her, desire came with a price and Wren was still very much afraid the price was too high.

Still, in a secret corner of her heart, she allowed herself the pleasure of knowing that Drew had looked at the artwork painted on her stockings and liked what he saw—not only the flowers and the wood nymphs, but the legs inside the silk. She'd recognized the expression on his face, and the knowledge that Drew hadn't bothered to hide his admiration, or his lust, excited her.

She hadn't appreciated his honesty or the humor in the situation at the time, but remembering the look of boyish innocence on his face when he'd asked, *Would you have lifted your skirts and shown me your stockings if I'd asked?* and the way he'd shrugged his shoulders and replied, *That's why I didn't ask,* when she'd avowed her refusal made her shake with quiet laughter. It reminded her of those long ago days when she'd been carefree and innocent and madly in love with him.

A knock sounded at the cottage door, startling Wren

out of her mirth. She turned away from her easel, slid off the stool, and crossed the room to open the door. As she reached for the doorknob, Wren realized she was still cradling Erin against her chest. She slipped the hedgehog into the pocket of an old three-quarter pelisse hanging by the front door, wiped her hands on her skirt, and opened the door.

The footman, the same one who'd delivered Drew's ultimatum the day before, stood on the threshold. "Mr. Newberry sent me to tell you that his lordship asks that you join him at the stables, ma'am. And he told me to tell you that you might want to bring your sketchbook."

Wren thought about refusing the request, but curiosity got the better of her. "All right," she said. "Let me get my sketchbook."

The footman glanced at the short, puffed sleeves of her dress. "Better get a wrap, too, ma'am. The afternoon's turned chill."

Wren nodded to let him know she'd heard him before she returned to her worktable for her sketchbook. She stuffed the book and a few sticks of charcoal into her knapsack and pulled on the pelisse as she walked out the door.

Chapter 13

When Love's delirium haunts the glowing mind,
Limping Decorum lingers far behind.

—GEORGE GORDON, 6TH LORD BYRON,

1788—1824

Kit was near to bursting with excitement as he took Miss Allerton's hand and followed her down the hall toward the eastern portico. He glanced over his shoulder to make certain Drew was keeping pace and tugged impatiently on his governess's hand, urging her to hurry.

As soon as the stables came into view, Kit pulled his hand out of Miss Allerton's and streaked across the lawn toward the fenced paddocks.

"Whoa there, Master Kit." Riley, Swanslea Park's head groom, intercepted the little boy as he ducked beneath the bottom fence rail. "You're to stay on that side until I tell you it's safe to come inside the paddock."

Kit stuck out his lip and pouted, but he did as Riley told him and stayed outside the paddock, hanging on to the fence rail, watching as the groom put a bay Dartmoor through its paces.

"I like that one!" Kit pointed toward the Dartmoor. "May I ride that one?"

Riley shrugged his shoulders. "You'll have to ask his lordship about that." He nodded toward Drew and Miss Allerton.

Kit turned to Drew. "May I ride that one, his lordship?"

"Your lordship," Miss Allerton corrected.

"Drew," Drew replied. He dropped to his haunches to meet Kit on the child's level. "Other people may call me your lordship or his lordship," he explained. "As my br . . . as part of my family, you're entitled to call me by my given name." He smiled at Kit. "Understand?"

Kit solemnly shook his head.

"My name is Andrew," Drew said. "But you may call me Drew."

"Okay," Kit agreed. "My name is Christopher." He stumbled over the pronunciation of his name. "But you can call me Kit."

"Agreed." Drew extended his hand, waited while Kit shook it, then stood up and spoke to the head groom. "How's the Dartmoor?"

"He hasn't been properly trained," Riley said. "But he shows promise."

"And the others?" Drew nodded toward where the grooms were walking the other ponies around the stableyard.

"I brought the best of the lot," the groom told him. "But most of them will need work."

Drew shrugged. "I never expected to go into the pony business, but we've plenty of room in the stables for them and . . ."

"You have a weakness for the stubborn, shaggy little blighters," Riley teased. "Especially when you know that two or three of them would have been sent to the mines or the rendering pot."

A frown marred Kit's forehead as he turned to Drew and asked, "What's a render pot?"

"Nothing you need worry about," Drew assured him. "None of these little beauties is going to the mines or the rendering pot."

Miss Allerton smiled at Drew. "I believe you *must* have a fondness for ponies if you're willing to take the whole lot of them."

"I'm afraid I may not have a choice," Drew said wryly, "now that Kit's seen them. If he's like most boys, he's going to want them all. But he won't be able to ride them all. If the pony he falls in love with isn't the one most suitable for him to ride, he ought to be able to have both."

Suddenly Kit looked up and saw his mother making her way toward the stables. He raced toward her. "Mama! Come look!" He grabbed hold of her skirts with one hand and pointed toward the ponies in the paddock with the other.

Wren smiled at the look of pure joy on Kit's face as he moved closer and closer to the ponies. He tugged on her dress and Wren followed him until they stood side by side, pressed against the fence, admiring the ponies.

"Still think I'm going to disappoint him?"

She was so enthralled by Kit's reaction to the ponies that Wren jumped when she felt a hand on her shoulder and warm breath against her neck. She dropped her knapsack on the ground and reacted automatically, jabbing her elbow as hard as she could into the hard wall of muscle at her back before bracing for retaliation.

He let go of her and grunted in pain. "What the devil was that for?"

"I don't appreciate being frightened out of my wits. I don't like being accosted."

Drew met her searching stare with one of his own. "Accosted?"

She nodded.

He narrowed his gaze. "I didn't accost you. I placed my hand on your shoulder to get your attention."

"I don't like being touched."

"By anyone? Or just me?"

"By strangers."

His voice, when he spoke, vibrated with unspoken emotion. "I'm hardly a stranger, Kathryn."

"I know."

"Then, you don't object to my touch?"

The hopeful note in his voice made her uncomfortable, so Wren ducked her head and evaded his question by saying, "I didn't hear you approach."

"My fault," he told her. "In the future, I'll be sure to make enough noise to make my presence known."

Miss Allerton lifted an eyebrow and looked at Wren askance. They'd been talking from the time they left the mansion until they reached the paddock. He hadn't sneaked up on Wren. She'd simply been so absorbed in her own thoughts and in watching Kit watch the ponies that she hadn't heard any of their conversation or realized he wasn't alone.

Relief spread through Wren's veins when she realized she'd overreacted. She couldn't foresee the moments when blind panic would overtake her, couldn't always keep herself from reacting—or overreacting. But she knew Drew and she knew that no matter how angry or frustrated he was, no matter what he said to the contrary, he would never physically hurt her. He was safe in the way that her father and Bertrand and George had been safe, but he was so much more. He was young and handsome and he made her aware of her body in ways she'd forgotten. He made her want, made her ache with wanting. He made her feel alive and beautiful and desirable for the first time in four years. And she trusted him.

Wren reached up and flung her arms around his neck, hugging him tightly in a spontaneous gesture of joy. "Oh, Drew, you did it! You kept your promise. Thank you so much!"

"You're welcome." Drew returned her embrace. "I asked Miss Allerton to join us for the selection."

Wren felt a flush heat her face. "Oh, Ally, I apologize, I didn't . . ." A feeling of foolishness swept over her as Wren realized she'd flung herself into Drew's arms while Kit, Miss Allerton, Mr. Riley, and several stable hands looked on. She dropped her arms to her sides and would have stepped back, but Drew held her close. Wren pressed her hands against his chest and turned her face away in embarrassment. "I'm so sorry."

"For hugging me or hitting me?" Drew rubbed his ribcage.

She stared up at him, studying his face for any hint of anger. "For hitting you. I didn't mean to hurt you."

"Seeing you smile and having you hug me was worth a moment of pain." He bent to retrieve her knapsack, then straightened to his full height and handed it to her.

She smiled as she accepted the canvas bag and the rest of the world seemed to fade away. It was as if they were the only two people on earth. Drew stood mesmerized by the warm look in her eyes.

"Drew!" Kit tugged on the hem of Drew's jacket and began pointing at each of the ponies, repeatedly asking the same question, "Is he mine?"

Drew looked down at the boy. "That's up to you. Mr. Riley went into the village and collected all the ponies that needed a good home and a little boy to love. These are the ponies he found."

"Truly?" Kit's eyes were as big and round as saucers.

"Truly." Drew grinned.

"Are they all mine?" Kit asked.

Drew looked over at Riley, his head groom. Riley shook his head. "We'll keep the one you like the best and the one best suited for a lesson pony. The rest of them will stay here until we find good homes for all of them."

Kit frowned, clearly not happy with the idea that some of the ponies might go to other homes one day. "What about Mama? She doesn't have a pony. Can she have one?"

"Your mother is welcome to have one of these ponies." Drew met Kathryn's knowing gaze. "If one of them proves to be a suitable mount for her. But," he warned Kit, "she may prefer one of the mares in the stable."

"Mama, which pony do you want?" he asked.

"Kit, darling, Mama doesn't ride," Wren answered.

Drew raised an eyebrow at that. "You don't enjoy riding?"

"It's not that I don't enjoy it," Wren answered a bit defensively. "I like horses and ponies very much. I've just never been around them. I grew up in university towns and my father never owned a horse. We always walked or hired vehicles."

"You can have one to draw," Kit told her.

"That's true," she agreed. "But I don't have to own one to draw it. And it wouldn't be right for me to deprive a pony of a loving little boy or girl who would ride it."

The idea that Kathryn might not know how to ride had never occurred to Drew. He suddenly recalled her London Season and all the times she'd declined his invitations to accompany him on his morning rides in Rotten Row by saying she was sure he would much prefer his friend Julian's company to hers that early in the morning. All the women of his acquaintance were equestriennes. He never dreamed Kathryn wasn't. "I remember inviting you to ride with me in Rotten Row every morning," he said, softly. "And you always refused."

Kathryn didn't answer.

"I thought you were being coy," he continued. "I thought you repeatedly turned me down to whet my appetite so I'd step up my courtship of you."

"I've never been coy," she told him. "Even during my London Season. And while I confess to wanting to whet your appetite, I must admit that I had no idea my refusal to go riding with you might have that effect. You were such an accomplished horseman that I simply couldn't stand the thought of embarrassing you in front of your friends."

Drew looked at her with new eyes. "You don't ride at all?"

Wren bit her bottom lip. "I've never even sat on a horse."

"Then that's something we shall have to remedy." He turned to Riley. "What do you think?"

"Well," Riley said as he took off his cap and scratched his head. "There's Addy. You retired her to stable companion a few years back. She's old and calm, but she can be a mite stubborn and settled in her ways."

"Addy's *too* old and fat and set in her ways," Drew commented. "She's safe, but her top speed is a walk. Mrs. Stafford would be bored to tears. I think Felicity might be a better choice."

Riley agreed. "Aye. Felicity's sweet, well trained, even-tempered, and sure-footed, and she doesn't mind hours under saddle."

"Really, Drew," Wren interrupted, "I don't think that my learning to ride is necessary. Besides, Mr. Riley will have his hands full teaching Kit. I'd just get in the way."

"Oh, no, ma'am." Riley opened the paddock gate and exchanged the Dartmoor for another pony a groom brought forward, this one an old black Shetland pony, with a wide white blaze on his face, white stockings on both back feet, and a small patch of white on his chest. "I won't be teaching the youngster. I'm a trainer, but I'm no equestrian. I'll train the ponies, but Master Andrew—I mean, his lordship will teach young Master Kit and you to ride."

"What about Ally?" Kit turned to his governess. "Are you going to learn to ride, too? Which pony do you want? 'Cause I think that one"—he pointed to the Shetland—"likes me the bestest."

Miss Allerton smiled. "You needn't worry about me choosing that little fellow," she said to Kit.

"Why not?" Kit demanded, indignant at the idea that Ally found his choice lacking.

"Miss Allerton is one of the finest horsewomen in all of England," Drew said. "She needs something bet—bigger—than your old fellow. He's too small to carry an adult."

"Good!" Kit turned to Drew. " 'Cause he's the one I want."

Drew studied the pony. He was old; his face and shaggy black coat were mottled with flecks of white and gray. "He favors my old pony, Galahad. What do you think of him, Riley?"

The groom grinned. "I thought you'd like him." He patted the old pony on the shoulder and gave his ear a fond scratch. "He should look like your old Galahad. He's a good ten years younger than Galahad, but he had the same sire and dam. I found him awaiting a buyer at the stockmen's sale. He's well trained and well mannered for a Shetland, but he's pushing twenty and if he didn't find a buyer . . ." Riley let his words trail off. "His name is Lancelot."

"If he's half as good as Galahad, he'll be the best horse Kit will ever own." Drew blinked quickly to remove the bright sheen in his eyes. "You've made a fine choice, Kit. He's the perfect horse for you. If your mother agrees, then you may have him."

"Please, Mama." Kit turned to her. "Can I keep him?"

"*May* I keep him," Wren corrected automatically.

"May I keep him?"

Wren met Kit's pleading gaze, then turned to meet Drew's equally entreating gaze. "I suppose every little boy ought to have a pony to love and ride and take care of."

"Thank you, Mama!" Kit threw his arms around her legs and hugged her tightly.

"But you must promise to listen to Drew and Mr. Riley while they instruct you and do exactly as they tell you. Agreed?" She loosened Kit's grasp on her legs, then lifted him into her arms so that she could look him in the eyes.

"Agreed," he promised.

"Then, it's settled," Drew pronounced. "We'll put Lancelot through his paces on the ground, then we'll let Kit get the feel of him. And once we're done with Kit, we'll introduce you to Felicity."

"So soon?" There was an edge of fear in Wren's voice.

"There's no time like the present." He turned to his head groom. "We'll need to check to make certain the ladies' saddles are in good repair and in a few days, we'll need to find a child's saddle for Kit."

"I'll set one of the grooms to polishing up Galahad's old saddle."

"You kept it?" Drew was surprised.

"Of course I kept it," Riley said. "I knew we'd have use for it one day. It just needs a bit of polishing. The same goes for the ladies' saddles your mother used. 'Course, I'll have the groom check the rigging just to be sure." He looked at Wren. "Don't worry, missus. Felicity's sweet as an angel. She'll treat you right. We'll have you riding in no time."

"I don't have a riding habit." Wren turned to Drew. "Or boots."

"Your half-boots will be fine," he said. "And we'll have the seamstress make up a habit for you while she's making up one for Miss Allerton and riding breeches for Kit. But you won't need it right away. For now, you can hike up your skirts."

"I couldn't possibly . . ." Wren sputtered.

"Why not?" His expression was one of boyish innocence, but his words were meant for her ears alone. "Are you afraid to reveal more of your infamous artwork?"

"To you?" she snapped. "Yes!"

"But, my dear Kathryn, surely that's why you painted it," he drawled. "After all, art is meant to be seen and enjoyed." A smile played on the corners of his lips. "And I do enjoy it, Kathryn. I enjoy it immensely."

Wren heaved a frustrated sigh. "I wish you would forget you ever saw it."

"Not bloody likely," he murmured, "for I'm not that noble or that forgetful."

Chapter 14

Never promise more than you can perform.
—Publius Syrus, 1st Century b.c.

Despite Drew's intention to begin immediately, the afternoon chill grew decidedly colder and a light mist began to fall. The miserable conditions weren't favorable for the beginning pupils or the instructor, so Drew reluctantly agreed to postpone the lessons until early the following morning.

Wren didn't mind postponing the lessons until morning. In fact, she would not have minded postponing them forever, but Kit was inconsolable. In a show of unyielding determination that would have made the previous fifteen marquesses of Templeston green with envy, Kit refused to leave the stables until he'd had his first riding lesson.

Wren attempted to explain why the lessons would have to wait until morning, but Kit didn't care about explanations. He wanted to ride his pony.

"It's the Ramsey in him," Wren muttered when Miss Allerton tried placating the boy by promising that from

now on, they would begin the day with riding lessons
and leave his schooling until afternoon.

Drew suspected that the governess's last offer was
meant more as a reward for her forbearance than it was
for Kit's cooperation. He watched the negotiations between the child and the two women with a mixture of
amusement, admiration, and impatience. Kit had worked
himself up into a fine temper and showed no sign of
cooperating with his mother or governess. There was
only one thing left to do.

"That's enough!" Drew used the same tone of voice
he'd used on his soldiers.

Kit was stunned into silence. He gave Drew a cautious
look, suddenly unsure of what to do or say. No one had
ever raised their voice or spoken to him so sharply.

Drew addressed the little boy. "Am I to understand
that you refuse to leave the stables and return to the
house with your mother and governess until you've had
your first lesson in horsemanship?"

Kit nodded.

"Speak up," Drew ordered.

"Yes," Kit replied softly.

"Yes, *sir*," Drew corrected.

"Yes, sir," Kit repeated.

"All right, young man." Drew paused to glance at
Riley, then opened the paddock gate and stepped inside.
The light mist had turned into rain and the heavy drops
glistened on Drew's hair. "You shall have your first lesson in horsemanship."

Kit squealed with glee.

"Drew!" Kathryn protested. "You mustn't reward him
for misbehaving. You'll spoil him and encourage his
willful streak."

"I have no intention of rewarding him for misbehaving," Drew told her. "But I do intend to instruct him in his first lesson in horsemanship just as Riley's father instructed me."

"Then I must have my first lesson as well," Kathryn told him.

Drew looked her over from head to toe. The rain was beginning to saturate her pelisse and Kathryn shivered with cold. "I think it best we postpone your lesson until tomorrow when you're more suitably dressed."

Kathryn shook her head. "No. If Kit gets a lesson so do I."

Kathryn might choose to blame Kit's willfulness on his Ramsey forebears, but Drew knew otherwise. Kit's mother was every bit as willful as he was—despite the fact that she was literally shaking in her boots at the prospect of riding a horse. Drew grinned. One couldn't help but admire the measure of undiluted courage concealed beneath her palpable trepidation. "Forgive me for stating the obvious, Kathryn, but Kit has shown a great deal more enthusiasm for learning to ride than you have."

"Nevertheless, I insist."

Miss Allerton studied the battle of wills going on between the three of them—Kit, Mrs. Stafford, and Lord Templeston—and attempted to intervene. "Sir, I must protest. Conducting a lesson in this downpour cannot be safe and you'll all catch your death of cold."

"Not to worry, Miss Allerton," he said. "I assure you there's no danger. We'll be fine. But there's no reason for you to suffer the weather. Why don't you return to the house and ready a hot bath and something to eat for Kit, as he's certain to be tired, hungry, and dirty when we're done. And please, take Mrs. Stafford's knapsack inside with you; she won't need it now. We'll join you when Kit and Mrs. Stafford complete their first lessons."

He turned to Riley. "Clear everything except Lancelot out of the paddock. I'll give Kit ten minutes to get acquainted with the pony, then I'll bring him to you for the remainder of his lesson."

Riley motioned for the grooms to do as Drew instructed.

Moments later Lancelot stood alone in the paddock. Drew leaned across the top rail and lifted Kit over the fence. He taught Kit to introduce himself to the pony, how to stroke his neck, and how to lead him. When he was satisfied that Kit could manage the pony on his own, Drew handed the little boy the lead rope and motioned for him to lead the pony around the paddock. Kit was soaking wet and grinning from ear to ear as he brought the pony back to Drew. "Look at me, Mama!"

"I see you, darling." Wren leaned against the top rail of the fence and watched as Kit proudly led the pony around the small enclosure several more times.

"All right," Drew said. "That's enough for today. Lancelot is tired and hungry."

"No, he's not." Kit poked out his lower lip and threatened another tantrum.

"None of that." Drew squatted on his haunches until he was eye level with Kit. "The first rule of a good horseman is that his horse's comfort always comes before his own. You may not be tired or hungry, but Lancelot is. You only walked as far as the house to the barn, but your pony had to walk all the way from the village and put up with strangers along the way. He's had enough." Drew stood up and patted Kit on the shoulder. "You've done a fine job with the first part of your lesson. I'm proud of you. Now, I'll walk beside you while you lead Lancelot into his new home." He turned when Wren started to follow. "No," he said. "You wait here. I'll bring Felicity. You can get acquainted with her while Kit completes his lesson in the barn."

"Drew, I think I should—"

"Don't think," he said. "I'm the teacher here. Please do as I ask."

"I would if you ever bothered to ask," Wren grumbled.

Drew raised his eyebrow. "What was that?"

"All right," she said. "I'll stay here." She watched as Drew opened the paddock gate and showed Kit how to lead the pony through it. She kept watching, straining to hear the steady stream of questions Kit fired at Drew, as man, boy, and pony disappeared inside the massive stone barn.

Drew emerged from the barn some time later wearing a sealskin cape and with a beautiful bay filly in tow. Wren was immediately impressed by the regal set of Felicity's head and neck and the sweet, intelligent expression in her dark eyes. Wren also noticed that, unlike Lancelot, Felicity carried a saddle. Wren sighed in relief when she realized it was a man's saddle. "She's beautiful."

"Uh-huh," Drew grunted in agreement. He led Felicity into the paddock and motioned for Wren to join them.

Wren hesitated.

"Come meet her, Kathryn," he urged. "She won't hurt you."

Wren entered the paddock and took several steps in Drew's direction. She kept a safe distance from the horse, making no attempt to approach her.

"Kathryn." Drew's voice was gentle, but firm. "You said you liked horses."

"I do."

"Then step closer." He reached out a hand to her and

Wren grasped it. Drew pulled her closer. "I promise Felicity won't hurt you."

Up close, the thoroughbred looked huge and although Felicity had nice eyes, Wren wasn't completely convinced the horse was as gentle as Drew claimed.

"You've been around carriage horses," Drew reminded her. "And I've seen you pet Samson and drive the pony cart. What's frightened you about Felicity?" He brought Wren's hand up and began to stroke Felicity's neck with it.

"She's so much bigger than I expected."

"She's much smaller than a carriage horse."

"I know, but I thought she'd be more the size of Lancelot or perhaps the size of Samson." She shrugged her shoulders. "Besides, carriage horses wear harnesses that are attached to a carriage or a wagon and Samson is harnessed to the pony cart, while she's . . ."

"Wearing a saddle?" he suggested.

Wren nodded. "I thought I would have the same lesson Kit had. I thought I'd pet her and lead her around like Kit did."

"You will." He repeated the lesson he'd given Kit, showing Wren how to introduce herself to the filly, how to pet and how to lead her. As soon as Wren relaxed and began to enjoy the experience, Drew handed her the lead rope and told her to walk Felicity around the paddock.

Wren led the thoroughbred around the paddock until Drew motioned for her to stop. Wren smiled at him, her eyes sparkling with the prospect of more challenges. "Are we going to return to the barn for the rest of my lesson?"

Drew shook his head. "No."

Wren frowned. "But Kit—"

"Kit's a little boy whose first lesson was designed to

teach him to obey instructions and think of his pony before himself. You know the importance of obeying instructions and thinking of your horse before yourself." He opened the paddock gate and motioned for Wren to proceed. "Step through the gate. Felicity knows not to crowd you."

Wren led the horse through the gate and into the stable yard without incident.

"You did very well." Drew followed her into the open yard, where a stable boy appeared almost immediately with a leather bridle. The stable boy gave the bridle to Drew, then reached for Felicity's rope. Wren relinquished her hold on the filly, stepping back out of the way and watching as Drew replaced the horse's halter and rope with a bridle and rein. "The most important thing for you to learn is to trust your instructor, your horse, and yourself—and to enjoy the new experience."

"How?"

"By riding."

"You didn't allow Kit to ride."

"That's because I refuse to reward Kit for bad behavior and because I don't want him on the pony's back until I've seen more of Lancelot's groundwork. I'll allow him to ride when I'm certain Lancelot is safe enough for him." Drew smiled at Wren. "I know Felicity's safe."

"She may not be safe enough for me," Wren said. "I told you that I've never been on a horse." She eyed the leather saddle. "And I've certainly never been astride one."

"It's no different from being astride a man."

Wren gasped. "I've never . . ." She let her words trail off.

"What?" He pretended shock. "Straddled a man?"

She blushed. "This conversation is quite improper."

"So is riding astride," Drew said. "But we aren't going to let a little impropriety stop us." He placed his left foot in the stirrup, swung effortlessly up onto the saddle, and maneuvered Felicity close to the stone mounting block. "Come on, Kathryn," he said. "Gather your skirt in your right hand and climb onto the mounting block."

Wren glanced at the stable boy.

"He won't look," Drew assured her, then he turned to the lad and asked him to close his eyes.

The stable boy did as Drew asked and Wren gathered her skirt in her hand.

Drew eyed the delicate yellow rosebuds painted on Kathryn's black stockings as she climbed onto the mounting block, then shifted his weight, settling as far back on the saddle as possible. "All right," he continued, "move as close to Felicity as you can and turn around."

Wren hesitated.

"Trust me."

Wren turned around. Drew hooked his left arm around her waist and lifted her from the mounting block, across the saddle and onto his lap, cradling her between his arms and against his chest.

"You follow instructions very nicely," he whispered. "The yellow rosebuds are very becoming. I thank you for my extraordinary view of your secret artwork, but you can let go of your skirt now."

Wren let out an outraged gasp and immediately let go of her skirt. "I thought you were going to have me ride astride," she said.

Drew's face glowed with boyish mischief. "I am," he promised, "once we finish our horseback ride."

Chapter 15

License my roving hands, and let them go
Before, behind, between, above, below.

—JOHN DONNE, C. 1572–1631

Wren would recall that rainy afternoon ride through the forests and across the meadows of Swanslea Park for the rest of her life. It would remain firmly embedded in her heart and on her soul as the day she fell in love for the second time in her life.

Drew pulled her close against his body, enveloping the both of them in the generous folds of his sealskin cape. Their clothing was already soaked through, but the cape kept the worst of the cold and rain at bay as they meandered over the estate.

"I never understood the allure of the hunt or of galloping a horse across the meadows," she told him. "I didn't understand the sense of power and freedom being on a horse gives one. Until now."

"Walking a horse doesn't compare to the freedom of galloping it across the meadows on your own, but sitting this way should approximate the feel of riding in a ladies' saddle," Drew told her.

"A ladies' saddle doesn't offer the warmth or the support and protection your body affords," Wren replied.

"No, it won't," he agreed, "but it offers other protection."

"Such as?"

"Well, there's no danger of slipping off." He tightened his arms around her. "Falling backwards, perhaps, but not slipping off." He smiled at the flash of alarm that lit her gray-green eyes. "And there's no danger of anyone taking liberties with your person."

Wren arched her eyebrow in an uncanny imitation of Drew. "I didn't realize I was in danger of having anyone take liberties with my person."

Drew leaned forward and nuzzled her ear. "No one but me."

"Really?" She flirted with him, her voice low and softly seductive. "Tell me, Lord Templeston, if you were to take liberties with my person, what might I expect them to be?"

"If I were to take liberties," he drawled, "I might begin by slipping my hand beneath the folds of this cape so that I might unbutton your pelisse." He followed his words with action. Shifting the rein to his left hand, he bit the fingers of the leather riding glove covering his right hand and pulled it off. He unbuttoned the deep flap pocket on the outside of his cape and shoved the glove into it, then repeated the procedure to remove his other glove. When his hands were bare, Drew carefully eased the right one beneath the folds of the sealskin cape to unbutton Kathryn's pelisse.

Wren captured her bottom lip with her teeth and barely breathed as she waited for Drew to unbutton the last in the long line of onyx buttons fastening her jacket closed.

"And once I freed the buttons from their buttonholes, I might slip my hand inside your pelisse and continue my exploration of your person." His voice rumbled in his chest, his words hypnotic and deeply arousing.

Wren turned until she sat between his legs, her bottom wedged against his groin, her back resting heavily against Drew's chest. Her new position allowed him greater freedom to explore, but her seat was precarious. Wren weighed the impropriety of what she was about to do against the impropriety of what she was allowing him to do.

Sensing her indecision, Drew leaned close and whispered, "There's no one around for miles in any direction except me and I'll not be disclosing your breaches of propriety."

"Bother propriety!" Wren shifted her weight from right hip to left, hiked her skirt as far up as it would go, and maneuvered her right leg over Felicity's neck until she sat straddling the saddle, her legs resting against Drew's on either side of the horse.

"My sentiments exactly." He kissed the back of her neck.

Wren shivered with delight.

"Cold?" he asked.

"Not at all," she replied. "So tell me, Lord Templeston, if you were granted greater liberty to explore my person, what would you expect to find upon it?"

"I would expect to find two of the most extraordinary things any man could hope to find." Drew ran his hand over the front of her gown. The damp muslin clung to her body like a second skin, revealing the intriguing curves and bumps along the way. He paused to toy with the ends of the satin ribbon on the bodice of her gown before he gently palmed her left breast. "There's one." He whispered the words in her ear while he applied firm pressure in a rhythmic circular motion against the hard nub of her nipple. "Standing his post through rain and

chill and deliberate invasion like a good little soldier."
Her clothes created a tantalizing friction as he moved
his hand over her. He ran his thumb over her nipple once
again, then cupped her breast, plumping it, measuring
the weight of it in his hand. Wren groaned her pleasure.

Guiding the horse with his legs, Drew let go of Felicity's rein, shifted his weight in the saddle, and slipped
his left hand inside her jacket. "There's the other one,"
he noted, taking full measure of her other breast. "Just
as straightforward and as steadfast in his duty as his
mate." He pressed the flat of his hand against it and
began to knead it in the same circular motion he'd used
before.

The feeling of pleasure was like nothing she'd ever
experienced except the wondrous feel of her baby at her
breast. She wondered, suddenly, how it would feel to
have Drew suckle at her breasts. The idea released an
embarrassing surge of moist heat in her most feminine
places. Wren pressed against the saddle in an attempt to
assuage the ache.

"So, milady, have you any complaints about the feel
of my hands upon your person?" he asked.

"Only one."

"Indeed?" He flicked his thumbs against the steadfast
soldier and his mate, eliciting a series of husky groans
from her lips. "And what might that be?"

"Only that my clothing prevents me from feeling your
bare flesh upon mine." She broke off the teasing, flir-
tatious banter and replied honestly in a soft, shy tone of
voice.

Drew's groan was louder than any of hers. He was
rigid with desire at the image her words evoked. Drew
shifted in the saddle to relieve the pressure in his groin,
but it did no good. Kathryn snuggled closer; the feel of

her firm, rounded bottom pressed to him was sheer torture.

She closed her eyes and relaxed against his chest. "May I ask you something, Drew? Something personal?"

"Of course."

"Will you promise not to laugh or take offense?"

He smiled. "I'll do my best not to."

"I'm serious, Drew. You must give me your word."

"Not to laugh?"

"Not to mention a word of what I'm about to ask you to anyone. Or to laugh at me for asking."

"All right," he agreed. "You have my word on it." Her willingness to trust him took Drew by surprise. He ceased his exploration of her breasts, but he didn't remove his hands from her jacket. He simply cupped his hands over her.

"I've given birth to a child." She made the announcement as if Kit's birth were a revelation to him.

"Yes, I know," he replied, dryly.

"I carried him in my body and, after he was born, I allowed him to receive nourishment from my breasts."

That was a revelation. Noblewomen didn't feed their own children; they hired wet nurses to handle the chore for them. "And . . ." he prompted.

"I enjoyed it," she whispered. "It gave me the same feelings of pleasure that you're giving me. And I thought . . . I mean . . . I wondered if other people might feel the same way."

"I don't know," he said. "I've never been acquainted with a lady who nursed her own child, so I've never been in a position to ask."

"Oh." She was silent for a moment. "Well, what about you?" she asked. "If you had the opportunity, do you think that you might enjoy—that you might find pleasure in . . ."

"In what? Suckling a child?"

"No, in suckling me."

He didn't think it was possible for his member to become more rigid or insistent upon relief, but Kathryn's question proved him wrong. "God's nightshirt, Kathryn! What kind of question is that to ask a man?"

"An honest one," she said. "I was curious as to whether or not I might be unusual. I know the *ton* frowns upon women who wet-nurse their children. And I've been told that a great many women find it unpleasant, even shocking and revolting. So, I wondered if men . . . if you . . ." Embarrassed, she allowed her words to trail off.

"If I what?" The suspense was killing him. "Come on, Kathryn, say what you want to say. Spit it out. Don't turn missish on me now."

"You give such incredible pleasure with your hands," she said, "that I wondered if the same would be true if you used your mouth and tongue and teeth like a baby does. I wondered if there were men who would consent to perform such an intimate task or if they found the prospect as shocking and unpleasant and revolting as the women of my acquaintance seem to."

Drew didn't laugh out loud, but the relief he felt was so great that he couldn't keep from laughing on the inside—or prevent his body from shaking from the effort of holding it in.

"Drew, you promised!"

"I know. And I'm trying, but I can't believe you don't know the answer to that question."

"I'm gratified to know that you find me so amusing," she snapped.

"I find you desirable," he corrected. "And I'd consider it an honor and a privilege to suckle you." So would most every other man in England, but Drew didn't feel it necessary to reveal that bit of information.

"You would?" Wren heaved a sigh of relief. "You wouldn't find it disgusting or unnatural?"

"I'd find it the most beautiful and natural thing in the world," he assured her. "And if we weren't riding in the rain in plain sight of those tenant cottages"—he nodded toward a row of cottages lining the road that led to the village—"I'd be happy to prove it."

Wren followed his line of vision. They had ridden across the parkland, followed the stream through the forest, and emerged near a group of tenants' houses. "I thought you said we were miles away from anyone."

"We were when I said it, but Felicity took a shortcut when I wasn't paying attention, and now we're within a half mile of those tenant cottages. But don't worry. No one will suspect we're doing anything except riding. You're completely covered."

She glanced down to make sure and discovered that Drew was telling the truth. Her head was bare and her hair was soaked, but his sealskin cape covered her from her neck to her ankles. No one looking at them from a distance would ever suspect that he had his hands on her breasts.

"But," he added, "in order for me to taste you, you would have to face me and I'm afraid we'd both tumble off the horse in the process. But if we attempted it and somehow managed to stay on, there would be no way for me to get to you without concealing myself beneath the folds of my cape or exposing you to other eyes and the elements. And your reputation would be in shreds if anyone happened to see us because there would be no disguising what we were doing."

Wren chuckled. "In case you haven't noticed, my reputation is already in shreds."

"In London, perhaps, but not here." Drew amazed himself by telling her what he'd already realized. "Everyone on Swanslea Park and its environs thinks very highly of you."

"Not everyone."

"Everyone that matters," he amended.

"Despite the fact that I'm the mother of your father's child."

"Yes. Despite even that."

Wren shivered. "Thank you, Drew."

"For what?"

"For saying that and for this afternoon and my riding lesson."

"You're welcome." He ran his right hand down her ribcage and over her firm stomach. "Now, may I ask you something personal?"

Wren braced herself. "Y-yes, of course."

"Has there ever been a time you regretted not marrying me?"

"Every day of the past four years."

"Thank *you*." Drew pulled her closer and hugged her tightly—so tightly that her clothing began to emit an angry-sounding, high-pitched squeal. Felicity reacted to the unfamiliar sound by stamping her feet and taking several sidesteps. Wren held on to Drew for dear life while he withdrew his left hand from the folds of the cape and reined the horse to a stop. Drew took a few precious moments to calm Felicity before asking, "What the devil was that?"

"Erin!" Wren gasped. "Merciful heavens, I forgot about Erin! I put her in the pocket of my pelisse before I left the cottage. We must have dislodged her."

Something furry scrambled over his right forearm and down his hand. "And Erin would be . . . ?"

"Short for *Erinaceus eropaeus.*"

"Which is . . . ?" Struggling to remember his Latin, Drew grabbed the furry creature and pulled his hand out from under his cape. He opened his fist to reveal Erin, curled tightly into a defensive ball, her quills pricking his skin and her teeth firmly clamped in the webbing between his thumb and index finger.

"My hedgehog."

Chapter 16

We attract hearts by the qualities we display;
we retain them by the qualities we possess.
—JEAN-BAPTISTE ANTOINE SUARD

•

"*But of course.*" *Drew threw back his head* and laughed.

"Drew? Are you all right?" Wren reached for the hedgehog and gently pried the animal's teeth out of his hand. "It isn't like her to bite. *Erinaceus eropaeus* are normally quite gentle unless they're frightened."

"I'd venture to say that this one is frightened." He continued to laugh, the sound of it rumbling from deep in his chest before bursting forth in beautiful clear tones.

Drew couldn't seem to stop laughing and Wren couldn't seem to stop apologizing. "I'm so sorry, Drew. I can't imagine why you're laughing. Her teeth are very sharp. I know that must have hurt." Erin relaxed in her hand and Wren reached inside Drew's cape to return the animal to her pelisse pocket.

"It hurt like bloody hell," Drew said, finally able to speak without laughing. "It still hurts." He realized Wren's intent and stopped her. "No, my love, don't put her back in there. Give her to me." He held out his hand for the hedgehog.

Wren hesitated. "Are you certain? She may bite you again."

"I'm not going to hurt her," he said. "And I'm not going to frighten her. I'm simply going to put her in one of my cape pockets. They're deeper. And, more importantly, they're outside your clothing."

"Oh."

"Yes, oh." He carefully placed the hedgehog in the deep outside pocket of his cape, covered her with his leather glove, and buttoned the flap. "She'll be perfectly comfortable in there," he said. "And I'll be safe as well."

"Let me see your hand," Wren said.

Drew held out his hand, splaying his fingers so she could see the hedgehog bite. Erin had bitten through the flesh and it had hurt like the very devil, but he was quite proud of the fact that he'd managed to suppress his automatic urge to fling the creature off his hand and to its death. The wound hadn't ripped. There were only two beads of blood. "I've had worse wounds. I'll live."

Wren cradled his hand in hers as she studied the wound. "If you hadn't removed your riding gloves, she would have bitten the leather and wouldn't have punctured your skin at all."

"If I hadn't removed my riding gloves, I wouldn't have been able to feel you nearly as well. Suffering an *Erinaceus eropaeus* bite is a small price to pay for the pleasure of caressing you." He wiggled his fingers. "No damage done. They all work."

Wren wiped the droplets of blood away with the pad of her thumb, then pressed a kiss in the palm of his hand. "There," she pronounced when she lifted her head. "All better."

Drew closed his fist around the kiss and held it while

it worked its way from his hand to his heart. "I haven't had a kiss to make a hurt all better since I informed my mother that young men didn't need them." He snorted. "I believe I was ten at the time."

"Poor Lady Templeston," Wren said. "How that must have wounded her. I know it will break my heart the day Kit decides that he's too old for my hugs and kisses."

"Kit will never grow too old for your hugs and kisses. I pray to God that we'll somehow be able to make him understand that." Drew slipped his hand inside the seal-skin cape and placed it against her stomach.

"Oh, Drew," she whispered. "All boys go through a period of thinking that they're too old to be kissed and cuddled—especially by their mothers."

"But it's their mothers they cry for when they're lying wounded and dying in the mud and gore on the battlefield." Drew shook his head in a vain effort to dislodge the battlefield memories stored there. "You can't imagine, and I pray you never know, what it's like to hear thousands upon thousands of young men crying for their mothers. I don't think I'll ever forget it," he said softly. "The sound of all those men and boys calling for their mothers in English and French and German and Spanish and Italian. I never heard a single soldier call for any father—except the heavenly one. They all cried for their mothers and I'm afraid the memory of it is going to stay with me forever." Drew closed his eyes and leaned his forehead against the top of Kathryn's head.

"I prayed for you," Kathryn said softly. "I prayed that you would return home safe and sound."

"And so I have."

"But not without scars."

"Physical scars are the least of what I brought home with me," Drew said. "The memories, the nightmares, the fear—the guilt—are far worse than scars. I returned to England and was hailed a hero, but I still wake up shaking at night." He gave a little snort of derision. "Some hero. For the first two years after Waterloo, I spent every waking moment that I wasn't taking care of Julian, or overseeing his care, drinking myself into a stupor so I could forget. I still drink when I can't sleep. Ironically, my drink of choice is French brandy."

Wren took a deep breath. "I'll listen if you want to talk about it."

"War's not a topic a man should discuss with . . ." He almost said the words *his love*. "The fairer sex."

"I understand," Wren murmured. "I suppose it's something you could only talk about with your father, your confessor, or fellow soldiers and close friends."

"I never discussed it with my father and I haven't spoken about it with any of the other people you mentioned—with my confessor, my fellow soldiers, or my closest friend. Especially not my closest friend, for he knows all too well the horrors of war."

"Yes, I suppose he must." Kathryn's words were spoken so softly Drew barely heard them.

He didn't reply. Wren leaned against his chest. Drew held her close as he guided Felicity back around the parkland. It was raining harder, but they continued to ride in companionable silence until Drew began to talk.

The words seemed to pour out of him as he told Kathryn of the nightmare of war, the battles he'd survived and the horrors he'd endured. It was the first time he'd ever spoken to anyone about the things that lived in his memory and haunted his dreams at night. Drew exhaled when he finished relating his experiences, more relaxed and at ease with himself than he had been in years. He knew the memories would stay with him for the rest of his life, but he could make peace with them now. He

could come to terms with what he'd seen and done in
the name of war and eventually Drew knew that he
would manage to sleep soundly once again. Kathryn
would never be able to banish the pain he carried with
him, but she had been willing to share it and that meant
all the difference to a man who had spent the past four
years refusing to live the life he'd had spared.

"All better," he said, at last.

"Without a single hug or kiss," she teased.

"With something even more powerful than a hug or
a kiss," Drew said. "The compassion of a very special
woman." He leaned forward and kissed her neck. "I wish
to God I could go back to that day when I was ten and
let my mother kiss away the pain of that childhood
scrape. I wish I could tell her I'm sorry for hurting her."
He swallowed hard, once and then once more. "I wish
I could tell her how much I loved her."

"You already have," Wren said. "She hears you,
Drew. She knows what's in your heart."

"Perhaps," he admitted. "But I should have told her
then. I should have let her hug me and kiss me all she
wanted. I should have collected as many of her hugs and
kisses as I could, so I'd have more of them to remember
now that she's gone. I shouldn't have shrugged out of
her embrace and pushed her away."

"She forgave you the moment you did it."

"How can you be so sure?"

"Because I'm a mother," Wren told him. "And that's
what mothers do."

"I should have persisted with you, too," Drew whispered against her wet hair. "I should have waited at your
front door until you agreed to see me or else broken it
down and gone in anyway. I should have done more,
Kathryn. I gave up too easily. I ran away with Wellington and his army instead of staying in London with you."

"I wasn't your responsibility."

"You were the woman I loved, the woman I was going to marry."

"I was the woman who stood you up in front of the whole of London. You had every right to sue me for breach of promise."

"I thought about it," he admitted. "But what good would dragging both our names through the mud have done? I didn't feel the need to supply the ton with more fodder for gossip and I certainly didn't need to sue you for money. I had plenty of money. What I didn't have was you. And you're the only thing I wanted, Kathryn."

"I'm sorry I failed you, Drew."

Drew inhaled, then slowly expelled the breath. "I know you didn't do it on a whim to hurt me, Kathryn. I know something happened that made you feel as if you had no other choice." The moment he said the words, he knew they were true. The pain and the anger he'd carried since his wedding day lingered like the smoke from a flame, but it wasn't quite as acrid as it had once been. The lacerations on his heart were still evident, but the bleeding had finally slowed to a trickle. Time with Kathryn might one day provide the miracle cure he'd been searching for. "I only hope that one day you'll trust me enough to tell me what it was."

"Oh, Drew," she whispered in a voice thick with tears and trembling in pain.

"It's all right," he told her. "You don't have to tell me anything until you're ready. And whenever you're ready to tell me, I'll be ready to listen." He squeezed Wren tightly. "It's time to go home." Drew turned Felicity toward home.

Wren nodded.

"I usually ride alone every morning before breakfast," he told her. "If you'd like to join me."

"Will I have to ride my own horse?"

Drew shook his head. "Until you gain a bit of experience in sitting a horse, I think this might be the best way for you to ride."

"Then I'd be delighted to join you."

"There is one other thing I'd ask of you," he drawled.

"What is that?" Wren turned to meet his gaze.

"Your word of honor that you won't ask any other man if he'd enjoy tasting your breasts." The look he gave her made Wren hot all over. "That's one honor I want reserved exclusively for me."

"When?" she asked breathlessly.

"Any time you'd like," he answered. "I'll always make myself available for that."

Chapter 17

While the boy is small you can see the man.

—ENGLISH PROVERB

Kit came running out of the stable as soon as Drew and Wren rode up. "Mama, Mama, did you get to ride your horse?"

Riley grabbed Kit by his shirttail to slow him down and keep him from startling Felicity.

"I certainly did," Wren called down to Kit.

"By yourself?" Kit asked.

Wren shook her head. "Oh no, his lordship rode me around."

"Was anything amiss, my lord?" Riley asked.

"No," Drew answered succinctly as the groom reached up to help Wren dismount.

"You were gone so long I was afraid Felicity might have stumbled in a foxhole or thrown a shoe," Riley said.

"Felicity is fine, Riley," Drew told him, swinging down from the saddle and handing over the reins. "Mrs. Stafford and I covered the estate. That's all. What about

Kit?" He ruffled the boy's hair. "How did he do on his first lesson?"

"He did very well," the groom answered. "His governess came to collect him from the barn about an hour ago, but he begged her to let him stay until you got back."

Kit grabbed Drew by the hand. "Come look, Drew. You, too, Mama. Come see what I did." Kit pulled Drew down the aisle of the barn, pointing out the horses in each of the stalls until he reached Lancelot's. Wren followed close behind. "This is Lancelot's stall. See?" Kit bounced up and down on the balls of his feet, trying to see through the bars in the stall. "And that's Jem." He pointed to a stable boy cleaning the last stall. The boy looked to be about eleven or twelve. "He helped me groom Lancelot and clean his stall," Kit was saying, "and then I helped him to clean two other stalls."

Drew made a big show of inspecting the stalls Kit had helped clean and of checking to see that Lancelot had been properly groomed and fed and watered. He lavished praise on Kit for his hard work and on Jem for taking Kit under his wing and teaching him the proper way to care for his pony.

Wren smiled at Kit. He was filthy, covered from head to foot in dirt, and he smelled of horse droppings, but he was dancing with excitement and grinning from ear to ear.

"You helped clean three stalls?" Wren asked him.

Kit nodded. "Mr. Riley says a true horseman must learn to take care of his horse before he earns the right to ride him."

Wren looked at Drew with renewed admiration. "Kit's first lesson in horsemanship was mucking out stalls?"

Drew winked at her. "As was mine when I decided

to throw a tantrum in order to persuade Riley's father to let me ride Galahad. Riley and I were no older than Kit is now. Riley's father was head groom here and he put the both of us to work brushing horses and cleaning stalls. Do you remember, Riley?"

"Yes, sir. My pa began every riding lesson with a lesson in mucking and grooming."

"Mama?" Kit asked. "You can help me 'n' Jem clean Felicity's stall if you like."

Wren smiled at her son. "I'd love to help you and Jem clean Felicity's stall." She turned to follow Kit to the stall Jem was cleaning.

"Oh, no, you don't." Drew took Wren by the hand. "You may be wearing black, but it isn't suitable for stable work. And those"—he pointed to her half-boots— "will be ruined in a matter of minutes." He bent low in order to look Kit in the eye. "Why don't we wait until your mother isn't dressed in her fine ladies' clothes?"

Kit frowned.

"You can teach her how to muck stalls after your riding lesson tomorrow morning," Drew told him.

"All right," Kit agreed. He looked up at his mother. "Are you going to wear a dress tomorrow, too?"

Wren nodded. "Ladies aren't allowed to wear anything but dresses."

Kit turned to Drew, a serious look on his face. "All my mama's dresses look like that." He pointed to Wren's mourning dress. "Will I still get to teach her how to muck the stalls?"

"Of course." Drew bit the side of his cheek to keep from smiling. "I'll see what I can do about finding your mama something other than ladies' dresses to wear."

"You promise?" Kit fixed his gaze on Drew's face.

"I promise." Drew crossed his heart. "Now, it's time

for us to return to the house for tea. Say good night to Jem and Mr. Riley and Lancelot."

"Do I have to?"

"I'm afraid so," Drew told him. "Because I'm sure Miss Allerton has a hot bath and supper waiting for you."

" 'Night, Jem," Kit called. " 'Night, Mr. Riley." He stood on tiptoes to see into Lancelot's stall, but the pony was too short. Wren was about to hoist Kit high enough to see through the stall bars when he turned to Drew. "Drew, will you hold me up so's I can say good night to Lancelot?"

Wren's heart caught in her throat as Drew lifted Kit into his arms. Kit wrapped his arms around Drew's neck and rested his head against Drew's. The resemblance was uncanny. There was no denying the fact that those two were closely related. Kit was a blond miniature of Drew. Anyone seeing them together that way would naturally assume they were father and son. Tears burned in Wren's throat and shimmered in her eyes. If things had worked out differently four years ago, they might have been.

"Mama! Come look!" Kit turned and reached out a hand to her. "Lancelot is eating."

"Which is exactly what you should be doing," she said, stepping forward to join Kit and Drew as they stood watching the Shetland pony devour a mouthful of grain.

Kit started to protest, but Drew stopped him with a look. "What did I say was the second rule of good horsemanship?"

"All good horsemen do what you say," Kit recited.

"And what did I ask you to do?"

"Mind my mother and Ally," Kit answered.

Wren glanced over Kit's head to smile at Drew.

Drew winked back at her. "Good boy. Now, say good night to your pony," he instructed, " 'cause I'm as hungry as a bear." Drew pretended to roar like a bear and Kit dissolved into a fit of giggles.

"Good night, Lancelot." He waved to his pony. "Come on, Mama. We have to go home now 'cause me and Drew are hungry as bears!" Kit did his best to imitate Drew's great roar and the contest to see who could roar the loudest began.

Drew won. But only because Kit fell asleep against his shoulder before they reached the house.

"Wait, Drew." Wren stood in the threshold of the main house. "Let me take him from here," she said. "You're soaked. You'll drip water all over the floor."

"Hang the floor," he pronounced. "You're as wet as I am. And he's too heavy for you to be carrying up and down the stairs." He flashed his most devastating smile at her. "Don't worry, Kathryn, I won't drop him. I'm very good with my hands."

"You're incredibly good with your hands," she agreed with a smile. "And I appreciate your help, but it isn't necessary. Ally and I are quite capable of putting Kit to bed."

"That goes without saying, Kathryn, but the fact is that I see no reason why you and Miss Allerton should have all the fun when I'm perfectly willing to do my part." He nudged Wren forward, then followed her into the house and up the stairs to the nursery where Ally was waiting.

The governess took one look at her charge and gave Drew a knowing smile. "I prepared a bath for him, but I don't see the sense of waking him when he's this tired. Put him down on his bed." She reached for a bathing cloth and dipped it into a small tub of water. Drew placed Kit in the center of his bed, then stepped back out of the way. Wren removed Kit's dirty clothes while Ally quickly washed as much dirt as she could off him and buttoned him into a clean nightshirt. "Tell me, my lord, is there any muck left in the stables or has he brought it all with him?"

Drew laughed. "There's a little left. Kit insisted on saving some for his mother to shovel in the morning."

"Really?" Ally glanced at Wren.

"Yes, indeed," Wren confirmed. "He's to teach me how to muck stalls after our riding lesson tomorrow."

"Well," Ally said, clucking her tongue in satisfaction, "he had a grand time then." She sighed. "He's all boy, after all. I must admit I've been worried about Kit's lack of a masculine influence."

"You've worried needlessly," Drew told her. "Young Master Kit set a new all-time record for Ramsey heirs. He groomed his pony and helped clean three stalls. I only managed to help clean one and a half when I was his age."

Miss Allerton was properly impressed. "Then it's no wonder he fell asleep! We'll celebrate the accomplishment in the morning." She focused her gaze on Drew and then on Wren. "I can take care of things here. And, if you don't mind me saying so, your lordship, you and Mrs. Stafford should get out of those wet clothes and into warm baths yourself."

Wren leaned over the bed and placed a kiss on Kit's forehead. "Good night, sweetheart." She tucked the covers around him. "Sleep tight." She straightened, said good night to Ally and Drew, and left the nursery.

Drew caught up with her on the stairs. "Where are you going?"

"To the cottage."

"It's raining again."

"A little more rain won't hurt me," she told him. "I'm

already wet and I've got to see to the animals."

"The animals can wait until morning. Why don't you make use of your room here and forgo the rainy journey across the garden?"

Wren frowned at him.

Drew shoved his fingers through his wet hair. "I know there's a room kept in readiness for you here," Drew said. "Mrs. Tanglewood told me that my father asked her to keep one ready for you to use whenever you wanted it. Why go back to the cottage at all? Wouldn't you like to be closer to Kit?"

Wren nodded. "I'd love to be closer to Kit, but I gave George my word that I'd give Kit more independence by allowing him to stay in the nursery with Ally."

Drew was puzzled. "Why did he ask you to do that?"

"Because he was afraid that I doted on Kit more than I should and that hovering over him every moment of the day wasn't healthy for either one of us." She made a face. "And he was right. Kit has blossomed under Ally's care. He's become a lively little boy instead of an anxious, fretful one. I'm so proud of his progress."

"That's all the more reason for you to go back upstairs, take off those wet things, and soak in a hot bath. You'll be here first thing in the morning to help him celebrate his accomplishment." He gave her his most persuasive smile. "I'm having a bath sent up to my room. It's just as easy for the maids to bring up hot water for two baths as for one. If you return to the cottage, you'll have to heat and haul all that water yourself."

She showed no sign of capitulating so Drew added, "I'll send someone to ask Isley to take care of your menagerie for you."

"Please don't," Wren said. "He's getting old. I'd hate to have him come out in the rain on my account."

"Then I'll go with you."

"Drew, thank you, but it's not necessary."

"I'll help you tend your menagerie and then we'll return here for hot baths and dinner."

"I don't think that's such a good idea."

"But I do," he insisted. "And it will give me a few moments to speak privately with you. I have a favor to ask of you."

"What is it?" she asked.

Drew smiled. "I'll tell you on the way to the cottage."

Chapter 18

After kissing comes more kindness.

—ENGLISH PROVERB

"*What was the favor?*" Wren turned to Drew as soon as they entered the cottage. Margo yipped a greeting and padded over to welcome them before she raced out the front door, down the gravel path through the garden, making a beeline to the kitchen of the main house. Drew closed the front door behind her, then leaned against it, waiting as Wren lit the lamps to dispel the evening gloom. Soon the cottage was alive with activity—the chirps and squeaks of the animal inhabitants and the rustle of bedding and of tiny feet scurrying across the floors of their houses.

"This," Drew murmured. He didn't wait for her answer; he simply took her into his arms.

The touch of his lips against hers set Wren's heart racing and her nerves jangling. She leaned into him, wrapped her arms around his neck, and tilted her head back to better accommodate him. Drew cupped one of her breasts in his hand as he teased the seam of her lips with his tongue, tasting, probing until she parted her lips and allowed him entrance.

Wren shivered as Drew used his tongue to woo her. He deepened his kiss. Wren tasted him, feeling the roughness of his tongue as he raked the warm recesses of her mouth and taught her tongue how to answer his demands. She lost herself in his kiss—lost herself in the warmth of him, the scent of him, the feel of his hard body pressed to hers. If kissing was an art, Drew was the master of it and she his most avid and ardent student, willingly learning everything he wanted to teach her.

Wren burrowed her fingers into the thick hair at the nape of his neck and held on—wanting more of him, needing more of him. Overwhelmed by her response to his unexpected kiss, surrounded by his arms, his mouth, his hard masculine body and the taste and touch and smell of him, Wren melted against him. She inhaled his scent and nuzzled closer to its source. Drew groaned again. Wren tilted her head back as Drew brushed his lips against her closed eyelids before trailing down her neck to place hot, wet kisses behind her ear on the spot where her pulse hammered to keep pace with her raging emotions. He darted his tongue into the warm recesses of her ear and Wren gasped in reaction, tightening her grip around his neck when her legs abruptly refused to support her weight.

Suddenly, Drew broke the kiss. His breathing was heavy and irregular and his heart seemed to beat at a much faster rate than normal as he backed up a few steps to put some distance between them. Drew stared down at her. She was so beautiful. More beautiful now than she'd been as a girl. He was amazed that he'd nearly forgotten how beautiful. Her lips were red and swollen from his kisses, the expression in her gray-green eyes

slightly dazed, dreamy, and emotional. She looked as
thoroughly kissed and as well loved as a new bride—
even the creamy skin of her cheeks was suffused with
color and slightly abraded by his unshaven jaw.

"Well," he breathed. "I've waited all afternoon to do
that." He reached out his index finger to gently trace a
line along her cheekbone. "And it was well worth the
wait."

"That was the favor?" Wren asked when she'd caught
her breath and collected her wits well enough to give
voice to the thought. Because kissing him or allowing
him to kiss her was a favor Wren was more than willing
to grant on a daily basis.

"One of them. I have another to ask of you."

"Anything."

Drew smiled down at her, but the expression in his
eyes was serious as he touched her on the nose with the
tip of his index finger. "Where's your sense of prudence?
Don't be so eager to agree until you hear what it is."

"All right. What is it?" Wren asked as she turned to
feeding and watering the animals and tidying their cages.

Drew reached into the pocket of his cape and retrieved
Erin. He offered the hedgehog to Kathryn. "I believe
you're missing one."

Wren took Erin from him and placed the hedgehog in
her pen for the night. "You said you had another favor
to ask," she prompted.

"What about Margo?" Drew changed the subject.
"Are you sure you should let her out?"

Wren nodded. "She won't be gone long. It's raining
and Margo hates rain."

"Where does she go?"

"To your house," Wren said. "Cook puts out a nice
supper for her every evening. Margo knows to go to the
kitchen at the mansion. When she's done eating, she

patrols the garden, then returns to the cottage and her basket." She pointed to the basket near the fireplace, then walked across the main salon and down the short hall to the cottage kitchen, where she unlatched a small hinged door cut into the larger kitchen door. It was large enough for a fox or a small terrier to go through, but too small for larger animals. "Mr. Isley put it in for me," she explained, "so Margo could come and go." She turned to face him. "Now, what's the other favor?"

"I'd like you to accompany me to the village tomorrow afternoon. I've an appointment with Reverend Pool and I'll need to see the undertaker, Mr. Smalley, to make arrangements for the funeral procession." He paused. "I've handled a great many things in my life, but nothing like this. I have no idea how to go about it or what must be done and I thought that you . . ."

"There must be someone else you'd rather have accompany you." A shaft of disappointment so keen she could taste it shot through her. She didn't know exactly what favor she'd hoped he would ask of her, but Wren knew it had nothing to do with a trip to the village to confer with the local rector or the undertaker.

She opened the back door and stepped out into the rainy night. Drew followed close on her heels.

"Whom would you suggest? Newberry? Mrs. Tanglewood? Miss Allerton?" he demanded.

"Ally is a lady," Wren replied. "She is the younger daughter of a viscount."

"She's also in service. I need someone who is not."

"Don't you have any friends in the county?"

"If I did, I've lost touch with them," he answered. "I haven't been to Swanslea in four years." Drew studied the expression on her face. "What about you? Do you have any friends in the county?"

"Only Ally."

Drew raked his fingers through his hair. "I cannot take Miss Allerton with me to visit the rector or the undertaker. She's a governess in my employ and she's unmarried. There is no one left to ask."

"Except me." Wren knew it was unreasonable to feel hurt at being asked because he'd run out of choices, especially when she didn't want to go. But it hurt all the same. "And I'm . . ." She bowed her head, unable to meet his gaze.

"You're a widow," he pronounced. "But you were also my father's . . ." He cleared his throat and tried again. "Friend. I thought that since you and my father were . . . close . . . you might want to play a part in the process." Drew lifted her chin with the tip of his finger and looked her in the eye.

"I thought you came to Swanslea to prevent me from playing a part in the process," Wren reminded him. "I believe you said you couldn't have one of George's mistresses presiding over the funeral of another." She followed the gravel path around the cottage toward the mansion.

Drew overtook her on the path, his longer strides covering more ground than hers. He took hold of her elbow and forced her to look at him. "I did. Because I wanted to avoid more scandal. But I've never planned a funeral or had cause to deal with an undertaker, whereas you—"

Wren cut him off. "Have a great deal of experience planning funerals."

"I didn't mean to sound callous," Drew said.

"But that's what you thought?" She looked up at him. He nodded. "I'm afraid so."

"Well, why shouldn't you think that? I've been in mourning almost as long as Kit's been alive. I've arranged the funerals of my husband, my father, my aunt, my s . . ." Tears of self-pity stung her eyelids and clogged her throat. "My son has never seen me in any color but black." She wiped her eyes with the back of her hand. "There's no doubt that I have a fair amount of experience with funerals. It's been so long since I've worn colors that I don't remember what it was like."

Drew reached inside his coat, pulled a handkerchief of fine Irish linen from his waistcoat pocket, and handed it to her. "I remember how you looked," he told her gently. "You were beautiful. You wore thin muslin dresses in soft colors. Rose pink, blue the color of robins' eggs, butter yellow, and apple green. I remember them all—especially that pure white one you wore to the countess of Beresford's ball the first time I saw you and that incredible silver tissue dress you wore to Vauxhall two nights before our wedding day."

"The night you were recalled to the War Office."

He reached out and brushed away a wisp of dark blond hair that had stuck to her damp cheek. "Yes," he said. "The night Lieutenant Colonel Grant summoned me to the War Office to help decipher messages that helped reveal Bonaparte's plan of campaign." The expression in his eyes softened. "I knew I could count on my father to see you and your aunt safely home, but leaving you at the concert that night was the hardest thing I'd ever done."

She whispered her reply so softly, Drew strained to hear her. "Was it?"

He nodded. "Yes, it was." He thought that leaving her that night was even harder than standing alone at the altar two days later. Not because he hadn't trusted Kathryn, but because he'd known from the moment he left her that he'd made a terrible mistake. Drew remembered the overwhelming feeling of resentment and a tremendous sense of foreboding he'd felt at being forced to answer his commanding officer's summons almost literally on the eve of his wedding—especially since his commanding officer had kept him waiting for nearly two hours after issuing that urgent summons and had seemed more than a little surprised to see him at all.

It was ironic when Drew thought of how many times he'd contemplated returning to Vauxhall to collect her before he reached Grant's office. Another war with France was looming on the horizon and although he was marrying Kathryn in two days' time, Drew had been very much afraid that his dream for their future together was slipping out of his grasp.

"For years, I've blamed you for what happened to us," he said. "But now, I can't help thinking that if I'd gone back for you at Vauxhall our lives would be different now."

Wren understood what he was asking even though he didn't ask. "Yes," she agreed. "Our lives would have been very different."

He waited for her to continue, to reveal her secret, her reason for leaving him waiting at the altar, but she didn't say anything more and because he had promised patience, Drew was willing to wait. "Then I'm doubly sorry," he said. "But I want you to know that while you were beautiful then, you're more beautiful now. I don't mean to say that black suits you," he hastened to add. "Only that it does you no harm. Colorful dresses could never make you more beautiful to me than you already are."

"Thank you, Drew." She stood on tiptoe to press her lips against his.

Her spontaneous gesture surprised and pleased him. He would have preferred a real kiss from her instead of a chaste peck on the corner of his mouth, but Kathryn hadn't initiated a kiss with him in four years and Drew was willing to take what she offered. He waited until she stepped back, then touched the corner of his mouth with his fingers. "Was that a yes?"

Wren shook her head. "That was a thank-you."

"Oh."

"But since I can't bear to think of you alone and at the mercy of Mr. Smalley, I'll accompany you into the village. On one condition."

"What condition?"

"That you leave me plenty of time to bathe and dress before we visit the rector." She smiled impishly. "I have a riding lesson in the morning and a stable mucking lesson afterward."

"I'll have you in the bath in plenty of time," Drew promised, leaning forward to place a kiss on the corner of *her* mouth. "Thank you, Kathryn. Now, let's follow Margo's example and get out of the rain and find our supper." He started to reach for her elbow again, but thought better of it and reached for her hand instead.

He was still holding her hand when they entered the house and he didn't let go until they parted company at the top of the stairs.

Chapter 19

If all the world and love were young,
And truth in every shepherd's tongue,
These pretty pleasures might me move
To live with thee, and be thy love.

—SIR WALTER RALEIGH, 1552–1618

Wren emerged from her bedroom before sunrise the following morning and ventured downstairs to break her fast. She shuddered involuntarily as she passed the rooms that were normally designated as the twin salons and the music room. The doors connecting those massive rooms had been folded back to form a ballroom. The furnishings in the music room, including the pianoforte and harp, had been removed to other parts of the house and nearly every inch of the polished wood floor that made up the area of the ballroom had been covered in thick carpets to muffle sound. The massive dining table was draped in black crepe and placed in the center of the room to form a bier for George's coffin.

"You're up early."

Wren turned to her left and found Drew standing in the doorway of the breakfast room, a cup and saucer in hand.

"You said you usually rode early in the morning."

He stepped back to allow her entrance and caught a whiff of her perfume. "So I did." Drew refilled his cup from a silver pot on the buffet, then set it down and picked up another cup and saucer. "Coffee?"

"No, thank you." Wren approached the buffet. "I don't care for the taste. I prefer tea." She glanced at him from beneath the cover of her lashes. "Unless I'm feeling wildly decadent—then I prefer hot chocolate with whipped cream in bed."

Drew lifted a smaller silver pot from a warmer and filled the cup with steaming hot chocolate. He added a dollop of whipped cream, stirred it with a cinnamon stick, and handed it to her. He picked up his cup of coffee and raised it in salute. "Here's to feeling decadent."

"I'm impressed," Wren murmured, "but you forgot the most important element of feeling decadent."

"And that is . . . ?" He drank from his cup and returned it to the saucer sitting on the table beside his plate.

"Indulging in hot chocolate with whipped cream without leaving the comfort of one's bed." She savored the aroma, then took a sip of her chocolate.

"I didn't forget," he told her, the look in his eyes betraying a sudden smoldering surge of pure desire. "But I thought it best if we saved that particular form of indulgence for another morning."

The expression he gave her sent a wave of heat through her body. Wren blushed and tried to cover her reaction by turning her attention to her drink. She gulped the liquid, her hands shaking so badly that she bumped the rim of the cup against her teeth, spilling chocolate down her chin and creating a whipped cream mustache on her upper lip. She lowered her cup, rattling it against the saucer as she placed it in the center depression.

"All done?" he asked.

Wren nodded.

"Then allow me." He took her cup and saucer from her and set it aside before he stepped closer, ducked his head, and licked the drops of chocolate from her chin and the froth of creamy whipped cream from her top lip.

Wren felt the heat from his body, but it was nothing compared to the heat of his mouth. Her whole body quivered as he removed the last bit of cream from her lips before nipping at the bottom one, encouraging her to open her mouth. And when she complied, he deepened his kiss.

She marveled at the unique flavor of his kiss. It tasted of coffee—a taste she'd never learned to appreciate—and Drew Ramsey, a taste she appreciated more than any other. She felt the rasp of his tongue against her teeth as it slipped between her lips into her mouth. She understood the urgency of his mouth and echoed it, moving her lips under his, allowing him greater access.

Wren moved her own tongue, experiencing the jolt of unadulterated pleasure as it found, and mated with, Drew's. She tightened her grip on his wide shoulders, drawing tiny circles against the fabric of his riding coat, and then trailed her fingers up the column of his neck, burying them in his thick salt-and-pepper hair.

Drew caressed her back. The cloth of her borrowed riding habit frustrated him. He wanted to feel the softness of her flesh beneath the layers of clothing. He wanted to move his hands over her, count her ribs, and test the weight of her wonderful, pear-shaped breasts, but all he could really feel was clothing. Too much clothing, masking the curves pressed against him. He moved his hand down her back, over one firm buttock, to the back of her thigh and back up again, resting the palm of his hand against the curve of her bottom while his mouth ate at hers. Over and over again.

Drew stopped kissing her mouth only long enough to press warm, wet kisses against her jawline, her neck, and beneath one ear.

Hot, breathless, and light-headed, Wren turned her face toward his and sought his mouth once more.

Drew took that as a sign of encouragement. He became bolder, his kisses more fervent.

"What are you doing?" she murmured against his lips.

"I want to touch you," Drew groaned. "I want to undress you and spend the morning kissing you all over. Your lips, your eyes, your breasts." Belatedly realizing that he was kissing Kathryn in the breakfast room in full view of anyone who happened to be up and about, Drew untangled her arms from around his neck and stepped back to look at her. His dark brown eyes lingered on each part of her he listed. "But I believe we have a date to go riding."

His grin was so wickedly inviting Wren thought that she might agree to let him take her riding to the ends of the earth as long as he continued to kiss her.

He shuddered, fighting to regain control of raging desire while he sought a safer subject. "Did I tell you that you look as fetching this morning as you taste?"

Wren did her best to hide her disappointment that he had stopped kissing her. "Thank you for the compliment, my lord, but I think you rush to judgment." She glanced at him from beneath her lashes, encouraging him to resume his kisses with a bit of flirtation. "For there are parts of me you've yet to taste."

He was rock hard in an instant. "That color suits you."

"Thank you again for the compliment and for providing the riding dress." She wore an old-fashioned riding dress in burgundy with gray velvet lapels, a high waist, a double plaiting of Valenciennes lace around the neck, and a row of tiny dyed-bone buttons in the front.

Drew had retrieved the garment from a cedar-lined trunk in his mother's bedroom before he retired for the night. He'd had the garment aired and pressed and laid out for Wren to find when she awoke. The dress had included a pair of gray riding breeches to be worn under it and matching gloves and a pair of purple Spanish riding boots. Kathryn wasn't wearing the gloves or the purple boots, having chosen her black half-boots instead, and Drew sincerely hoped she had forsaken the breeches as well.

"It's years out of fashion," Drew admitted, "but it was the only one of my mother's habits that I could find that wasn't black." *It was also one of the few that buttoned in the front instead of the back.*

"Who cares how out of fashion it is?" she asked. "It's *burgundy*. Oh, Drew, it's so nice to wear something with color. I'll destroy what's left of my reputation and scandalize the county if anyone sees me, but it's worth it."

Privately, Drew thought that the color of her dress would cause less of a scandal than some of the things they'd already done. It would certainly cause less of a scandal than what he planned to do once he had her on his horse and in his arms. *If* he got her on his horse and in his arms. His current state of arousal made the idea of mounting a horse and sitting a saddle painful. "The reason I generally ride at the crack of dawn is because there are fewer people about. Riley will see you, of course, and perhaps one of the other grooms, but Riley's an old friend and the soul of discretion and I'm sure the rest of the staff will prove just as close-mouthed."

She smiled. "I've no regrets about agreeing to ride with you. I only regret the fact that the purple boots didn't fit." Wren held out her hands. "I thought my hands were small, but I feel like an Amazon compared to your mother. The gloves and boots were too small and the breeches were too big."

"I don't remember her being quite as slender of build as you are," Drew said. "I can't say I regret the breeches, but I'm truly sorry about the boots because I'm afraid your boots will be ruined."

"I'm sorry, too." She had confined her hair into a slick chignon, but several unruly curls had escaped and fallen onto her forehead. Wren shoved her hair off her face and laughed. "You can't imagine how much I looked forward to wearing those purple boots. I became enamored of them the moment I saw them."

"Do that again," Drew ordered suddenly.

"Do what?" She put her hand up to her forehead to check for more stray curls.

"Laugh," he said. "I always loved the husky sound of your laughter and you don't seem to do it as often as I recall."

Wren was thoughtful. "No, I don't guess I do, but the world is a different place now and I'm not the girl you knew. I've been in mourning for nearly four years and nearly everyone I cared about is gone. There wasn't much for me to laugh about." *And no one to share it with.*

"I've missed hearing it," he admitted.

Wren favored him with a beautiful smile. "Then I promise to try to do it more often."

"I promise to see that you do." Drew leaned forward and brushed her lips with his, and then straightened and handed her a plate. "Eat up. You can't ride or clean stalls on an empty stomach."

Although Drew had hoped for rain so he'd have a reason to wear his sealskin cape and enjoy the cover it gave him to unbutton those burgundy buttons and take as many liberties with Kathryn's person as possible, his hopes were dashed. The sky was clear and, despite the early hour, most of Drew's tenants were going about their daily business.

The riding paths on Rotten Row would have been deserted at this time of morning but the tenant cottages on Swanslea Park were beehives of activity.

They rode across the same part of the estate they'd ridden the day before. Because he was denied the opportunity to take liberties with Kathryn's person, Drew paid more attention to their surroundings and took care to maintain a safer distance from the more heavily populated regions of the estate. He held her close, but kept his hands in plain view and away from her breasts.

Drew had chosen a different horse for this morning's ride. Wren leaned forward and carefully patted the horse's neck. "She's every bit as nice as Felicity."

Drew laughed. "She's a he."

"Oh."

"Anyone who's working as hard as you are to produce a definitive illustrated edition of *Flora and Fauna Native to Britain* should know that."

"Unlike a bird or a butterfly," Wren said, "there's no obvious difference in coloration between the male and female of the species."

"That's because there's an even more obvious difference." He laughed harder.

"Ladies are taught to avert their gazes from that part of a stallion's anatomy," she replied primly.

"Abelard thanks you for the compliment." The horse flicked his ears at the sound of his name. "But he's not a stallion."

Kathryn wrinkled her nose. "Poor Abelard. Not a stallion and not native to Britain." She didn't say it, but the implication in her voice was that she'd have known of his gender and his altered state if he'd been a native of Britain.

Drew laughed even harder than before. "You didn't know he wasn't a she. So how do you know he isn't native to Britain?"

"He's not a pony. The only members of *Equus callabus*, in the family *Equidae,* native to Britain are ponies." Her voice took on a professorial tone as she attempted to recover from her blunder on his horse's gender by dazzling Drew with her knowledge of biological classification.

"Actually none of the large mammalian herbivores with an odd number of toes on each hoof who constitute the horse family are thought to be native to Britain." Drew grinned at her obvious surprise. "I became a senior wrangler and matriculated from Cambridge, Kathryn. I even managed to acquire a working knowledge of biology, Greek, Latin, and practical anatomy while I was there." He guided the horse onto the lane that circled the lower part of the estate.

"Touché," Kathryn complimented him. "But of course you have the advantage of being the eldest *son* of a wealthy peer who saw to your advanced education by sending you to school and to university."

"And you are the daughter of a forward-thinking, highly educated *naturalist.*"

"Who had me educated in the traditional ladies' arts, which do not include biology, Greek, or Latin." She frowned, suddenly uncomfortable criticizing her father's belief that females required a far different education than men. "In all fairness to Papa, he never censored my reading material or barred me from the company of learned scholars and colleagues, but he refused to provide me with formal instruction in biology, Greek, and Latin until he needed my assistance with his definitive work."

"Not to mention the fact that he apparently omitted practical anatomy lessons altogether," Drew teased.

"I believe my *naturalist* father felt that since I'd been married and borne a child, I'd *naturally* received adequate instruction in practical anatomy."

His breath tickled her ear and Drew leaned forward and nuzzled her neck with his chin. "That just proves my theory that your highly educated naturalist father wasn't the most observant of men. Especially where his daughter was concerned."

"You think my father was unobservant?" She couldn't believe her ears. "He was one of the most revered naturalists in England."

"He called you Wren." Drew said those words as if no other explanation were necessary. "After a rather dull, common little bird, and you've never been dull or common. He couldn't have been too observant or he'd have seen how beautiful and uncommon you are."

"You've never called me Wren." She marveled at the fact that Drew had discerned the truth about the way her father viewed her and the way she yearned to be from the moment they met. Wren was rather dull and ordinary, but Kathryn was refined and elegant.

"I've never thought his appellation suited you. You've always been a Kathryn, never a Wren."

"Stop the horse," she ordered.

"Why?"

"I want to kiss you."

"Here? Now?" Drew's mouth went dry. They were close enough to the village and to Swanslea Park to be seen and recognized. And while Kathryn claimed that she no longer cared what happened to what remained of her reputation, Drew realized that he did.

"Why not?"

"Because we're in view of half the village." They meandered through the copse of trees by the stream near the mill where he'd delivered Kathryn's luncheon the day before, and Drew discovered the roaring in his ears wasn't entirely due to Kathryn's announcement. The mill was in operation. The waterwheel was turning. The miller and his apprentice were working. Several people from the village waited for flour and a man driving a horse and buggy turned onto the lane.

Wren looked over her shoulder. "No one is paying any attention to us."

"They will if I stop to kiss you."

"I don't care."

"I do," he said softly. He surprised himself with his words, but after taking a moment to think about them he knew they were true. "Strangely enough I do. And I see no reason to court folly by giving anyone cause to gossip about either one of us or to cast aspersions on your good name."

Wren sighed. "I suppose I should be grateful for your change of heart," she said. "But all I can think about is how much I want to kiss you and how much I want you to kiss me—and to taste me."

"Hell and damnation, Kathryn! If I don't allow you to kiss me, I'm a fool and if I do allow it, I'm a bounder and an opportunist."

Drew pulled Abelard to a halt and turned Wren in his arms to face him. Her face was so close to his he could feel her breath. He inhaled sharply.

"So," she whispered, "to kiss or not to kiss. That is the question."

At any other time Drew would have smiled at her

interpretation of Hamlet's dilemma and would have promptly settled the question, but her sudden capitulation scared him. "One of us has to keep his head." Drew released the breath he was holding. "And I may be the biggest fool of all time, but I'm not going to be the man who ruins your good name."

"My good name has already been sullied," she reminded him.

"Not by me," he said. "And not here among the people who count."

"Less than a week ago, you gave me a fortnight to get used to the idea of becoming your mistress." Wren leaned closer. "And I have."

"I haven't," he pronounced.

"What?" Wren was truly surprised.

"Kathryn, I was wrong to try to coerce you. My only excuse is that I was hurt and angry," he admitted. "I made that proposition in the heat of anger. Now, I'm not sure that it's what I want."

"I see."

"I don't think you do." He reached up and brushed a lock of hair from her face and leaned forward and pressed a chaste kiss to her forehead. "It doesn't mean I don't crave your kisses." He managed a painful smile. "I do. Very much. It just means that I'm an idiot, not a cad. Now," Drew said as he turned her back around in the saddle, "let's get you home. You've a riding lesson to attend to this morning and a son who is eagerly looking forward to teaching you how to shovel horse dung."

Chapter 20

Her great merit is finding out mine—there is nothing so amiable as discernment.

—GEORGE GORDON, 6TH LORD BYRON, 1788–1824

Wren's first riding lesson on Felicity was progressing nicely by the time Kit and Ally arrived at the paddock.

"Look at my mama!" Kit shouted, hopping up and down and excitedly pointing to Wren.

Wren turned her head to acknowledge him and saw Ally's eyes widen in shock at the sight she presented in her burgundy riding habit. She sat atop Felicity, her back ramrod straight, her hands lightly resting on the reins as Drew controlled the horse from the ground.

Attached to a long length of rope, Felicity circled the paddock in a walk. It probably didn't seem like much to an accomplished rider like Ally, but after the instruction in bridling and saddling and the tortuous lesson in mounting and remounting, of learning to time her boost into the saddle, balance her weight, and hook her right leg over the horn without falling backward, Wren was extraordinarily pleased with her progress.

"Head up. Eyes forward," Drew called out. "Loosen

your grip a bit and widen your hands." He nodded approvingly as Wren followed his instruction. He circled the horse twice more before ending the lesson.

"Whoa." Felicity stopped in her tracks and Wren rocked backward in the saddle.

"I think that's enough for today," Drew declared. He dropped the long line and stepped forward to help Wren dismount. "You both did very well." He rubbed Felicity on the neck and praised Wren as he lowered her to the ground.

Wren's right leg was numb and she leaned heavily against Drew, the sharp pins-and-needles feeling in her leg and hip sending tears to her eyes. Wren took a step and sucked in a breath.

"That's one of the hazards of riding aside," he told her.

"How would you know?" Wren snapped.

Drew bit the inside of his cheek to keep from smiling. "I learned to ride aside as a boy in order to help the grooms exercise my mother's favorite horses. She wouldn't allow them to be ridden with a man's saddle. I guarantee the numbness will subside in a moment. Walk it off." He leaned close enough to run his finger down the buttons on the front of Wren's dress and whisper in her ear, "I'd offer to massage the pain away, but we'd scandalize Riley and Miss Allerton."

"I'm afraid Ally's already scandalized," she murmured. "She's never seen me in anything but mourning colors."

Drew turned to the paddock rail. "What do you think?"

"Mama looks pretty," Kit chirped.

Drew grinned. "Indeed she does. What about you, Miss Allerton? What do you think of Mrs. Stafford's first lesson?" He didn't wait for the governess to reply, but continued, "I'm pleased with her progress and I must admit that producing one of my mother's old riding habits made all the difference. I know it isn't in keeping with her mourning, but until a proper habit can be made up for her, this one will have to do. I don't think a lady can relax enough to seat a highly sensitive horse if she's worrying about showing too much ankle." He shrugged his shoulders. "I hope we haven't offended your sensibilities by our seeming disregard of mourning customs, but I assured Mrs. Stafford it was temporary and that a fine horsewoman like yourself would understand the necessity."

Wren bit her lip to keep from dropping her jaw at the way Drew took complete responsibility for her inappropriate attire. And while it was true that he had provided it, he hadn't forced her to wear it.

"N-not at all, sir," Ally replied. "I think the burgundy is most becoming and that you made a most sensible choice."

Drew blew out a breath. "Then, if you've no objection, I took the liberty of ordering the rest of my mother's riding things aired and pressed and made available to both you and Mrs. Stafford. Feel free to make use of any or all of them."

"Thank you, sir." Ally gave him a bright smile. "I appreciate your kind generosity."

Drew smiled at the governess. "You're welcome, Miss Allerton, and your kind generosity is equally appreciated." He waited for Wren to walk off the numbness in her leg, then handed Felicity's reins to her.

"Take her to Riley. He'll see that she's unsaddled and cooled down."

"Shouldn't I do that?"

Drew shook his head. "I want you to know how because an emergency might demand it one day, but the grooms at Swanslea would never allow a lady to saddle and unsaddle her own horse." He opened the paddock gate. "Besides, we can't disappoint Kit. He'll want his mother at the fence cheering him on."

Wren led Felicity to Riley, then made her way back to the fence in time to watch Jem lead Lancelot into the paddock. The pony was already bridled and saddled and Kit was bouncing with excitement.

"Are you ready, Kit?" Drew asked.

"Yes, sir." Kit nodded his head.

Drew grinned. "Then, come on. I'll give you a boost up." He fastened the long line to Lancelot, boosted Kit onto the saddle, and began issuing the same instructions he'd given Wren.

Wren's heart swelled with pride as she watched her little boy striving to obey Drew's commands and win his praise. Tears shimmered in her eyes. She stood by the governess and watched as Drew put the pony and the little boy through their paces.

When Kit's riding lesson was over, Ally commented, "Remarkable, isn't it?"

"What?"

"How very alike they are." She nodded toward Drew and Kit.

"They should favor," Wren answered. "Brothers generally do."

Ally shot her a skeptical look. "You're his mother and in a much better position to know than I, but I heard you have a history with the current Lord Templeston and I want you to know that it makes no more difference to me than your *supposed* relationship with the late Lord Templeston did. The late Lord Templeston was the current Lord Templeston's father and it wouldn't be the first time an engaged couple anticipated their vows with long-lasting results. Or the first time a grandparent stepped in to avoid scandal."

Wren turned to the governess and Ally had the grace to blush. "Others may think Kit is the new Lord Templeston's son. They may even have heard of our broken betrothal, but Kit isn't his son and nothing anyone says or does can ever change that. No matter how much they might wish otherwise."

The governess's eyes were full of compassion at the wistful note in Wren's voice. "Forgive me for asking, but does that include you?"

"Me most of all," she whispered.

Ally cleared her throat. "I apologize for prying, Wren, but I can't help but notice the way you look at his lordship and the way he looks at you. And Kit bears such a remarkable resemblance. . . . I value our friendship and I know I shouldn't have presumed upon it, but I admit to a certain amount of curiosity." She paused, then cleared her throat once again. "My London Season was three years before yours, but my sister came out the same year you did."

"I didn't realize," Wren said. "Is your sister a governess as well?"

Ally shook her head. "She married Lord Telland. I lived with them before I became a governess, but, well . . . Lord Telland's, shall we say, private appetites tended toward sisters. I left his household because I found the idea repellent. I love my sister. And she loves her husband. The very suggestion that he . . . would break her heart. But we were close before she married, and Lord Templeston's courtship of you was the primary topic of conversation that Season. So naturally when he waited for you to appear at the church . . ." She shrugged. "There's been a great deal of speculation."

"I can imagine."

"So, if you want to dismiss me without references for my impertinence, I would certainly understand."

"Dismiss you?" Wren laughed. "Don't be absurd, Ally. I couldn't do without you. Kit loves you and I love you. You're my friend and a member of my family." She wrinkled her nose at Ally. "Friends are entitled to a healthy curiosity about each other's lives."

Ally nodded toward Drew. "Were you in love with him?"

"Then, now, and always."

"And the late Lord Templeston?"

"The late Lord Templeston saved my life by giving me a son."

"Come on, Mama!" Kit demanded her attention. "It's time to groom Lancelot and clean his stall. Drew said he'd help us. Hurry, Mama, afore you miss it!"

Ally laughed. "A grubby little boy is the only one in the world who would look forward to shoveling horse droppings."

"I'm not so sure the horse droppings are the major attraction," Wren mused. "Look at him, Ally. He's reveling in his brother's attention. I'm sure Kit thinks that shoveling horse droppings is a reasonable price to pay for his lordship's companionship."

Ally smiled. "I'm not one to ever poach on another's preserves, but I am human and, at the risk of sounding very forward, I'd have to say I'd agree wholeheartedly with Kit."

Wren winked at her friend. "So would I."

Chapter 21

By my faith, the fool hath feathered his nest well.
—THOMAS MIDDLETON, 1580–1627

After a hot bath, a change of clothes, and a light luncheon, Wren stopped by the nursery to help Ally tuck Kit into bed for his nap. Kit hugged her tightly as she kissed him and wished him sweet dreams.

"I love you, Mama." He yawned widely as she pulled the covers up around him. "And Drew and Lancelot and Felicity and Jem and Ally and Mr. Riley and Papa."

"I love you, too, angel."

He fingered the fabric of her black dress. "And you love Drew and Lancelot and Felicity and Jem and Ally and Mr. Riley and Papa like me?"

"Yes," she whispered. "Just like you." She frowned when she realized that Ally and George had fallen several rungs below a Shetland pony and a Thoroughbred filly.

Kit yawned once more, closed his eyes, and drifted off to sleep.

Wren tiptoed out of the nursery. She met Drew in the marble foyer at the bottom of the stairs.

His hair was still damp from his bath and he had changed into dark, formal mourning clothes for his meeting with the rector and the undertaker. Newberry stood at his elbow with a snifter of brandy on a silver tray. She watched as Drew lifted the glass from the tray and tossed the contents down in a single swallow.

"Thank you for accompanying me, Kathryn," he said. "You look very nice. Very pr—"

"Proper?" She wore black. From the top of her plumed hat and veil to the tip of her black kid shoes.

"I was going to say pretty." Drew set the empty brandy snifter on the silver tray Newberry held and offered Wren his arm. "But perhaps prim and proper are more appropriate to the occasion. You look very prim and proper and regal and every inch the lady of the house."

Newberry deposited the tray and the empty glass on a small Duncan Phyfe table in the foyer and crossed the marble floor to open the front door. "Your hat and stick, sir." Newberry produced Drew's hat and cane.

Drew took the proffered items in his left hand, then escorted Wren through the front door and down the steps. A coach with the Ramsey coat of arms emblazoned on the door waited on the circular drive.

"Shall we?" he asked before handing her up into the coach.

"If we must," Wren muttered, perching on the edge of a deeply cushioned velvet seat in the darkened interior of the coach.

Drew climbed in the coach, took the opposite seat, rapped the end of his stick on the ceiling of the coach, and ordered the coachman to lay a path for the village rectory. "Is something wrong?" He stared at her, noting her discomfort.

"I thought you'd drive your curricle into the village."

"I'm afraid not," Drew told her. "This is an official visit—a state visit, if you will—by the new marquess of Templeston upon the local rector. I have to go in full livery in order to announce the orderly transition of power from the fifteenth marquess to the sixteenth one." He peered into the darkness surrounding her. "Kathryn, are you all right?"

"Of course I am." She managed a thin, hollow-sounding laugh. "Why do you ask?"

"Because you're sitting on the edge of the seat with an expression on your face that says you may bolt at any minute and because you've gone as white as a sheet. Are you ill? Shall I take you home?"

"I don't like being closed up in a coach." *Especially the marquess of Templeston's state coach.* It brought back too many unhappy memories. The sickening lurch and sway of the springs, the pressure in the middle of her back, the smell of dusty velvet cushions pressed against her face and nose, the feel of a cold, brass door handle against her arm and rib, the heavy panting and the grunts and groans.

The edge of barely controlled panic in her voice and the memory of another explanation alerted him. *I don't like being accosted.* Her voice had sounded exactly the same and she'd worn the same look on her face. Maybe what she really meant to say was: *I don't like being accosted while I'm closed up in the marquess of Templeston's coach.*

Drew edged closer to her until their knees were touching. He reached for her hand. It was ice-cold beneath the kid leather of her glove. He pressed it between his palms. "There's no need to worry, Kathryn," he spoke in a soothing tone of voice. "I won't hurt you and I won't let anyone else hurt you. I promise."

She looked up at him and tried to pretend that nothing was out of the ordinary, but it was a very unconvincing performance. "We're paying calls, Drew," she said in a carefully steady voice. "I know I'm quite safe in your company. Reverend Pool and Mr. Smalley may be unpleasant, but you can rest assured that I've nothing to fear from them."

"All right," Drew suddenly agreed with her. "I'm reassured." He gave her his most handsome smile as the coach pulled to a stop in front of the rectory.

The footman opened the door of the coach and unfolded the steps.

"Take a deep breath." Drew unfolded the veil attached to her hat and dropped it into place over her face. "Now, blow it out."

She did as he instructed.

"Better?"

Wren gave him a quick nod as he climbed out of the coach and reached up a hand to help her down.

"Good. Remember I'll be right beside you."

Seconds later, she was standing beside Drew at the door of the rectory. He rapped on the door with the head of his cane. A maid answered.

"Don't announce me," Wren whispered urgently.

Drew cast a sharp glance at her from the corner of his eye, but he did as she asked. "The marquess of Templeston to see the Reverend Mr. Pool," he said.

The maid ushered them into the sitting room of the rectory.

Drew removed his hat and motioned Wren toward the settee. She sat down, pushed her veil up off her face, and folded her hands in her lap.

"Good afternoon, my lord," the reverend declared as

he entered the room. "It's a pleasure to meet you, my lord. I'm honored to be the first in the county to offer you my heartiest of congratulations on the assumption of the marquessate. I'm delighted by the prospect of conducting the late marquess's funeral and I'm quite certain that you'll be relieved to know that I've already prepared much of the text." Ignoring Wren, the minister extended his hand to Drew.

Drew disliked him on sight.

The Reverend Mr. Pool was a big, blustery fellow full of his own importance. He might be considered attractive in some circles, but with his weak chin, receding hairline, and pasty skin, Drew thought him a reptilian schemer oozing insincerity and oily charm. His deep booming voice was his greatest asset and although he had yet to attend a service, Drew already knew that it would be a long, drawn-out, incredibly boring pontification on the pious virtue of Reverend Pool and the damnable vices of everyone else.

Drew met the minister's cold, unblinking gaze with a look of hauteur designed to remind the fellow of his place. He stared pointedly at the reverend's outstretched hand, making no attempt to accept it. "I mourn my father, the late marquess, sir. I don't consider your hearty congratulations appropriate for so solemn an occasion."

Mr. Pool withdrew his hand without offering an apology. "Nevertheless," he replied in a dismissive tone, "you're here to conduct business. May I offer you refreshments in the library?"

"You may acknowledge the lady and offer her refreshments," Drew responded in kind, although he fervently hoped Kathryn wouldn't take the pompous ass up on his offer. He didn't want to spend any more time in the man's presence than necessary and Drew certainly didn't intend to allow him to conduct his father's funeral service.

Pool made a show of ignoring Kathryn while he glanced around the room as if searching for the lady in question. "I don't see a lady," he sniffed and then leveled his gaze at Drew. "I see your father's whor—"

"Be very careful, Mr. Pool," Drew warned.

"So, that's how it is. Like father, like son."

"I won't warn you again." Drew's voice was a low, rumbling growl. "You don't own your benefice. You're here to minister to the needs of the parish because the village needed a rector and because the late marquess allowed you to make use of the Swanslea glebe and tithes *gratis*."

"I am *not* a charity case," Mr. Pool retorted. "Your father refused to sell me the living because I would not allow his wh—concubine—to attend services or participate in the parish and I would not acknowledge his bastard, but as this parish had no spiritual guidance the bishop persuaded the late marquess to offer me use of the living."

"Why any bishop worth his salt would institute a pompous ass like you to the rectory here at Swanslea is beyond me." Drew didn't bother to mince words. "And how my father could allow himself to be persuaded to grant you use of the house, two hundred acres, and the large and small tithes, after meeting you, is just as puzzling."

"We never met," Mr. Pool said. "The late marquess tended to be an absentee landlord."

"That explains why my father allowed you to remain," Drew commented. "He didn't know you. It doesn't explain why the bishop instituted you."

"The bishop is my uncle." His reply was smug. "He made an agreement with your father allowing me to hold this living until another of equal value becomes available. Until that happens, I'll remain rector of this parish, whether you like it or not. You aren't the only one with connections, Lord Templeston."

Drew's stare was unflinchingly direct. "So, we understand one another. Now all that remains to be seen is which of us is the better connected."

"Am I to take that as a threat, Lord Templeston?"

"I don't give a damn how you take it, Mr. Pool, as long as you understand that your days as rector of Swanslea are numbered," Drew told him.

"In the meantime," the reverend sneered, "the rectory is mine and I have work to do within it. I'll thank you to remove yourself and your rather shopworn whore from my house so that I may finish preparing the text of your father's funeral service. Finding the right passage has been rather a challenge—even for one as well versed in the Holy Scriptures as I." He paused for effect. "Tell me, Lord Templeston, what admirable things does one find to say about a blatant whoremonger destined to suffer eternal damnation?"

"Drew, no!"

Wren's warning came too late as Drew caught Mr. Pool on the jaw with a vicious uppercut.

The rector hit the floor hard.

" 'Many have fallen by the edge of the sword,' " Drew quoted. " 'But not so many as have fallen by the tongue.' "

"Y-y-you hit me," the rector sputtered. "I'll see that you live to regret that."

"Consider yourself lucky that's all I did." Drew walked around the fallen clergyman and offered his arm to Wren. "I already regret my blow didn't break your jaw."

"It didn't," Mr. Pool spat. "And I can promise you

that the text I preach at your father's funeral will be your undoing! Yours and your whore's!"

Drew kicked the other man's foot aside to clear a path to the front door. "You pompous ass! You're not going to offer a sermon over my father. I didn't come here to conduct business with you. I came as a courtesy to inform you that someone else would be performing my father's rites."

"The bishop will hear about this! You cannot usurp my rights. I'm the rector of Swanslea. I'm entitled to conduct services for the peerage!"

"The bishop will most definitely hear about this," Drew agreed. "Because my godfather, the archbishop of Canterbury, asked to perform my father's rites and I granted him that favor. I chose to explain in person so that you would know my decision to grant His Grace's favor was not meant to slight you." He turned to look at the man still sprawled upon the floor. "Had I known of your character, I would not have done so. You, sir, are beneath contempt and when this sad business is over, your time here will be at an end. I will not provide a living to a man who offers me congratulations instead of condolences upon the death of my father or a man who casts aspersions on his name and reputation as well as the name and reputation of the lady to whom I was once, and am again, betrothed."

Wren sucked in a breath.

The rector laughed. "You expect me to believe that you're serious about marrying her? Why bother, when you can have her without benefit of vows?" He narrowed his gaze at Drew. "Or can you? Did she refuse you, too?"

"Good day to you." Drew gave the rector another vicious kick in the leg as he stepped over him to open the front door. "And good riddance."

"Remember me when he tires of you," the rector shouted after Wren. "I have need of a whore and I'm not too proud to take a randy widow into my bed—especially a widow who's been mistress to two marquesses!"

Chapter 22

Temper gets you into trouble, pride keeps you there.

—ANONYMOUS

"*That went well,*" *Wren commented dryly as* soon as they reached the privacy and close confines of the coach.

"What did you expect me to do?"

"I didn't expect you to brawl with a clergyman. Have you taken leave of your senses?"

"He called you a whore and my father a whore-monger."

"He said to our faces what others would say behind our backs. You hit a rector. A man of the cloth!"

Drew laughed. "He may be a man of the cloth, Kathryn, but he's a pompous ass and his holy raiment is so thin it might as well be imaginary. Hit him? I should have killed him." He tapped his stick against the ceiling of the coach and instructed the coachman to drive them to the undertaker's.

"But, Drew . . ."

"I thought you were upset because I informed him of our betrothal before I discussed it with you."

"There's no reason for me to be upset about your announcement, because we aren't betrothed." She used that prim, dictatorial tone of voice he loved.

"Yes, Kathryn, we are," he insisted.

"No, *Andrew,* we are not."

"Why not?"

"Because it's impossible."

Drew leaned forward and took both of her hands in his. "Why, Kathryn? Tell me why it's impossible."

"Because."

"That's not a reason."

"You heard the reason!" she hissed. "You heard what Mr. Pool said about me. I'm the local concubine. The fallen woman. The only one in the county who isn't received at church."

"Thank your lucky stars for that!" He gave her his most engaging grin. "Who wants to listen to the gospel of hypocrisy and snobbery according to the ill bred, ill mannered, rude, and pretentious Mr. Pool?" Drew shuddered in mock horror. "The idea that I might be required to sit and listen to that bag of wind for hours on end sends shivers up my spine."

"You can laugh, Drew, because you don't understand what it is like not to be received. At church or in any of the homes of the villagers. I'm not received anywhere respectable women are. When I offer to help with the church bazaars or visit the sick or provide charity for the needy, my efforts are met with hostility and scorn. The deacons' wives refused to accept the Christmas and Easter hampers I donated for the poor. Everything I do must be done through Mrs. Tanglewood or Ally. The only place I'm accepted is Swanslea Park. When I leave the grounds, I'm a social pariah—an outcast." She closed her eyes and bowed her head. "I despise Mr. Pool, and I don't care to listen to his sermons. I *do* care that I'm barred from attending them. I do care that Kit isn't allowed to attend services or receive the religious instruction he's going to need later in life. I can teach him the catechism, but I can't force the rector to confirm him. I can't legitimize him."

"I can," Drew said.

Wren opened her eyes and stared into his chocolate brown ones. "Please, don't tempt me with the one thing you know I can't refuse. My reputation is ruined. Do you want to have your good name destroyed as well? Do you want to listen to the gossip about my relationship with your father? Or pretend to ignore the whispers of your friends and colleagues? Because that's what will happen if you marry me. You may be able to overlook my past, but they won't. Find someone else, Drew, because I can't be the kind of wife—the kind of marchioness—you need."

"You're the marchioness I want," he told her. "The one I desire."

"For how long?" she demanded.

Drew recoiled. "I don't deserve that."

"You think not, but less than a week ago you wanted to throw me off your land and out of my home and you wanted to take my son. And that was before you offered me the dubious honor of becoming your mistress."

"And I apologized for acting in anger."

"Isn't that what you're doing now?" she asked.

"I don't think so." He removed his hat and placed it on the coach seat, then raked his fingers through his hair. "God's nightshirt, Kathryn! I'm offering to marry you."

"Because you've inherited the title? Because you have a duty to your family and the people who depend on you for their living? Because you must marry and sire a Ramsey heir?" She bit back the tears.

"Yes."

"Because, as my husband, you'd regain the dowager cottage and the settlement George gave me? Because it's convenient?" she asked.

"Yes," he continued. "Because it's convenient to desire the woman you marry and sensible to marry the woman you desire." He expelled a long, frustrated breath. "And because we could both keep what we want."

"What do you want, Drew?" she asked.

"You."

"You heard the good reverend." She managed a derisive snort. "You don't have to marry me for that. And if that's all you want from me, you shouldn't marry me."

"Why not?"

"There are any number of reasons," she said softly. The main one being that he hadn't mentioned loving her. And if she married him knowing that he no longer loved her, it would certainly break her heart.

"Name one," he challenged.

"You need a wife who can give you children. I can't do that. I can't have any more children."

Drew felt as if he'd taken a fist in the solar plexus. He sat back against the cushions of the seat, struggling to breathe and to make sense of what she'd told him. "What?"

"I can't give you a legitimate heir. I can't give you sons of your own." Wren took a deep breath. "You do want children, don't you?"

"I always saw them as part of my future, yes."

"Then forget about marrying me. Because having more children cannot be a part of my future." She turned her face away from his and stared out the window in a futile attempt to prevent him from knowing that she was crying.

"Kathryn." He sat beside her, put his arm around her,

and gently guided her head to his shoulder. "I already
have an heir in Kit."

"He's not your son."

"No, but he's *your* son and my half-brother. And he
could be *our* son. Once we're married, I'll adopt him.
I'm very fond of Kit. He's as much a Ramsey as I am
and the family name would continue through him."

"That kind of marriage wouldn't be fair to you. We
cannot be intimate . . ." She blushed. "Because I dare not
risk conceiving another child. . . ."

"Would conceiving a child endanger your life?" he
asked.

"No," she whispered. "But I cannot carry another
child for fear of it dying."

"Who told you this?"

"My father. He said it was the same with my mother."

Drew tilted her chin up with his index finger and bent
to kiss her. "There are ways to prevent conception. I
know a number of them and we can learn other ways.
Say you'll marry me, Kathryn. It's the perfect solution
for all of us."

She couldn't refuse him. She couldn't refuse the protection marriage to Drew would provide for her and for
Kit. She couldn't deny Kit his chance for legitimacy.
But Wren couldn't help but worry about Drew. What if
he regretted his decision later? What would happen to
them then? Could she be sure that he'd forgiven her?
Could she face marrying him knowing that he might one
day look at her with contempt?

She took a deep breath and asked Drew the hardest
question she had ever asked in her life. "Knowing everything you know about me, knowing everything that your
friends and colleagues are likely to say about me, knowing that there are things in my past neither of us can

change, can you forgive that past and marry me without regret?"

Drew stared deep into her eyes and knew that their future happiness depended on how he answered. She had a past and she still kept secrets from that past, but he'd never wanted to marry anyone else. "The past is dead and buried, Kathryn. We can't change it, but there's no reason we can't learn to live with it and build a home for Kit and a future together." He leaned forward and pressed his lips against her brow once. "Without regrets."

"Then, I accept."

He pulled a handkerchief from his pocket and handed it to her. She hadn't made a sound and she might not even have been aware of it, but a continuous line of tears were rolling down her cheeks. "All better?"

"Yes, thank you."

"We've arrived at the undertaker's." Drew squeezed her hand in a comforting gesture. "I can attend to the details alone if you'd rather not face Mr. Smalley."

Wren shook her head. "Mr. Smalley's the only undertaker for miles around. He may be the only undertaker between here and London. If you attend to him in the same manner you attended to the rector, you may have to send to London for another undertaker."

"Mr. Pool deserved what he got."

"Mr. Pool deserved far worse. My concern is that you may conclude the same about Mr. Smalley."

Drew groaned. "He can't possibly be that bad."

"He's not as arrogant as Mr. Pool, but he's every bit as unctuous and lecherous."

"Has he made improper advances toward you?" Drew opened the door of the coach.

"I'm a widow," Wren reminded him. "And widows are considered fair game. Nearly every widower or single man in the county has made improper suggestions or advances toward me—including you." She glanced at him to gauge his reaction. "Why do you think George offered me his protection?"

Drew handed her down from the vehicle. "I had hoped it was because he loved you."

She turned to him and smiled a dazzling smile that reminded Drew of all the reasons he'd fallen in love with her so long ago, a smile that gave him hope for a bright future. "He did love me," she said, at last. "But you should know that any love he felt for me paled in comparison to what he felt for you."

Chapter 23

Of all things upon earth that bleed and grow,
A herb most bruised is woman.

—EURIPIDES, C. 480–406 B.C.

Drew decided that he'd rather face a charge of French cavalry than ever have dealings with another undertaker. Especially if the undertaker was Denton Smalley.

The man had questioned every decision he'd made, from the length of the lying-in-state and the place of burial to the number of vehicles and guests in the funeral procession. Almost every decision. It seemed the unctuous undertaker was thrilled to learn the archbishop of Canterbury would conduct the services. The rector of Swanslea wouldn't have been nearly as good for future business.

And Drew soon discovered that business was Mr. Smalley's primary concern. When they'd finally settled on the order of precedence for the honored guests and the servants in the late marquess's households, the number of coaches and horses required, and the number of farmers, laborers, tradesmen, and tenants on foot in the procession and decided upon the arrangements and the cost, the undertaker had had the gall to suggest that the *ton* would think him cheap unless he selected the finest quality gloves and scarves for the guests. He was required to supply at least two pairs of gloves per guest and two sets of mourning clothes for all of the late marquess's servants.

Once they'd settled those details for his father, the entire process had begun again for his father's companion. Only this time the undertaker had argued that because the young woman in question had no near relatives, more mutes would have to be hired to act as mourners.

When Drew sarcastically remarked that they might as well hire the opera chorus at the Haymarket Theater to act as mourners, Mr. Smalley had leaped at the opportunity to extend an invitation. It proved easier to go along with the ridiculous idea than to fight it.

Drew gave in, throwing up his hands in frustration, and Kathryn had entered into the negotiations.

From that moment forward, Drew refused to allow the undertaker to steer him where he wanted him to go, deferring instead to Kathryn. She had dealt with the man before and she was more adept at handling him. She had an innate ability to make the right decisions and the patience to do so. She understood the importance of honoring the late marquess and the need to keep the funeral a family affair. George Ramsey had been a man with two very disparate lives. His public life had been spent as King's Bench, a member of the House of Lords, a peer of the realm, but his private life had included several mistresses Martin Bell was currently tracking down, one of them a young woman named Mary Claire who had remained largely unknown.

There would be no lying-in-state for Mary Claire, no great funeral procession, only family and known friends from the opera chorus. There would be no additional mutes or ostentatious funeral gifts. The guests who attended Mary Claire's funeral would receive the same gloves and scarves George's guests received along with a simple mourning brooch. Her funeral would take place after the marquess's. It would, in effect, take place while George's funeral feast was underway.

Kathryn had taken control and quietly, efficiently finished working out the details of his father's funeral and arranging Mary Claire's. Drew shook his head in amazement. The thing he'd feared most—the scandal he'd been sure would ensue if he allowed one of his father's mistresses to oversee the funeral of another—was without merit.

Oh, he knew that there would be talk. There was always gossip among the *ton*. But there would be no scandal. Because the mistress arranging the funeral was Kathryn. And Drew frankly didn't know what he would have done without her.

She was magnificent.

And he wanted her now more than ever before.

Drew turned from his silent contemplation of the fire in the hearth and walked over to the secretary. Kathryn had fled to the safety of her dowager cottage the moment they'd returned to Swanslea Park. She'd made a feeble excuse about needing to see to her menagerie and he'd let her go. Not because he wanted to, but because she needed him to.

The call on the rector had to have been one of the most humiliating experiences of her life, doubly humiliating because he'd been witness to it. Drew opened the glass doors and poured himself a snifter of brandy from the decanter. Kathryn had known what to expect, yet she'd willingly agreed to accompany him. She'd subjected herself to the minister's abuse simply because he had asked her to help him. A muscle began to tick in his jaw. Out of love for his father? Or out of friendship to him?

Drew took a swallow of his brandy and stared at the pull-down desk of the secretary. The message from Martin lay open on the writing surface. It had been delivered to Swanslea Park while he and Kathryn were paying calls on the rector and the undertaker. He reread the words Martin had written: *Having concluded our sad business in Ireland, I am returning home with the bodies of the fifteenth marquess of Templeston and his companion. Am expected to arrive on the twenty-third. Your loyal friend and servant, Martin Bell.*

Drew glanced at the calendar. Tomorrow.

Drew took several sheets of stationery out of the top drawer. It was time to decide.

Could he forgive her her past? Could he forgive her for disappointing him the last time? She'd asked him if he could marry her without regrets. And he'd promised that he could.

But he wasn't so sure. Could he be that noble? Could he forget that she'd been his father's mistress and had borne him a son? Could he put aside his dream of children of his own? Could he make those sacrifices in order to build a lasting relationship with her?

He did love me, she had told him. *But you should know that any love he felt for me paled in comparison to what he felt for you.*

Drew had always taken his father's love for granted and accepted it as part of his due. He was an only son and heir. A beloved son and heir. He'd believed that wholeheartedly until he'd learned of his father's death—and of Kit, his father's other son. Now he wondered how the father who had loved him so much could have taken Kathryn as his mistress. She said he'd done it to protect

her from men like the minister and the undertaker, but
Drew wasn't so sure. Was it possible that his father—
his beloved father—had wanted her for himself four
years ago? Something had happened to Kathryn that
made her change her mind about marrying him. Had his
father taken what he wanted? Had he seduced her or
forced her?

And would Kathryn have remained loyal to a man
who had forced her—even if that man had been a marquess?

*Knowing everything you know about me, knowing
everything that your friends and colleagues are likely to
say about me, knowing that there are things in my past
neither of us can change, can you forgive that past and
marry me without regret?*

Was she asking too much of him? Or was he expecting too much from himself?

Because Drew knew in his heart of hearts that he
would have regrets—too many regrets—if the only relationship he managed to build with her was built on the
need to protect Kit and on mutual desire. Would he be
able to keep his regrets to himself? Would he be able to
hide the truth from her? Could he live with himself if
she disappointed him once again?

And how did Kathryn feel about him? What did she
want from him? What did she need? But most of all,
why had she left him four years ago?

Drew sighed. He had asked himself these questions a
thousand times over the past two days, never daring to
look too close for the answer. Until now. Because now
he needed more from Kathryn than physical release. He
needed redemption from the long, empty existence his
life had become. He had gone in search of death when
she abandoned him and he'd found every manner of
death imaginable—except his own. Now he needed to

learn how to live. And he was very much afraid that Kathryn was the only woman who could teach him how.

He'd risked his life the last time she'd disappointed him. Shouldn't he be willing to risk his future on the chance that she wouldn't a second time? Drew took a drink of his brandy, then sat down at the secretary and began to write a heartfelt letter to his godfather, the archbishop of Canterbury, enclosing the twenty-eight guineas necessary for a special license.

A knock on the door interrupted his writing. "Come in."

Harriet Allerton opened the door. "I'm sorry to disturb you, sir, but Kit wanted to know if you'd come up and tuck him in."

Drew smiled. "I'd be happy to. Please, come in. That is, if you don't object to being alone with me. You may leave the door open if you like."

Ally's shy smile transformed her rather plain features. "That won't be necessary, my lord. I'm over thirty and employed in your household. I have no objection to being alone with you."

"I had hoped Mrs. Stafford would join me for dinner but she retired to the cottage with a headache after we returned from Mr. Smalley's." Drew shuddered. "I can certainly understand why. The rector was bad enough, but the undertaker is a ghoul."

"A lecherous ghoul," Ally corrected.

"I take it you've met the man," he replied dryly. He walked over to the secretary, poured a small glass of sherry, and offered it to her.

Ally accepted the drink. "Unfortunately. And I've heard quite a bit about what happened this afternoon."

Drew looked surprised.

"Belowstairs is up in arms, sir. The coachmen heard nearly everything and what they didn't hear Mr. Pool's maid has been repeating all over the village." She paused. "Don't be so surprised. Mr. Pool and Mr. Smalley view all women as vessels for their improper suggestions. Including me." She took a sip of sherry, studying Drew over the rim of her glass.

"The rector acted abominably," Drew said angrily.

"So did you when you first arrived," Ally reminded him. "The truth is that he desires her and he despises her for his weakness." The governess looked him in the eye. "You must realize that it took a great deal of courage for Wren to accompany you to the rectory and to the undertaker's place of business. They've hounded her mercilessly."

"I had no idea," he said.

"The world has always been friendlier to men than women," Ally said. "And some men take that idea quite to heart. They believe they should be able to have whatever or whomever they want."

"She handled herself very well." He frowned. "She conducted herself with a great deal more decorum than I did."

"A woman in Wren's position has little choice except to learn how to exercise restraint."

"She was magnificent."

"You still love her." Ally hadn't realized she'd spoken her thoughts aloud until she saw the expression of wonderment on his face.

"Yes, I believe that's a possibility," he answered. "Tell me, Ally, has she been in to say good night to Kit yet?"

Ally nodded. "She came up right after his supper. She didn't stay long. She listened to him recount this afternoon's adventures, kissed him good night, and returned to the cottage." Ally hesitated. "She appeared to have been crying."

Drew set his glass on a side table and raked his hands through his hair. "Damn. I knew I should have killed that pompous ass." He looked up and remembered Ally was in the room. "I beg your pardon, Miss Allerton."

"There's no need," Ally assured him. "I'm very fond of Wren and if it were possible for me to do so, I would have dispatched that odious man months ago. I cannot believe he's going to conduct the late marquess's funeral service. He sees his lordship's death as an opportunity to impress the *ton* with his rhetoric. He views his position here as rector as a society coup instead of an opportunity to serve the village."

"There's no need for you to get worked up about it, Ally," Drew told her. "Apparently the coachmen didn't hear everything. For if they had, they would have known that the reason I paid a call on the reverend in the first place was to inform him that my godfather, the archbishop of Canterbury, had asked if he could conduct the services and that I had naturally agreed."

Ally clapped her hands in delight. "The archbishop of Canterbury is coming to Swanslea?"

"Yes."

The governess's eyes sparkled despite the solemnity of the occasion for the archbishop's visit. "That means . . . Oh, my lord Templeston, but that would be a splendid time to . . ."

"Purchase a special license?"

Ally nodded.

"I'm one step ahead of you, Miss Allerton." Drew held up the sheet of paper he'd been writing on when she entered the study. "I've already requested one." He showed her the twenty-eight guineas he planned to enclose. "Paid in advance."

"I wish you both every happiness, my lord." Ally finished her sherry and rose from her seat. "I'm very pleased and proud to be a part of the staff here."

"You're not a part of the staff," Drew said. "You're part of the family. Please tell Kit I'll be up momentarily." He winked at the governess. "Just as soon as I conclude this letter."

Wren looked up from her desk, the lines on the pages of illustrations and watercolor drawings scattered across her worktable blurring in the lamplight. She squeezed her eyes closed, then wearily pinched the bridge of her nose between her thumb and index finger to ward off the headache threatening to form there. It was no use. She couldn't keep her mind off Drew long enough to concentrate on her work.

She had returned from Mr. Smalley's and gone straight to the cottage. She told Drew she needed to tend to the animals, but that was only partly true. Wren needed time alone to think about what she'd done in the midst of an afternoon that had turned nightmarish in the extreme; Andrew Ramsey had proposed marriage once again. And she'd accepted once again.

Wren put her drawings away and got up from her worktable. She went into the kitchen, built a fire in the hearth, and heated water for a hot bath. She dragged the big copper tub from the alcove and filled it halfway with water from the pump. She sat down on a wooden stool and, while she waited for the rest of her bathwater to heat, reflected on what might prove to be the greatest folly of her life.

He hadn't said he loved her. He'd talked about duty and convenience and a marriage that would make Kit legitimate and provide a measure of protection for him against the cruel gossip and the stigma of being born a bastard. He'd told her he wanted her and assured her that he could marry her without regret.

What he hadn't told her was how he knew marrying her without regret was possible. Had he truly forgiven her?

Wren sighed. Drew had wanted to know if his father had loved her. And she'd told him half the truth when she'd said that he had. But George had never loved her romantically. He'd loved her like a daughter. Or, more precisely, he'd loved her like a daughter-in-law. He had loved her because Drew had loved her. Because he had loved his son.

She closed her eyes and remembered the desperation in her father's eyes the morning after the coach—a coach identical to the one they'd ridden in this afternoon—had deposited her at the front door of her Aunt Edwina's town house. Wren shuddered involuntarily. The coach she and Drew had used this afternoon had brought back a flood of memories she'd thought she'd finally managed to forget. But some things were impossible to forget and the fear and pain and terror of rape was one of them.

The household had been asleep when the coach dropped her off. Wren remembered stumbling into the kitchen and doing exactly as she was doing now. She'd dropped her ruined gown and underclothes on the floor, drawn a scalding hot bath, sank down into it, and scrubbed her skin until it was raw.

She'd managed to remove the scent of him, but she'd never quite erased the feel. It never went away no matter how often she washed or how hard she scrubbed. The humiliation she'd suffered this afternoon evoked the same feelings. And here she was, four years later, attempting the same remedy.

Wren got down from the stool, lifted the pot of boiling

water from the hook above the fire, and poured it into
her tub. She gathered her bath things—a washcloth, a
bottle of scented oil, a bar of soap, a length of toweling
from the alcove cupboard. She retrieved her flannel
nightgown and robe from the bedroom and returned to
the kitchen. Wren hung the robe and nightgown on a
peg by the door and set everything else within reach on
the stool. She poured a handful of scented oil into the
bathtub and swirled it around. The scent of tuberoses
filled the kitchen.

Wren added more coal to the fire, undressed, and
stepped into the tub. Easing herself into the water, Wren
soaped her body, then sank low in the tub, resting her
head against the rim. She closed her eyes, covered them
with her forearm, and sighed in relief as the water
soothed her aching muscles.

The hot water hadn't soothed her four years ago.
Nothing could soothe her then. Four years ago, she'd
climbed out of the bath when the water grew too cold
to bear, wrapped herself in her cloak, and crept into her
bed, curling herself into a tight ball and willing herself
to die.

A kitchen maid discovered the bathtub, still full of
water, the next morning. On the floor beside it lay
Wren's silver dress and her ruined undergarments. The
maid summoned the housekeeper, who summoned the
butler, who summoned her aunt, who sent someone to
rouse Wren's father before rushing to her niece's bedchamber.

She found Wren wrapped in her cloak, curled tightly
in a ball in the center of her bed, desperately clutching
a razor-sharp knife in her fist. Wren never remembered
taking the knife from the kitchen or what she intended
to do with it. She only remembered wanting to die.

Wren hadn't thought the marks were visible. She'd

fought him when he'd taken her unawares, but he'd only struck her once. He'd forced her face down into the cushions covering the hard wood of the coach seat and held it there while he pushed himself into her from behind. He hadn't meant to leave any marks—any sign that he'd ever been there. And he'd been surprised to discover that she was still a virgin, pleased that, despite her engagement, he'd been the first.

Wren had foolishly believed that what had happened in the dark confines of the marquess of Templeston's coach would remain a secret. But she'd been wrong.

Her father had cried when he saw her. He was able to see what had been done to her. And if he could see it, so could everyone else. She'd demanded a mirror and her father had reluctantly handed one over. Wren stared into it without emotion. The young woman with the bruised and swollen cheekbone, the black eye, and the scraped forehead was unrecognizable. She bore no resemblance to the Wren Markinson who had attended a Vauxhall Gardens concert on the arm of Drew Ramsey because that Wren Markinson no longer existed.

Her aunt had accompanied her to Vauxhall, but they'd become separated during the crush at intermission. Wren and Drew had remained in their seats, chatting with friends who came by while her aunt went to speak with friends of her own. When Drew received an urgent message summoning him to the War Office, he'd escorted Wren to his borrowed coach while he went in search of her aunt and someone to see them safely home.

Her aunt never appeared, but someone else had and he'd shoved her into the corner of the coach and raped her.

Aunt Edwina suggested they send for Drew.

But Wren refused to allow it, saying she didn't want to see him.

Despite repeated attempts to change her mind, Wren never relented. The prospect of seeing Drew terrified her. She made her father and aunt swear they wouldn't say anything. Made them promise never to breathe a word of what happened. And they'd agreed. For her sake, if not for Drew's.

She would only say that a man had attacked her in the coach and forced himself on her.

They told Drew she'd taken ill and offered no explanation for the illness.

On the day of her wedding, Wren remained in bed. She didn't cry. She didn't move. She didn't make a sound. She simply willed herself to disappear.

She almost succeeded.

If she hadn't discovered that she was with child, she might have stayed in bed until she died. But while she could wish for her own death, she could not condemn an innocent child to that same fate. By the time she felt strong enough to face Drew, he had gone to Belgium with Wellington.

When she confided in her father, he had sent for George and the two of them had set out to secure a husband for her.

Bertrand Stafford had been the perfect man for the job.

He was older and scholarly, he had known Wren from the time she was a little girl, and he sincerely wanted to be her chevalier. Bertrand proposed a marriage of convenience and Wren reluctantly but gratefully accepted. In exchange for Bertrand's name and protection, she agreed to take care of him and his house in his waning years.

The marriage was chaste and companionable and the agreement worked well right up until Bertrand's death when her son was nearly five months old.

Chapter 24

I arise from dreams of thee
And the spirit in my feet,
Hath led me——who knows how?
To thy chamber window, Sweet!

      —PERCY BYSSHE SHELLEY,

                1792–1822

"*Kathryn?*"

Wren lowered her arm and opened her eyes. Drew stood in her kitchen looking down at her. She had no idea how long he'd been there or how long he had watched her while she attempted to soak away the bad memories. "What are you doing here?" She crossed her arms over her breasts, but there was no way to cover up the rest of her.

He cleared his throat. "I was worried about you. When you didn't come to the house for dinner, I decided to see if you were all right." He tried to keep his eyes on her face, but her shapely legs and the triangle of downy curls between her thighs beckoned to him. He swallowed hard.

"I'm fine," she said.

"I can see that." His words carried a double meaning.

Wren blushed. "Hand me the towel, please." She nodded toward the wooden stool. "And turn around." The look in his eyes warmed her almost as much as it frightened her. "How did you get in?"

"The front door was unlocked." Drew handed over the towel and turned his back to the tub. His heart pounded in his chest and the front of his trousers became unbearably tight. He heard the splash as she rose from the bathwater and his imagination took flight. He imagined her stepping out of the water and bending at the waist to dry her feet, before running the towel up her shapely legs, over the soft skin of her stomach, and between her thighs. He imagined droplets of bathwater clinging to her downy blond triangle and secreted in her navel and he envied the length of toweling she held in her hand. He shifted his weight from one foot to the other, seeking a more comfortable position to accommodate the swelling in his trousers.

"You can turn around now."

Her invitation surprised him. Drew half-expected her to order him out of the kitchen and out of the house. When she failed to order him out of the house, Drew turned around. His breath caught in his throat at the sight of her.

She had wrapped the length of towel around her body and tucked the ends into the valley between her breasts. Although the towel managed to cover the essentials, it gaped open from her left hip to her waist and only reached to upper thigh length. Damp in places, the towel clung to her womanly curves, revealing as much as it concealed.

"Thank you," he breathed in a reverent tone of voice.

"For what?" she asked.

"For allowing me this." He wet his lips as his gaze took in every nuance of her appearance. "I've dreamed of seeing you like this for four years," he admitted. "And I'm dying to touch you."

Wren looked down at the towel. Her pulse beat in the hollow of her throat. She trembled with emotion and a touch of fear. She had dreamed of their wedding night. Four years ago, she had dreamed of having him see her, touch her, and love her—dreamed of seeing him, touching him, loving him. And even though she knew those dreams would never come true, she had continued to dream them. Wren took a deep breath, gathered all of her courage, and whispered, "Don't die. Just touch me."

She loosened the knot at the valley of her breasts and let the cloth fall to the floor.

The husky timbre of her voice sent shivers down Drew's spine. He didn't wait for a second invitation. He closed the distance between them and dropped to his knees. He didn't touch her, he simply positioned his mouth within a hair's-breadth of the pink nub crowning her right breast. Glancing up at her, he asked, "May I?"

"Please," she whispered.

Drew brought his hand up and caressed her breast, then kissed it, gently, reverently, as if it were the most precious thing in all the world.

Wren couldn't describe the feelings of tenderness that overwhelmed her as Drew suckled at her breast. She pressed his head closer, urging him to take whatever nourishment he needed. He sucked her eagerly, lapping at her nipple with his tongue like a greedy kitten at a bowl of cream, then nipped it with his teeth before pulling it into his mouth once again. The moment Wren thought she'd die from the pleasure of it, he let go of that breast and lavished affection on the other.

The touch of his lips was electric. She gasped in response, as the warmth seemed to flow from his mouth through her breasts and down to her most secret woman's place. She burrowed her fingers into his thick hair and held him tightly. His tender care and his sweet caresses melted her fear and unleashed the torrent of emotions she'd kept hidden. Drew made her feel. Drew made her ache and burn with wanting. Wren knew in her heart that Drew was the only man she had ever wanted and that only Drew could heal her.

Drew took her response as encouragement. He increased the suction, teasing her sensitive nipple with his teeth before pulling back to lave it with his tongue. Drew groaned. He trailed his other hand from her waist to the underside of her other breast, feeling its shape, measuring its weight and warmth.

She wasn't afraid any longer. She was ready to love him and be loved in return. "Please," she said again.

"Tell me," he ordered, his breath teasing her nipple. "Tell me what you want."

"More," she answered. "Touch me. Kiss me. Love me, Drew."

Those were the words he wanted most to hear. "With pleasure," he murmured, before he lived up to his promise by touching and teasing, fondling and sucking at her breasts, offering her the pleasure she craved. He kissed his way over her breasts and down her stomach until he reached the dark blond curls at the juncture of her thighs.

Wren's knees nearly buckled when he combed his fingers through her downy curls, dipping two of them inside her warmth, smoothing the hot honeyed liquid over her womanly folds and the tight little button hidden there.

She gripped his hair reflexively as he bent lower.

"What are you doing?" Her voice was an achy, breathless sigh.

"Kissing you," he answered, his voice a whisper of

warm breath that tickled her curls and triggered a rush of more hot liquid.

"Drew . . ." Wren reached for him.

"Let me." He looked up at her, his eyes a deep, dark brown shining with the desire to give her something very special. "Pretend it's our wedding night and that you're a new bride eagerly anticipating the joys of the marriage bed."

"We can't turn back the clock," she said, blinking away the sudden sting of tears.

"Yes, we can," he answered firmly. "We can and we will. For you. For me. For us."

She believed him. "What do you want me to do?"

"Close your eyes and enjoy. Believe in me. Believe I'll never hurt you." Then he licked her there on the soft folds of flesh hidden by the hair. She pressed her legs together in reaction, before opening them again to allow him access.

Drew took advantage, deepening his kiss, tasting the most secret part of her.

Wren squirmed as the myriad of incredible sensations surged through her body—all of them emanating from the place Drew lavished with attention. She moaned her pleasure and gasped out his name as the pressure within her body began to build. "Stop, please . . ." She thrust her hips upward, seeking a release from the sensations flooding her body and her mind.

Drew tried to pull away to gauge her reaction, to see if she wanted him to stop but Kathryn held him close, her fingers still tangled in the strands of his hair. He kissed her again, gently, softly, then harder.

She screamed. "God, Drew, don't stop, please."

He had no intentions of stopping, not until she found completion.

"Drew?"

He heard the question in her voice, knew she was desperately close to finding satisfaction, knew she didn't understand what was happening to her. He paused in his ministrations to reassure her. "It's all right, my love, let go, let it happen. I'm with you." He plunged his tongue inside her, and lavished his attention on the sensitive button, lavishing it with her nectar.

Her muscles relaxed, then tightened, quivered, and finally relaxed completely as she cried out his name. Drew caught her around the hips as her knees gave way, pressing his face against the softness of her belly, supporting her, cradling her in his arms while she shivered in the aftermath of her magnificent climax.

Chapter 25

Full nakedness! All my joys are due to thee,
As souls unbodied, bodies unclothed must be,
To taste whole joys.

—JOHN DONNE, c. 1572–1631

Kathryn opened her eyes. Drew looked up at her face. Her gray-green eyes were round and wide-eyed with wonderment. She didn't realize she was crying until he reached up and caught one of her tears on his fingertip and tasted it. Her face crumpled at the sight and she began to cry in earnest.

"What is it, love?" he asked. "What's wrong?"

"Nothing. It's ... it's just that I've never ..." She paused to catch her breath. *I love you.* Wren felt an almost overwhelming need to tell him that she loved him—that she had always loved him and always would—but when she managed to speak, other words came out. "You should have been the first."

Drew managed a sad smile. He hadn't expected her elderly husband to be much of a lover, but Drew would have thought that his father was a better lover than was evidenced by Kathryn's reaction. Drew shrugged. "Judging from what just happened, I think maybe I was."

He could tell from the expression on her face that she

didn't understand what he meant. "Hasn't anyone . . . ?" He didn't finish the question because he didn't want to know the answer.

Drew let go of her. He pushed himself to his knees and took several steps backwards to allow her some distance. "Forgive me," he said at last.

"Why?" she asked.

He bent down and handed her the towel she'd let fall to the floor. "For not compromising you years ago. It should be a crime for an old man to initiate a beautiful young woman like you into the joys of lovemaking."

Wren sighed. *It had been a crime.* A crime that had precluded joy and lovemaking. The only good thing to come out of her initiation had been her son. "Until a few moments ago, I didn't realize there were any joys to lovemaking."

Drew groaned in agony. "Christ, Kathryn!"

"Are there more?"

"Many more."

"Show me."

Drew shook his head. "Kathryn, I think we should wait."

"For what?"

"A minister. I'd be a first-class bounder if I bedded you now before we exchange our vows. You deserve a wedding and a proper wedding night."

Wren smiled. "I had a wedding once and a proper marriage," she told him. "And they weren't all they were cracked up to be. What I haven't had is a very improper wedding night. So, if you don't mind, that's what I'd like."

"You want . . . ?"

She wanted to feel loved and cherished and wanted before she became a means to an end, a necessary convenience. "To be your mistress before I'm your wife.

Drew, I want very much for you to be the first-class bounder I need you to be. Make love to me. Now. Tonight." Wren stared at him. She couldn't bring herself to beg, so she willed him to understand.

Drew found he wasn't noble enough to deny her. "Are you certain that this is what you want?" he asked.

"Very," she replied.

"No regrets?"

"Not if you want to marry your mistress in the morning," Wren answered.

"Fair enough." Drew bent at the knee, scooped her into his arms, and carried her into the bedroom. "We'll make love tonight and let tomorrow take care of itself." Drew placed her in the center of her bed, then followed her down, shifting his weight at the last moment, until he lay beside her instead of on her. And when he lay next to her he began to pat the bedding—the pillows, the sheets, and the blankets around her.

"What are you doing?" she asked.

Drew traced the contour of her mouth with the tip of his finger, feeling the words as she formed them. "I'm about to take great liberties with your person and I'm making sure I won't be bitten by one of your companions for my efforts."

Wren snuggled against him. "You may be bitten, my lord, but it won't be by an *Erinaceus eropaeus* or any other of my companions. Only yours." She sucked his finger into her mouth and gently, playfully bit it.

Drew felt the white-hot line of pleasure all the way to his toes. He pulled her close against him.

The buttons on his shirt pressed into her cheek. She stretched out against him, seeking the warmth of his body. Drew was lying beside her. Drew, who made her feel safe and secure and completely desirable; but he was still fully clothed and she wanted him naked beside her, touching her. Wren whimpered her dismay.

"What is it, love? Did I squeeze you too tightly?"

"No," she said, "but your attire is much too formal for this occasion." Wren grinned an impish grin. "You're wearing too many clothes."

His body reacted so violently to her words, Drew thought his heart might stop beating. He reached for the top button of his shirt.

"No." Wren placed her smaller hands under his and pushed him onto his back. "I've never undressed a man before. Let me."

"Feel free," he invited.

"I do." Wren unbuttoned the first button, then another, and another, until his shirt gaped open, exposing the hard muscles of his chest and stomach. She rubbed her hands over the furry mat of hair on his chest, then leaned over him, allowing the tips of her breasts to rub against the soft hair. She liked it so much, she repeated the action twice more.

He shivered, groaning at the tantalizing feel and scent of her. Drew reached for her and would have pulled her down on top of him, but she evaded his grasp. "Enjoying yourself?"

She paused to give his question serious consideration. "Yes, very much."

Drew gave a tight laugh. "Well, don't stop now. Be my guest."

"I don't know what to do," she admitted shyly. "Tell me what you want."

Drew forced himself to concentrate, forced himself to think about something other than her beautiful pear-shaped breasts hanging just out of reach. "Ride me," he ordered.

She did.

He sucked in his breath. His stomach muscles contracted as she settled herself atop him. He strained against the front of his trousers.

Wren wiggled again, moving up his torso until her bare bottom rested squarely on his stomach, then leaned forward.

Several of Drew's dreams came true at once. He struggled briefly, yanking free of his shirtsleeves, before raising his head to meet her.

She'd meant to kiss his mouth, but overshot her mark. Her lips brushed his forehead and his thick hair. She would've moved back, but Drew wrapped an arm around the curve of her buttocks, holding her in place while his other hand moved up to caress her breast and his mouth closed over the hard nub at its crown.

His blood rushed downward and the hard, male part of him throbbed with each beat of his heart. He ached to sheathe himself inside Kathryn's warmth. Desperate to end the exquisite torment, Drew tightened his grip on Kathryn and rolled her to her back.

He let go of her breast and found her mouth, kissing her as if his life depended on it. Wren tasted herself on his lips and on his tongue and realized she had marked him as her own, branded him with her essence. The idea excited her as much as it shocked her. She tangled her fingers in his hair, deepening the kiss.

Drew broke off the kiss. He braced himself on one elbow and worked his other hand between their bodies, caressing her stomach and the soft delta between her legs. He slipped his fingers between her soft, moist folds, and touched her there.

Wren jerked in reaction. She slid her hands down his back, over his tight buttocks, then back to the waistband of his trousers. She followed the strip of fabric from back to front. Drew groaned aloud as Wren brushed her fingers across his bulging fly. She searched for and located his buttons. Forcing each button through its hole, she opened his trousers and pushed them off his lean hips, over his buttocks, and as far down his long legs as she could reach. Drew kicked free of them, moaning his pleasure as the hard jutting length of him spilled into her waiting hands.

She marveled at the feel of him. She never dreamed anything so hard, anything capable of inflicting so much pain, could be so velvety soft and hot and enticing. She closed her fingers around him and before Drew could stop himself, he thrust against her hand.

She let go of him.

Drew took her hand in his and gently guided her back to him, showing her the motion he preferred. "It won't hurt you," he said. "*I* won't hurt you." He tried to smile, but the movement of her hand made a smile impossible. The best he could manage was a heartfelt groan that bared his teeth. "You're in control now. I may seem strong to you, I may appear invincible to the rest of the world, but this is the secret foolish men don't want women—especially virgins and wives—to know. You see, when you hold us like this, we're literally putty in your hands."

"How does it feel?" she asked, entranced by her new-found power over him.

"Like you felt when I put my fingers on you." He bit out the answer, barely able to form coherent thoughts.

Kathryn groaned. "As good as that?"

"Every bit." Drew shuddered, straining to regain a measure of his control. "Kathryn," he breathed her name. "God, I . . ." He wiggled his fingers against her.

She gasped out her pleasure.

"Take me," he ordered, "take me inside you."

She froze.

She didn't know how. She had no idea where to guide him or how. She'd given birth to a child, but she behaved as if she were a virgin. Those thoughts registered in a recess of his brain as Drew lifted her hips and guided himself into her welcoming warmth.

Wren cried out his name as he entered her. She lifted her legs and locked her thighs high around his waist.

Drew closed his eyes, threw back his head, and bit his bottom lip as he sheathed himself fully inside her warmth. His entire body shook with the effort of holding back the tide of pleasure he knew would come. Drew lost his battle to maintain control as her movement forced him deeper inside her. He began to move his hips in a rhythm as old as time.

Wren moved with him, her hips matching him thrust for thrust as she followed the primitive cadence of their pounding hearts. She clung to him, reveling in the weight and feel of him as he filled her again and again, gifting her with himself in a way she'd never thought possible. She squeezed her eyes shut. Tears of joy trickled from the corners, ran down her cheeks, and disappeared into her hair. He felt so good, so right. Wren gave herself up to the emotions swirling inside her, gave voice to the passion with the small moans that escaped her at each wonderful thrust. She tightened her muscles around him, holding on as the exquisite pleasure peaked. She muffled her scream against his shoulder.

"Kathryn!" Drew felt her tremors surrounding him and called out her name in a guttural cry wrung from the very depths of his soul. He shuddered as he collapsed atop her, completely spent, completely satisfied. He brushed his lips against her cheek and buried his face in her blond hair. Tasting the saltiness of her tears, Drew lifted his head and looked down at her beautiful face.

I love you. Her eyes were shining with emotion. He

touched his mouth to hers in a kiss so gentle, so loving, so precious, it brought fresh tears to her eyes.

"What's this?" he asked, kissing one away. "More tears?"

Wren nodded, pressing her lips against his shoulder. "Special tears," she said, "tears of joy."

Drew smiled down at her and took a deep breath. "When two people have shared kisses like ours, and lovemaking so exquisite the earth spins out of control, there's only one thing left to do."

"What's that?" A lump caught in her throat. She expected him to say something profound, something so incredibly beautiful that she could open her heart and declare her love for him, but when he answered her, all she could do was laughingly agree.

"Do it again," he teased. "As soon as possible."

Chapter 26

Busy old fool, unruly Sun,
Why dost thou thus,
Through windows and through curtains call on us?
Must to thy motions lovers' seasons run?

— JOHN DONNE, C. 1572–1631

The sun was peeking over the horizon, spreading tendrils of pink across the purple sky, when Wren awoke from a brief nap just after dawn. She rolled over in bed and came face to face with the man sharing her pillow. Drew. She smiled as he opened his eyes and reached for her.

"Good morning." She ducked her head, blushing with the knowledge that although her heart kept secrets from him, her body held none. "Time to get up."

"I'm already up," he said, reaching for her hand and guiding it to him. "I've been waiting for you to wake up and notice."

"Drew, it's morning. . . ." Wren pulled her hand away.

"Yes, it is," he agreed. "And this is an early morning greeting. A friendly reminder of the best way to start the day."

Wren giggled in spite of herself. "Is it possible for us to do this again after doing it twice last night?"

"Are you too sore?" he asked.

She blushed again. "No."

"Then, my love"—Drew took her hand and brought it back to him, wrapping her fingers around his shaft and covering her hand with his own—"it's not only possible, it's inevitable."

ᝈ

When they woke the second time, sunlight poured in the cottage windows and Wren's menagerie clamored for attention. Margo barked her frustration and scratched at the kitchen door.

Wren sighed. She shoved her hair out of her eyes, lifted her head from its resting place on Drew's shoulder, and looked down at him. "I latched her door last night because I didn't want her to bring mice inside and loose them in the kitchen while I was bathing."

"She does that?" He opened one eye and scanned the bed.

"Of course she does," Wren said. "She's a fox."

"I thought she was a pet." He toyed with one of Kathryn's long blond curls.

"She may be a pet, but she's still a fox and foxes hunt mice." Wren flipped back the covers. "I have to let her out."

"You stay put. I'll go." Drew gave her a sweet lingering kiss then rolled out of bed and strode from the bedroom to the kitchen naked.

Wren watched him, admiring the view of his firm buttocks and his long muscled thighs. "Well," she asked when he returned to the bedroom moments later, "any regrets?"

He knew what she was asking, but he couldn't help but tease her a little. "One," he admitted. "No, two."

"Oh?" She tried to sound nonchalant and failed miserably.

"That we can't stay in bed all day today and that I didn't catch a glimpse of your private artwork last night. You'd already removed your stockings before I got here."

Wren favored him with a brilliant smile and turned back the covers, inviting him to join her in the warmth of the bed. "I shan't need stockings if we stay in bed all day."

Drew chucked her under her chin. "I can think of a dozen reasons to wear stockings to bed—all of them carnal. How can it be that a notorious mistress like you knows none of them? My father was terribly remiss in your education." He bent and gathered his scattered clothing.

Wren blinked. Drew had just joked about her having been his father's mistress. And the joke was without rancor.

She couldn't bring herself to lie to him, so she settled on telling most of the truth. "George wasn't around me as often as you might think, and, when he was, I was either *enceinte* or taking care of a baby. My every waking moment was consumed with caring for my baby. Romance was the least of my concerns."

Drew pulled on his shirt and stockings, then stood up and stepped into his trousers. "I hope romance will play a much greater role in our relationship," he said. "But I'm sorry that I won't be able to see you with child. I would have liked that."

Wren frowned. "You can still save yourself from a childless fate."

"No." He framed her face with his hands. "I can't. I would rather have you than children." He leaned forward and kissed her. "Besides, we already have a son—who'll be expecting his riding lesson shortly."

Wren scrambled out of bed and began searching for her clothes. "What time is it?" She glanced at the sunlight pouring in the bedroom, trying to gauge the hour. "Will there be time for you and me to take our private ride before our lessons begin?"

Drew laughed. "I would think you'd had enough riding for one morning." He sat down on the edge of the bed and began pulling on his boots.

Wren opened the door to the armoire and took out her burgundy riding dress. She pulled fresh undergarments from the Queen Anne chest and added a pair of newly painted stockings. "I meant *horseback* riding."

"I know what you meant, my love, but I'm afraid we'll have to forgo our ride on Abelard this morning. If I don't hurry, Kit will come looking for me. I'll barely have time to change clothes and grab a bite to eat as it is." He retrieved his cravat linen from beneath the bed. It was hopelessly wrinkled, but Drew tied it around his collar anyway. It wouldn't do to be seen leaving the cottage less than fully clothed.

My love. He'd said it again. Drew called her his love. Wren held his words to her heart. His love. Even if he didn't declare it, he used the endearment. Surely that meant he cared. "What about my lesson?" Wren asked.

"You've had all the riding lessons you're going to get this morning," he said.

"What about this afternoon?" Now that she'd begun to learn how to ride Felicity, Wren was eager to improve.

Drew shook his head. "I'm afraid not. I'm expecting Martin to arrive this afternoon with the bodies of my father and his companion."

"Oh, Drew, I'm so sorry." Wren swallowed a sob. "I didn't realize . . ."

"Martin's message was waiting for me when we returned from the village yesterday afternoon. I would have mentioned it at dinner last night, but you didn't come to the house." He shrugged his shoulders and grinned a frankly boyish grin. "And I was too distracted to mention it later in the evening. Martin will want to go over the details of Father's will with us before the guests arrive for the funeral. And I must make certain all the preparations have been made for the funeral feast and for the guests."

"Ally and I will see to it."

"I'll have Mrs. Tanglewood prepare my mother's chamber for you."

"Drew, you can't."

"Yes, I can," he told her firmly. "Because we're going to be married by special license as soon as the archbishop arrives. I'll ask Martin to stand up for me and I'm sure Ally would be honored to stand beside you." He leaned against the doorjamb and watched as Kathryn returned the burgundy riding habit to the armoire and withdrew a black dress. "Have you any other color to wear for the wedding?"

Wren shook her head. "I couldn't wear it even if I did. I'm in mourning for your father," she reminded him. She walked over to the washstand and began her morning ablutions. She rinsed her face and reached for the towel. "If we get married, I'll have to do so wearing black."

Drew handed it to her. "We're getting married, my lady marchioness, never doubt it."

Wren pulled a clean chemise over her head and followed it with her black dress. She reached behind to button it and discovered Drew had other ideas. He brushed her hands away, then planted a kiss on the back of her neck before he buttoned her dress. "I thought you were in a hurry to leave."

"I'll leave," he drawled, "just as soon as you get to the good part."

"The good part?" she parroted.

He reached over and lifted one of her stockings from the bed. "I'm waiting for these."

Wren hiked up her skirts, then lifted her leg and began to smooth the first stocking over it. "In that case"—she cast a glance in his direction—"enjoy the show."

"Hedgehogs." He laughed when he saw that she'd painted an army of little hedgehogs marching on a path of white blossoms from her ankle to her garter.

"I knew you'd like them."

Chapter 27

The years keep coming and going,
Men will arise and depart;
Only one thing is immortal:
The love that is in my heart.

—HEINRICH HEINE, 1797–1856

*Martin Bell arrived from Ireland, as ex-*pected, later that afternoon. He brought the bodies of George Ramsey, the late marquess of Templeston, and his companion, Mary Claire, with him.

Drew met him at the front door.

Martin clutched the handle of his battered brown leather file case in his fist as he climbed down from the wagon and embraced Drew. "It's good to see you, my boy. I've brought your father home."

Drew signaled for the group of footmen who had been assembled to unload the coffins from the back of the hearse to begin their sad task. The larger coffin bore the standard of the marquess of Templeston, while the smaller one was covered by a simple panel of black silk.

"Thank you, Marty." Drew patted the older man on the back. "From the bottom of my heart, I thank you."

"Hardest thing I've ever done." Martin's voice was tremulous. His hand shook when he offered it to Drew and he looked a decade older than he had when he left

London and sailed to Ireland. "Brace yourself."

"I consulted with the local undertaker," Drew said.

"The bodies were prepared in Ireland," Martin told him. "I hired the hearse when we docked in London. The notices have already been posted there, so the only thing the local undertaker need worry about is the funeral procession and the funerals."

Drew ushered his friend up the steps and into the house. "Everything is ready." He opened the door to the study. "Go inside and sit down, Marty. I'll just be a minute."

Drew closed the door to the study and followed the footmen carrying his father's coffin into the ballroom, where the massive mahogany dining table that would serve as a bier lay draped in black mourning cloths. He helped the men lift the coffin into place.

"Shall we open it, sir?" Newberry stood at Drew's side.

"Not yet." Drew shuddered. "Keep it closed until the guests begin to arrive. Set up a stand of candelabras at each corner and provide a kneeling bench."

"What shall we do about the other?" Newberry nodded toward the footmen carrying the other coffin.

"Set up a bier in the chapel. Do the same for the young lady that you do for his lordship. I want candles burning at all times and I want someone there with her at all times. She was my father's companion, and although we cannot give her a state funeral, we can give her the same care we give my father."

"As you wish, milord." Newberry quietly issued instructions to the footmen, then turned back to Drew. "Shall we post notice that the young woman will be in the chapel?"

Drew shook his head. "No, we'll have someone greet each guest and provide remembrance cards at the door.

Guests who ask for her card should be directed to the chapel. And we need flowers," Drew remembered. "Fill the house with them."

"Very good, milord." Newberry bowed.

"Oh, and Newberry." Drew thought of something else. "The ballroom will be off limits to everyone in the household this evening. I intend to sit with his lordship tonight and I would appreciate complete privacy."

Newberry nodded. The new marquess would say his good-byes to his father in private. "I'll see that your brandy cabinet is stocked before I retire for the evening, milord. It will be available should you require it."

"Thank you." Drew dismissed the butler and returned to his study. Martin had made himself at home in one of the big leather chairs before the fire. "You look like you could use a brandy." Drew crossed the threshold and closed the door behind him.

"I may need an entire bottle." Martin propped his feet upon the leather footstool in front of the hearth and buried his face in his hands.

Drew walked over to the secretary and poured each of them a deep snifter of brandy. He carried Martin's drink over to him, then sat down beside him. "What do we know about Mary Claire?"

"Mary Claire O'Brien, aged eight and twenty, born in Limerick, Ireland. No family."

"She was older than I thought," Drew said.

"It surprised me as well." Martin was thoughtful. "She appeared to be much younger. She was a lovely girl."

"Is there anything I can do to make this easier for you, Martin?"

Martin unhooked the legs of his spectacles from his ears and carefully polished the lenses on the ends of his cravat. "Nothing can make this easier for me. Your father and I have been friends all our lives. I loved him like a brother. My duty to George didn't end with his death. This task was a part of it. The worst bloody part of it, but a part of it nonetheless." He paused long enough to put his spectacles back on, then turned to look at Drew. "What about you? Did you count your mission here a success?"

"Very much so."

"You evicted her?"

"No."

"Wasn't that your mission?" Martin asked. "How can you claim your trip here was successful if you failed to evict your father's mistress?"

Drew managed a lopsided smile. "My mission here changed as soon as I realized the mistress in question was Kathryn Markinson."

"Aah . . ." Martin gave a long, satisfied sigh. "So, I see."

"Of course you do," Drew agreed. "You knew what my father had planned. You knew I couldn't evict her even if I still wanted to. You knew who she was. You knew Kathryn was here."

"I knew."

"Why didn't you warn me?" Drew asked. He took a deep drink of his brandy and set the glass on the table between the leather chairs.

"I tried to warn you," Martin reminded him, "but you didn't listen to me. You heard only what you wanted to hear. And you didn't want to hear that the terms of George's will prevented you from evicting her."

Drew nodded in agreement. Martin was right. He hadn't listened to Martin's explanations or his warnings. He had heard exactly what he wanted to hear. "You drew up Father's will, so I assume you knew about Kit as well."

"Yes." The solicitor held up his hand to forestall any

comments or accusations. "I suppose you read the copy George kept here in the safe?"

"I read it," Drew told him. "He left the dowager cottage to Kathryn and the land it sits upon to me and he arranged for us to share custody of Kit. When I read the will, I couldn't decide if it was sheer genius or sheer madness."

"It was both," Martin answered. "Surely you realize there was a peculiar method to the madness."

"Of course I do. He tied us together. For better or for worse."

"George was attempting to put things right."

"The best way of putting things right would have been for him to marry Kathryn and ensure Kit's legitimacy." Drew stood up suddenly and began to pace the room.

"He couldn't marry her." Martin expelled his breath in a long exasperated sigh, unwilling to allow Drew to censure George's feelings or question his actions or his methods.

Drew nodded. "Kathryn told me that when my mother lay dying, my father promised her he would never remarry."

Martin was thoughtful. "I wonder how she knew about that."

"Her father told her," Drew replied. "Is it true?"

"Yes, it's true. George did promise Iris he would never remarry, but that was only a part of the reason he felt he couldn't offer to marry Kathryn."

"What was the other part?"

"Sit down, Drew, and I'll tell you," Martin said. "But your endless pacing is making me dizzy." The solicitor waited until Drew sat down before he continued with his explanation. "Your father couldn't marry Miss Markinson, I mean Mrs. Stafford, because a marriage between the two of them would prevent the two of you from marrying. The law states that a widower cannot marry his stepdaughter and the same is true for a woman. A widow cannot marry her stepson. If George had married her, you would have become Kathryn's stepson."

"There are exceptions."

"That's true," Martin admitted. "Upon occasion, the Crown grants an exception, but George didn't want to rely on the generosity of the government. Seeing you and Kathryn finally wed was your father's fondest wish." He paused. "George's method may have been a bit unorthodox, but how else could he guarantee that she wouldn't marry anyone else? Besides, George always believed that if you saw each other again, you'd rekindle the flame."

"Then he would have been very happy to learn he was right." Drew smiled. "I asked Kathryn to marry me and she consented. I'd like you to stand up with me, Marty."

"When?"

"As soon as the archbishop of Canterbury arrives with the special license."

Martin grinned. "Well done." He clapped Drew on the shoulder. "Well done." He rubbed his palms together. "Will you ask her to join us, Drew? She should be present at the reading of the will. The codicil to the will and the envelope he left for Kit in your keeping are for your eyes and ears alone. I'm not at liberty to share the terms of the codicil with anyone but you, but you may disclose the terms or do whatever you wish with them—except disregard them."

"What's in the envelope for Kit?"

Martin smiled. "All in good time, my boy, all in good time. Now, if you'll summon your intended, we can get on with the business of following George's final instructions regarding the dispossession of his property." The solicitor started to get to his feet, but Drew waved him back down onto the chair.

"Relax, Marty. Finish your brandy. I'll send someone to fetch Kathryn."

Wren arrived at the mansion a half hour later. Drew could tell from her appearance that she'd spent much of the afternoon working. She'd removed her painting smock, but the strong aroma of turpentine clung to her dress and hair and a splotch of reddish brown paint, the same color as the sprinkle of freckles dotting the bridge of her nose, bisected her right cheekbone.

Although she gave Drew a lingering glance when she entered the study, Wren's primary focus was Martin. Her heart went out to the solicitor, for he would be as lost without George as George had been without her father. She hadn't known until Bertrand died that the three of them—George, Martin, and her father—had been at school and university together. They'd been steadfast friends for more years than she had been alive and they had welcomed Bertrand Stafford into their midst because he was her father's friend and mentor. Martin started to get up from his chair, but Wren dropped to her knees and laid her head in his lap. Her throat ached and she choked on a sob. "Martin, I'm so sorry for your loss."

Martin patted her head the way her father had always done, stroking her shining blond curls. "Poor Wren," he said. "You and I have seen much too much of death in these past few years. And for me, this is perhaps the cruelest blow of all because it came so unexpectedly."

Watching them, Drew suddenly realized that Kathryn had grown up surrounded by her father's friends and colleagues. She had grown up listening to their stories, learning their histories, and she had become a surrogate daughter and a pet to all of them. He walked over to Martin's chair and offered his arm and his handkerchief to her.

She blinked back her tears as she took Drew's arm and pushed herself to her feet. "I apologize for my display, Drew," she said, "but Martin and I have been through so much together. As you can see, I'm quite fond of him and in truth, I don't know what I would have done if I hadn't had him—and George—to rely on."

"There's no need for you to apologize, Kathryn." Drew offered her his chair and got another from against the wall for himself. "I'm as fond of Martin as you are. He's been as much a father to me, in many ways, as my father was."

Martin cleared his throat. "That's because you and I are of a similar temperament. We are creatures of habit who like things neat and tidy with no surprises."

"That's true enough," Drew agreed.

"Whereas your father loved surprises," Martin continued. "And he loved creating them most of all. Which brings me to one of the reasons we're together." He hefted his leather file case onto his lap, opened the flap, and took out a sheaf of papers, then he reached into his waistcoat pocket to retrieve his spectacles and placed them on his nose. "The reading of George's will."

Martin glanced at Wren. "Did George share any of the terms of his will with you?"

Wren nodded. "He told me that I wouldn't have to worry about losing Kit or the cottage. He said that the next Lord Templeston would, of course, be Kit's legal guardian, but that as Kit's mother, I would have physical custody of him and be consulted in all matters that concern Kit. And George promised he'd make certain the next Lord Templeston understood his wishes by mentioning his bequest of the dowager cottage to my father in his will. George told me he used my married name in the document because he knew Drew wouldn't object to Mrs. Bertrand Stafford inheriting the cottage." She looked at Drew. "I've since learned that the wording of the will is not exactly as George led me to believe, but I haven't read the document or any portion of it."

"Is that so?" Drew remarked. "Because I could have sworn you'd read at least part of it."

"I told you I hadn't."

"Yes, but you threw so much of what was in it up in my face—on a number of memorable occasions," he drawled.

"I wasn't certain about anything," she admitted to Drew, "but I'd shared my concerns about Kit's future with George and I trusted that he would keep his word. Your ignorance of my presence here at Swanslea enabled me to bluff."

Drew turned to Martin with a wry smile. "Let that be a lesson to you, Martin. Don't play cards with her unless you like to lose."

"George did keep his word," Martin said. "He simply added a few more details." He cleared his throat and began to read the document.

Wren listened to the words and legal phrases as Martin read the will, but she didn't really begin to pay attention to the meaning of the words, through the long lists of the usual bequests to members of the households and the marquess's favorite charities, until her name was mentioned.

" ' . . . the gardens, tenants' houses, and the acreage under pasture that make up the estate of Swanslea Park will belong solely to my son and heir, Andrew Ramsey, but the main house is to be held in trust for the legitimate heirs or issue of Andrew Ramsey or the legitimate heirs or issue of Kathryn Markinson Stafford. The house is to be held in joint trust by Andrew Ramsey and Kathryn Markinson Stafford until the time that legitimate heirs or issue of Andrew Ramsey or Kathryn Markinson Stafford reach the age of majority. Should there be no living legitimate heirs or issue of Andrew Ramsey or Kathryn Stafford, the main house, gardens, tenants' houses, and the acreage under pasture will, upon their deaths, become the property of the Trevingshire hunt.

" 'As I gifted the dowager cottage to Wesley Markinson some years ago and the deed he held has been duly inherited by his daughter, Kathryn Markinson Stafford, I further deed to her, for her sole use for as long as she lives, the parkland surrounding the cottage, after which it will become a part of the estate held in trust for the legitimate heirs or issue of Andrew Ramsey or Kathryn Markinson Stafford. In addition, the Marquess of Templeston will provide ten thousand pounds per annum for the maintenance of the jointly held property and the dowager cottage.' "

"He gave me the park?" Kathryn was astonished.

Martin nodded. "George believed in you and the importance of the work you're doing. He wanted you to be able to continue that work undisturbed."

Wren exchanged a meaningful look with Drew. "You mean that *I* would have been within my rights to order the hunt off Swanslea Park land?"

Drew smiled. "As I recall, you *were* ordering them off Swanslea Park land, but since you were up a tree and powerless to prevent them from hunting, they refused to go. Now you know that you are within your rights to force them to leave. All you have to do is send for the sheriff or magistrate."

Martin dropped his chin and glanced over the top rim

of his glasses, a puzzled expression on his face. "The Trevingshire hunted here? When? They know better. George barred them from hunting three years ago."

"They seemed to think that since George was dead, the hunting could resume," Wren told him.

"Good heavens!" Martin exclaimed. "You were up a tree? What happened? Was anyone hurt? Is Margo—"

"She's fine." Wren explained the incident, ending her recitation by saying, "Drew arrived in time to rescue us."

Martin cleared his throat once again. "The master of the hunt clearly overstepped his bounds. Something will have to be done about that."

"Something has been done about it," Drew said.

"Really?" Wren was clearly surprised.

"You don't think I'd allow them to come onto our land and tree the future marchioness without reprisal, do you?"

She wrinkled her brow. "But I wasn't the future marchioness then."

Drew reached over and cupped her face with his hand, caressing her cheek with the pad of his thumb. "My dear Kathryn, don't you understand? You have always been the future marchioness."

The sexual tension in the room rose several degrees and Martin shifted uncomfortably in his seat. "Yes, well, you can continue your discussion about that later. But for now, we've a few more details to go over. . . ."

Drew rubbed his thumb over Wren's lips, then released her and sat back in his chair to listen while Martin read the remainder of the will.

" ' . . . I hereby name my son and heir, Andrew Ramsey, twenty-eighth Earl of Ramsey and sixteenth Marquess of Templeston, sole legal guardian for any and all of my children except Christopher George Ramsey, known to the family as Kit. Guardianship of Kit is to be shared with his mother, Kathryn Markinson Stafford. Kit shall not be removed from Kathryn's home or care without her knowledge and consent, nor shall he be allowed to travel without her knowledge and consent. The sixteenth marquess shall not hire or fire any nannies, governesses, or tutors without Kathryn's consent, nor can he send Kit to boarding school without the consent of the boy's mother. Furthermore, the sixteenth marquess shall not arrange any betrothals or marriages for Christopher George Ramsey without the consent and approval of Kathryn Markinson Stafford.' "

Martin finished reading the will. "So you see, my dear girl, George did everything he said he would do and more."

Wren sat very quietly. "He blamed himself."

Martin shook his head. "Not for what happened, but for his inability to do right by you. There was never any need for you to doubt him. You could always count on George to see to your future."

"Oh, George . . ."

Kathryn looked so stricken Drew thought she might faint.

"Is he in the ballroom?"

There was no need for Drew to ask whom she meant. Drew nodded.

"P-please, excuse me." She got up from her chair and rushed out of the study.

Drew followed her as far as the door and would have followed her into the ballroom, but Martin stopped him. "Let her go, my boy. Let her cry it out and say good-bye in private."

He hovered in the doorway, watching as Kathryn knelt beside his father's coffin. She slipped her bare hand beneath the Templeston standard and began to cry. She didn't make a sound, but her shoulders shook with the force of her grief and Drew's heart ached at the sight of it.

Wren leaned her forehead against the coffin. She felt the smooth polished wood beneath her fingers and the soft silk flag against her forehead. Martin's words echoed in her ears. *You could always count on George to see to your future.* Drew had used almost identical words the day he'd asked her to accompany him to the undertaker's—the day they'd talked about that fateful night at Vauxhall Gardens. *I knew I could count on my father to see you and your aunt safely home.* Drew had asked his father to see her and Aunt Edwina safely home. But George hadn't escorted either of them. Aunt Edwina had caught a ride with her friends and Wren had been raped and dumped at her aunt's front door. And after all the many kindnesses he had bestowed on her, after all the care and concern he had shown her father, after all these years, George had still blamed himself for what happened. Unable to stop the hot flow of her tears, Wren let them come. "Oh, George," she whispered, "you more than made up for anything that happened when you gave me Kit. Didn't you know that? Didn't you understand?"

"She'll be all right, Drew," Martin said as Drew made a motion to go to Wren. "Come sit down."

Drew hesitated.

"Come on," Martin urged. "I still have to read the codicil to George's will." He waved the addendum to the will in the air and showed Drew a bundle wrapped in heavy protective paper. "And I have a package for Kit addressed to you."

Drew returned to his chair and took the package Martin handed him.

"George gave it to me to give to you in the event of his death."

Drew unwrapped the paper and discovered a black

velvet drawstring bag containing a small teakwood box. He opened the intricately carved box to reveal a gold and diamond locket. Drew held it up for Martin to see. "It's a locket." On a piece of paper, written in Latin in his father's hand were the words, *You shall know they are mine by the likeness they bear.*

The solicitor nodded. "I thought it might be." He unfolded the legal papers and began to read. " 'Codicil to the last will and testament of George Ramsey, fifteenth Marquess of Templeston. My fondest wish is that I shall die a very old man beloved of my family and surrounded by children and grandchildren, but because one cannot always choose the time of one's Departure from the Living, I charge my legitimate son and heir, Andrew Ramsey, twenty-eighth Earl of Ramsey, Viscount Birmingham, and Baron Selby, on this the third day of August in the Year of Our Lord 1818, with the support and responsibility for my beloved mistresses and any living children born of their bodies in the nine months immediately following my death.

" 'As discretion is the mark of a true gentleman, I shall not give name to the extraordinary ladies who have provided me with abiding care and comfort since the death of my beloved wife, but shall charge my legitimate son and heir with the duty of awarding to any lady who should present to him, his legitimate heir, or his representative a gold and diamond locket engraved with my seal, containing my likeness, stamped by my jeweler, and matching in every way the locket enclosed with this document, an annual sum not to exceed twenty thousand pounds to ensure the bed and board of the lady and any living children born of her body in the nine months immediately following my Departure from the Living.

" 'The ladies who present such a locket have received it as a promise from me that they shall not suffer ill for having offered me abiding care and comfort. Any off-spring who presents such a locket shall have done so at their mother's bequest and shall be recognized as a child of the fifteenth Marquess of Templeston and shall be entitled to his or her mother's portion of my estate for themselves and their legitimate heirs in perpetuity according to my wishes as set forth in this, my last will and testament. George Ramsey, fifteenth Marquess of Templeston.' "

Drew opened the locket and stared down at the miniature portrait of his father.

"George wanted me to give you this, along with the package, after the reading of the will and its codicil." Martin got up from his chair and took an envelope out of his jacket pocket. He stared at the letter for a moment, then gave it to Drew. "I'll just go see if Mrs. Tanglewood has a room prepared for me," he said, patting his young friend on the shoulder, "while I leave you alone to read your letter."

Drew waited until Martin left the room before he walked over to his desk and broke the wax seal on the envelope and read:

My dearest son,

If you're reading this letter, then I've met my Maker a bit sooner than I'd planned. If everything is as it was meant to be, Martin or I would have already destroyed this letter, but if you're reading it, that is not the case.

I cannot rest easy in my grave until you know that I never meant to fail you. You counted on me and my momentary thoughtlessness drastically altered your life's path in a manner neither of us could have foreseen. I hope that, one day, you'll forgive me. I bear a heavy guilt for my misplaced trust.

I love you, son, and I have always been so very proud of you—as a boy and as the man you've grown up to be. Your mother and I always knew that you were our shining accomplishment and our greatest joy. You were the light of her life and you've been the light of mine.

I have entrusted to your care my second shining accomplishment and the joy of my old age, my son Christopher George Ramsey. Kit. He needs you, Drew. He needs a father to love and to look up to. Be that father. He cannot help the circumstances of his birth, nor should they matter. But in a country like ours, the order and circumstance of one's birth is everything. I claim him as my son because he is my son. He cannot claim legitimacy, but he can lay claim to something more important: blood. He is your half-brother, but I would ask that you raise him as your son for I do not want him to suffer for the actions (not the sins) of his parents.

I did not sin in loving his mother, nor did she sin in loving me. My sin was in putting a solemn promise to one love ahead of the needs of another. There are those who will view Kit as an accident or a mistake. He was never an accident or a mistake. I wanted him—loved him—just as much as I wanted and loved you. Accept him, with my blessings, and give him the family he deserves.

For you see, Drew, my fondest wish for you was that you would meet a young lady and have what your mother and I shared. I thought you had found it with Wren, but something terrible happened to prevent her from marrying you.

Don't blame her. She did what she did to protect you. She has never confided it to me. I guessed the truth. I didn't want to believe it, but I know it was true.

It is not my place to divulge her secret. She must be the one to do that. I can only say that no matter what you believe of me at this moment, know that I loved you and that I tried to atone for my mistake by watching out for the one you loved.

You should also know that all of the ladies with whom I have been intimately acquainted have my locket. The locket that accompanied this letter is the one I gave to Kit's mother. All of the ladies with whom I've shared a bed and pillow—including Kit's mother—have something else in common—a trait you cannot fail to notice should they decide to present themselves to you.

Trust in your heart, my son. Follow it. Let it lead you to Wren's door. Don't grieve too much for me, for I am with your mother now and we are both looking out for you and your family.

My love to you and to Kit and to Wren.

Your loving and proudest of fathers, George.

Drew refolded the letter and placed it in his jacket pocket close to his heart. He picked up the locket and held it tightly in his hand, warming the cold metal as he left the study and made his way to the ballroom.

Kathryn was gone.

But his father wasn't alone. Newberry stood a silent vigil over the corpse of his late employer. Drew dismissed him as he entered the room. "Close the doors behind you, Newberry, and lock them. I'll be here until morning."

Newberry did as he was asked, leaning against the heavy wooden door only once to listen as the current marquess of Templeston sobbed out his grief at the loss of his father, his hero, his friend.

Chapter 28

'Tis the last rose of summer, left blooming alone; all her lovely companions are faded and gone.

—THOMAS MOORE, 1478–1535

The guests began arriving for the marquess's funeral the next morning, but Drew wasn't aware of it until late afternoon. After spending the night locked in the ballroom with his father's body, he'd made his way wearily up the stairs to his bed. He crawled beneath the covers fully clothed except for his jacket and boots and slept, oblivious to the bustle going on downstairs.

Unaware of Wren's new status as the future marchioness of Templeston, Newberry quickly pressed Miss Allerton into service to act as hostess to the arriving guests. Polly, the youngest of the housemaids, was sent to the nursery to entertain Kit.

The lull before the storm had ended and the house was filled with the sounds of strangers arriving en masse—carriages rolling across the crushed gravel driveways, luggage being unloaded and carried to guest rooms, and the steady drone of conversation.

The activity continued throughout the morning and

well into the afternoon, when the lord of the estate awoke.

Drew washed at the basin, shaved a day's growth of whiskers from his face, and put on a fresh shirt and cravat. He pulled on the same jacket he'd worn the previous day, stepped into his boots, and left his room by way of the servants' stairs.

He emerged in the kitchen, where preparations for the funeral feast continued unabated. His presence startled a few of the kitchen staff, who started forward to see to his needs. Drew waved them away, tearing a chunk from a loaf of freshly baked bread cooling on a table and grabbing a wedge of cheese to assuage his hunger as he exited the house.

Avoiding the drive, which was crowded with carriages and coachmen and grooms, Drew followed the gravel path through the garden. He kept his head bowed, ignoring several acquaintances who had wandered into the garden, as he veered off the path and headed toward the cottage and Kathryn.

A feeling of unease began to permeate his senses when he discovered Kathryn gone and the cottage empty of wildlife. He wheeled around and began to retrace his steps, lengthening his stride until he was practically running back to the mansion.

"Milord," Newberry called to him as Drew entered through the servants' entrance, "Lord and Lady St. Jacque and His Grace, Lord Canterbury, have arrived. Lord Canterbury asked me to tell you that he brought the license as you requested and he wants to know if you've decided about the ceremony."

Drew paused. "How many guests have we?"

"A dozen so far."

"Tell Lord Canterbury I've decided on tomorrow

morning. I'd like to have it done before we've a large crowd. Tell me, Newberry, have you seen Mrs. Stafford this morning?"

"No, milord."

"When did you see her last?" Drew demanded.

"I don't recall, milord. Did you try the dowager cottage? She's usually there this time of day."

"I tried the cottage," Drew told him. "She's not there and neither are the animals. Think, man, when did you last see her?" Drew raked his fingers through his hair and muttered, "The archbishop is expecting a bride for the ceremony and I'll not allow her to disappoint me twice."

"Milord?" Newberry wasn't certain he'd heard correctly.

"Mrs. Stafford and I are getting married in my study tomorrow morning if I can locate her in time. That is why His Grace brought the license and why he asked about the ceremony. Your future marchioness is missing."

"About that, milord . . ."

"Yes?"

"I last saw Miss Wren beside the late marquess's coffin yesterday afternoon. I stayed with his lordship's body after she left, but I overheard her ask one of the maids if the chapel was ready."

Drew rubbed his eyes with the heel of his hand. "The chapel."

"Yes, milord."

"Thank you, Newberry."

"You're welcome, milord." Newberry shifted his weight from one foot to the other in an uncharacteristic display of unease. "About Miss Wren . . ."

"What is it, man?" Drew was impatient to find her.

"I didn't know of Miss Wren's change in status, milord, and as Miss Allerton was born a lady, I asked her to act as hostess in your absence. I meant no offense to Miss Wren and I beg your apology for my presumption."

"Think nothing of it." Drew clapped him on the shoulder. "I wouldn't have wanted Kathryn to face those vicious tabbies in the *ton* with her status in doubt, anyway. If the fates were kind, she would never have to face them, but as it is, the best we can do is ensure that when she does face them it will be as the marchioness of Templeston. As a lady, Miss Allerton was the most logical choice and I've no doubt that she's doing a splendid job." He clapped Newberry on the shoulder once again. "I'm off to the chapel. Tell Lord and Lady St. Jacque and His Grace I'll see them at supper."

The chapel was nearly as large as the rectory, for it had been built during the reign of Henry VII when the earl and countess of Munnerlyn, Drew's maternal ancestors, had been Catholic and the household had included a priest. The household staff and the villagers had attended mass every morning with the family in their private chapel. But that practice came to an end during the Civil War. The present house at Swanslea Park replaced the house that had been razed by Cromwell's Roundheads. Miraculously, the stone chapel had survived, even though the priest and the sitting Lord Munnerlyn had not, and the house was rebuilt in 1705, with the architect incorporating the original chapel in its design. Shortly thereafter, the Munnerlyns had restricted the chapel to family only and ordered a rectory built in the village.

Drew stared up at the rose window. The sunlight filtering through the stained glass cast colored patterns across the solitary coffin. Those spots of color and the two brace of lighted candelabra at the corners of the coffin provided the only light. Drew exhaled a sigh of relief. On the opposite side of the coffin, keeping silent vigil, sat Kathryn.

He walked over to where she sat. "Thank God I found you."

She stood up, immediately alarmed. "Why? Is something wrong? Has something happened to Kit?" She swayed on her feet.

Drew wrapped his arms around her. "Kit's fine. Everything is all right." He looked her in the eye. "Forgive me for frightening you."

Wren sagged against him, allowing Drew to bear her weight.

"I couldn't find you," he said. "No one had seen you since yesterday. The cottage is empty. Where are the animals? What's happened to your menagerie?"

"Mr. Isley is keeping them at his cottage. I thought it best, in case Margo should get loose while your guests are here."

Drew held her tightly, gently pressing her head against his chest. "God, Kathryn, I thought I'd lost you again."

Wren could hear the rapid beat of his heart against her ear. "I didn't leave you," she said. "I was here."

"All night?" He pulled back to look at her. Her eyes were red-rimmed and bloodshot and there were dark bluish-purple circles beneath them. She looked exhausted and extremely fragile. "You kept vigil in the chapel all night?"

Wren nodded. "You sat through the night with George. I thought someone should sit with his companion."

Drew stroked her blond curls. "Her name was Mary Claire," he said softly. "And I asked Newberry to have one of the staff stay with her."

"He assigned a trio of maids to relieve each other at

four-hour intervals," Wren said. "I came instead." She leaned back so she could stare into Drew's brown eyes. "Have you seen her, Drew? Did you look at her?"

"No. Did you?"

Wren nodded. "Martin asked me to see that she was dressed appropriately. I hope you don't mind, but I provided her with one of your mother's old gowns. A dress made of gold brocade to complement her coloring. The Irish undertakers left the dress she was wearing when they found her on her. Fortunately, Martin thought to ask me to check. I would have hated for her mourners to see her that way."

"I can't believe Martin asked that of you."

"I didn't mind," Wren told him. "I came down to the chapel, viewed her body, and went back upstairs to get a dress. When I returned, Cassie and I dressed her."

"Who's Cassie?"

"One of the maids Newberry asked to sit with her. When we were done, I sent Cassie back to help Mrs. Tanglewood and I stayed with Mary Claire. She was so young. . . ."

"She was eight and twenty," he said. "Older than you are."

"Well, she doesn't look it. She has long auburn hair and I'll bet her eyes are the same chocolate brown color as yours and Kit's. She was beautiful. I can't blame George for falling in love with her." Wren shrugged her shoulders. "After seeing her and performing such an intimate task for her, I couldn't stand the thought of having hired maids sit with her body. She deserved family—or at least someone who understood what it was like to be a part of the marquess of Templeston's life."

"What is it like?"

"I don't know what it was like for Mary Claire," Wren answered honestly, thoughtfully. "I only know what it's been like for me." She continued to look up at him.

"How has it been?" He leaned close and brushed her lips with his. "With this marquess of Templeston? So far?"

"So far it's been incredible."

Drew bent at the knees and scooped Wren up into his arms. "That's what I like to hear." He kissed her again. "Now, let's find a bed. You look exhausted. You need some sleep."

"You're part of the reason I haven't had any sleep," she teased.

"That's true," Drew said. "But this time I intend to see that you get some sleep."

"I don't know if that's possible as long as you're in the bed."

"It's not only possible," Drew repeated his earlier words, "it's inevitable."

He carried her from the chapel to the dowager cottage. He undressed her, lifting her dress and chemise over her head and peeling her drawers and the black silk stockings with the playful hedgehogs painted on them down her long legs. When he had her undressed, Drew turned back the bed linens and placed her in bed, then he rid himself of his clothes and climbed in bed beside her.

"I thought you said we were going to sleep," Wren murmured.

Drew cradled her against him. "We are." He kissed the top of her head and closed his eyes. Holding Kathryn in his arms gave him peace of mind he hadn't had since he went to war. For the first time in years, he could sleep through the night. She kept his nightmares at bay.

Drew awoke the following morning to find Kathryn snuggled close beside him, her head pillowed against his chest. "Wake up, my beauty," he whispered. "We have an appointment with the archbishop this morning."

Wren opened her eyes and smiled at him. "We do?"

Drew nodded. "He granted us a special license, so today is your wedding day." He touched the tip of her nose with his index finger. "Put on your prettiest black dress—and your prettiest black stockings."

She bit her bottom lip and frowned.

"What is it?" he asked. "What's bothering you?"

"I'm not sure that marrying me is the best thing for you, Drew. A virgin of impeccable reputation and fortune might be a better choice."

"Why would I want a virgin when I can have a beautiful young widow of property?" He focused his perfect white smile on her. "I'm sure that marrying you is the right thing for me. Unless you've had a change of heart?"

She wanted him to tell her he loved her. She wanted him to marry her because he couldn't envision life without her by his side, but she knew that was impossible. What Drew felt for her wasn't love. It was lust. Wren took a deep breath. "Of course I haven't." She feigned a sophistication she didn't feel. "Marriage to you will give my son legitimacy, repair my reputation, and make me a wealthy marchioness. What more could I want?"

Love, he thought. He'd like to hear Kathryn say she loved him. She'd told him she loved his father. Maybe asking her to love him as much as she'd loved his father was asking more than she was able to give. "I thought we'd meet in my study at ten this morning."

"All right."

"Miss Allerton will stand up for you, and Martin and Kit will stand up for me," he told her.

"Fine." Her voice sounded wistful. If he would only tell her how he felt about the wedding. If he would only tell her how he felt about her.

Drew kissed her one last time before he rolled out of bed and began to dress. "Then I suppose I'll see you at ten." His voice sounded wistful. If only she would tell him how she felt about the wedding. If only she would tell him how she felt about him.

"I'll be there."

Would she? After the last attempt, he couldn't help but wonder if she'd show up. "We'll have to postpone the wedding trip for a while," he said. "And remain in the country."

"Of course," she replied. "We're in mourning."

"But we'll take a trip later."

"That isn't necessary, Drew." She blushed. "We've already had the honeymoon and I'm perfectly content to remain in the country."

He finished dressing. "I'll see you at ten."

"I'll be there," she repeated. "I promise."

Chapter 29

Grant them the joy which brightens earthly sorrow;
Grant them the peace which calms all earthly strife,
And to life's day the glorious unknown morrow
That dawns upon eternal love and life.

—FROM HYMN 214 OF

THE COMMON BOOK OF PRAYER

"*We missed you at supper, Drew,*" His Grace, the archbishop of Canterbury, greeted his godson as he entered Drew's study a few minutes before ten o'clock. "Your friends, the St. Jacques and I."

"I'm sorry, Your Grace," Drew murmured, "but something came up to detain me." Drew stood alongside Martin, Miss Allerton, and Kit. He was trying to contain his nervousness, but his palms were damp with perspiration and he was fighting a desperate urge to pace the width and breadth of his father's study. The clock on the mantel was beginning to chime the hour and the bride had yet to make an appearance.

"Apology accepted." The archbishop glanced around the study. Everyone seemed to be present except the bride. "Are you quite certain that you want the ceremony performed in here? I believe Swanslea Park has a perfectly charming chapel suitable for the occasion."

Drew shook his head. "My late father's companion, Miss O'Brien, is currently lying-in-state in the chapel. I didn't think a wedding there would be appropriate under the circumstances. . . ." He glanced at the door.

"Quite right," the archbishop said to Drew. "The study is a more appropriate choice for a quiet solemnization of nuptials while the household is in a state of bereavement."

"Am I late?"

Kathryn stood in the doorway, a vision of serene beauty, dressed in a black velvet dress and clutching a bouquet of hothouse lilies and roses. Her blond curls were fashioned into an elegant chignon and she wore a small black velvet hat without feathers or veil.

She had never been as beautiful to him as she was in that moment and Drew released a heartfelt sigh as he stepped forward to greet her. "No, of course not." He led her forward to greet the archbishop. "Mrs. Bertrand Stafford, may I present you to His Grace, Lord Canterbury?"

The archbishop shook Kathryn's hand. "An honor to meet you, my dear."

"Thank you, Your Grace. The honor is mine once again."

Lord Canterbury raised an eyebrow in query.

"We met four years ago," Wren explained. "I was known to you then as Kathryn Markinson."

"You're the gel who . . ."

Wren bowed her head. "Yes, Your Grace. Your godson has a remarkable capacity for forgiveness."

If the archbishop was dismayed by Drew's choice of a bride, he showed no sign of it, beyond his initial outburst. "If you're ready"—he glanced at Drew before he straightened his vestments and opened his Bible—"shall we begin?"

Drew nodded his assent and Martin stepped forward. The solicitor stood at Wren's side and offered her his arm. "May I have the honor to stand in your father's stead, my dear?"

Tears sparkled in her eyes. "Thank you, Martin."

The archbishop cleared his throat and began the service. "Dearly beloved, we are gathered together here in the sight of God, and in the face of these witnesses, to join together this man and this woman in Holy Matrimony, which is an honorable estate, invented by God in the time of man's innocency, signifying unto us the mystical union that is betwixt Christ and his church; which holy estate Christ adorned and beautified with his presence, and first miracle that he wrought in Cana of Galilee . . ."

He stared first at Wren and then at Drew. "I require and charge you both as you will answer at the dreadful day of judgment, when the secrets of all hearts shall be disclosed, that if either of you know any impediment why you may not be lawfully joined together in Matrimony, ye do now confess it. . . ."

Although he'd first cursed his father for not marrying her, Drew looked heavenward and said a silent prayer of thanks to his father for his extraordinary forethought and wisdom. He remembered the words his father had written in the letter folded in the breast pocket of his jacket: *I can only say that no matter what you believe of me at this moment, know that I loved you and only tried to watch out for the one you loved.* For if his father had married her, then he would not be able to marry Kathryn now.

"Andrew Ramsey, sixteenth marquess of Templeston, twenty-eighth earl of Ramsey, Viscount Birmingham, and Baron Selby, wilt thou have this woman to thy wedded wife, to live together after God's ordinance in the holy estate of Matrimony? Wilt thou love her, comfort her, honor and keep her in sickness and in health; and forsaking all others, keep thee only unto her, so long as ye both shall live?"

"I will." Drew's answer was strong and firm.

He smiled at her and Wren saw the conviction in the depths of his brown eyes. Drew had promised to love her. Even if he could not bring himself to tell her, he had given himself to her before God and witnesses. He was hers for the keeping.

"Kathryn Markinson Stafford, wilt thou have this man to thy wedded husband, to live together after God's ordinance in the holy estate of Matrimony? Wilt thou obey him, serve him, love, honor, and keep him in sickness and in health; and forsaking all others, keep thee only unto him, so long as ye both shall live?"

Wren returned Drew's smile with one of her own. "I will."

The rest of the ceremony passed in a blur of tears for Wren as she listened to Drew repeat his vows and she repeated hers in kind. She stared up at his face and knew that she would love him until the day she died and beyond.

"With this Ring, I thee wed, with my body I thee worship, and with all my worldly goods I thee endow: in the Name of the Father, and of the Son, and of the Holy Ghost. Amen." Drew slipped a heavy gold and sapphire band onto the fourth finger of her hand.

Wren gazed at it as she bowed her head for prayer.

"Kathryn?"

She looked up from her woolgathering to find Drew looking down at her, a tender expression of concern on his face. "It's time to sign the register." He signed his name with a flourish and then watched as she followed suit: Kathryn Markinson *Ramsey*. She halted the pen in midmotion and Drew leaned close and said, "Marchioness of Templeston, countess of Ramsey, Viscountess Birmingham, and Baroness Selby."

She gave him a grateful smile.

"At last," Drew pronounced.

Yes, she thought, finally. For better or for worse, they were husband and wife—as they should have been for the past four years.

Newberry arrived with a trolley bearing a tea tray and a small bride's cake as the ceremony ended. There was no wedding breakfast or celebration. Indeed, there was to be no change in the household routine at all while guests were present—except that Wren would sleep in the master chamber with Drew and stand with him at the funerals. Once the funerals were over, Drew planned to post an announcement to the *Times* and to take Kathryn on a wedding trip, but until then, things would continue unchanged.

Neither the Church nor the State prohibited marriage between a man and a woman in deep mourning, but it was considered poor form to announce it until sufficient time had passed. For the next few weeks, news of their marriage would be kept quiet, known only to a select few and the household staff.

Wren and Drew stood side by side as Martin and Ally and Lord Canterbury offered them congratulations and good wishes. Ally leaned down and whispered something in Kit's ear and the little boy walked over to Drew.

Drew sat on his heels in order to put himself at Kit's level.

"Ally says to wish you happy 'cause you married my mama."

"Thank you, Kit," Drew answered.

"What's married mean?"

Drew grinned. "It means that you and your mama will live with me for always. From now on, I'll be your papa and you'll be my son and heir. If you've no objections."

"My papa's dead," Kit told him. "Are you dead, too?"

"No, Kit," Drew said. "I'm very much alive."

Kit seemed to digest that information. "Will I get to see you more than my other papa?"

Wren's heart seemed to catch in her throat. She had always suspected Kit hungered for George's company. Now, his innocent questions confirmed it.

"You'll get to see me all the time," Drew promised. "Because we're going to live in the same house."

"Are we going to live in Swanslea Park or in the cottage?"

Drew ruffled Kit's soft hair. "We're going to live at Swanslea Park and keep the cottage for your mama's work and sometimes we'll live in my houses in London and Scotland."

"Will Lancelot and Jem live there too?"

The fact that Kit's primary concern about the wedding was whether or not his pony and the young groom who'd become the boy's mentor would be able to live with him made Drew laugh. "I think that can be arranged."

Kit was satisfied. "Okay." He glanced over at his mother. "Can I have some cake now? Ally said if I was good I could have cake."

"May I have some cake?" Wren corrected automatically. "Yes, you may." She turned to Drew. "How does it feel to know that your new son only came to our wedding for the cake?"

"I was worried that he wouldn't accept the idea, so you can imagine my relief at knowing he can be bribed so easily."

Wren laughed. "The last time you bribed him it cost you a pony."

"Seven ponies," Drew reminded her. "But I'm learning to pace myself."

◠

"I have something that belongs to you," Drew said much later when he and Wren sat alone in the cottage sharing afternoon tea.

"Another wedding present?" she teased. He'd already made love with her and presented her with the marchioness of Templeston's extensive collection of heirloom jewelry. And she had given him an enticing view of her latest private artwork—white doves with olive branches in their beaks that graced the tops of her stockings—her father's gold watch, and an original watercolor she had painted of him astride Abelard.

"No," he answered. "Something contained in a package Martin gave me after the reading of my father's will." He pulled the locket from his jacket pocket and handed it to her. "He said it was yours."

"Drew!" she breathed. "It's lovely." She turned the gold and diamond locket over in her hand, then opened it and gazed at the miniature portrait of George. "But Martin was mistaken. This doesn't belong to me. I've never seen it before."

"Not Martin." Drew frowned. "My father. He said he gave it to Kit's mother."

"Perhaps he meant to give it to me," she suggested.

"No," Drew insisted. "He said that I should also know that all of the ladies with whom he had been intimately acquainted had a locket like this one."

Wren gasped. "I had no idea."

"He said that the locket accompanying his letter to me—this locket—was the one he gave to Kit's mother. It has to be yours."

She met Drew's gaze and slowly shook her head. "It isn't."

Drew looked at her. "You must have one like it then."

"No."

All of the ladies with whom I've shared a bed and pillow—including Kit's mother—have something else in common—a trait you cannot fail to notice should they decide to present themselves to you.

"Oh, Christ!" His father's words flooded his brain like a fever and suddenly all of the disparate pieces of the puzzle of his father's relationship with Kathryn made sense. Drew reached for Wren's hand. "Come with me."

He pulled her out of her chair and headed for the front door.

"Drew, we're not dressed!"

He glanced down and realized that he was shirtless and barefoot and that Kathryn was wearing only stockings and a chemise. He closed the front door and went in search of their garments. Drew returned to the bedroom and grabbed his shirt and coat from where he'd hung them on the bedpost and tossed Kathryn's black velvet dress and slippers to her. When they were dressed, he reached for her hand once again.

"Where are we going?" she asked.

"The chapel."

Drew lifted the lid on Mary Claire's coffin, slid it aside, and stared down at her face. The pain was so sharp and intense that he felt as if a huge fist were squeezing his heart. Suddenly, he was seventeen again, staring down at the pale, lifeless face of his mother. Drew pulled the coffin lid back into place and dropped to his knees on the chapel floor and began to shake.

Have you seen her, Drew? Did you look at her? She has long auburn hair and I'll bet her eyes are the same chocolate brown color as yours and Kit's.

It was true. Drew would have recognized Mary Claire O'Brien anywhere. He wouldn't have known her name, but he would have recognized her. He would have recognized the porcelain skin, the perfect oval of her face, the bone structure, the color of her hair, the shape of her nose and mouth. He carried an almost identical image in his mind and in his heart. For Mary Claire O'Brien was a younger, Irish version of his mother.

Wren dropped to her knees beside Drew and wrapped her arms around his shoulders. "What's wrong, Drew? Are you all right?"

"All of the ladies with whom I've shared a bed and pillow—including Kit's mother—have something else in common—a trait you cannot fail to notice should they decide to present themselves to you." Drew quoted that portion of his father's letter aloud, then turned and looked at Kathryn. "Looking in that coffin was like looking at the dead face of my mother once again. Father's mistresses will all resemble my mother. You don't. You are not Kit's mother."

Wren sat down on the stone floor and pulled her knees to her chest. She rested her chin on her knees and sighed. "I am his mother," she insisted. "The only mother he's ever known."

"But you're not the one who gave birth to him." Drew waited for her to contradict him and when she didn't, he felt free to continue. "You lied to me. You led me to believe that you were my father's mistress, but you were never intimate with him. You never shared his bed."

"No," she admitted.

"Yet you allowed yourself to be branded as his mistress. Why?" Drew demanded.

"I wanted Kit," she said simply. "And that was the only way to ensure that no one would ever question my right to him—until George could make it legal."

"Was Mary Claire his mother?" Drew asked.

"I don't know," Wren answered. "George never told me. He appeared at my house late one night three months after Ian died and—"

"Ian?"

"Ian Wesley Stafford," Wren said, softly, reverently. "My baby."

"Stafford's son?" Drew squeezed his eyes shut to hold back the tears burning his eyes. "How? Why? Why didn't you tell me?"

"Ian was born while you were in France. He was a beautiful baby but frail. He looked robust and healthy, but he bruised so easily. Sometimes just holding him was enough to bruise him. He was almost five months old when Bertrand died. And then—" She choked on her words and had to start again. "Three months later, I lost Ian. He was crawling about, pulling up on the furniture trying to learn to walk. One day he bumped his chin on a table. It shouldn't have been serious. Babies bump their heads and chins every day. But Ian began to bleed—from his mouth and his nose and ears. The doctor couldn't stop it." Her voice broke again. "He died two days later. In the space of two years, I lost you and Bertrand and Ian and I didn't think I could go on. I stopped eating and willed myself to die and I nearly succeeded, but one night three months after Ian died, George showed up on my doorstep with Kit in his arms."

She smiled. "It was love at first sight. George gave him to me. He told me that we were made for one another because Kit needed a mother as much as I needed a son. He placed him in my arms and told me that the best thing he could do as Kit's father was to give him to me to love. George saved my life that night and the only thing he asked in return was that I live at Swanslea Park and become Kit's mother. Everyone assumed I was George's mistress and I pretended it was true in order to keep Kit. I left Bertrand's house and came to Swanslea Park and moved into the dowager cottage with Papa. George made sure that no one here has any idea that Kit isn't my natural son."

"And you've no idea who Kit's mother was?"

"None." She looked at Drew.

"It doesn't matter," he said softly. "My father was right. You are his mother."

Chapter 30

The waters were his winding sheet,
the sea was made his tomb;
yet for his fame the ocean sea,
was not sufficient room.

—RICHARD BARNFIELD, 1574–1627

The morning of the marquess of Templeston's funeral dawned clear and cool. Wren, heavily veiled, stood with Kit alongside Drew as the pallbearers lowered George's coffin into the open grave. She watched quietly as the upper servants filed past carrying their staffs of office, which they ceremoniously broke and threw onto the coffin lid.

Despite Drew's best attempts to keep it small and quiet, the late marquess of Templeston's funeral was the grandest event the county had seen in ages. The death of a marquess was news. The scandalous death of a marquess was bigger news, and many people thought that George's alliance with his young mistress, and her death with him on his yacht, was scandalous.

People came from London and all over the rest of England to pay their last respects. Although custom usually dictated that a man of George's rank be allowed to lie in state for a fortnight or more, Drew decided that his father and Mary Claire would be laid to rest after only three days.

They had been dead nearly a month now and Drew refused to keep his father or Mary Claire on display a moment longer than necessary. The time to bury them was at hand. The guests had been arriving in droves and the tenants, neighbors, farmers, tradesmen, the local gentry and clergymen, and the staff of the late marquess's homes had been filing past the coffin for two full days. Members of the House of Lords and of Brooks's, George's gentlemen's club, even the members of the Trevingshire hunt, had come to offer condolences and pay tribute to George Ramsey.

But along with the crowds of guests and the personal and private tributes came the whispers.

Everyone knew the new marquess was a bachelor so who was the woman standing beside him? And who was the boy? Were the rumors to be believed? Was he the late marquess's bastard son or the new marquess's?

Ignoring the whispers, Wren slipped her gloved hand into Drew's and squeezed it. He was burying his father today and nothing would ever be the same.

Kit shifted his weight from foot to foot and fidgeted. He looked up at Wren and tugged on her sleeve. She bent to lift him, but Drew intervened. Leaning forward, he lifted Kit into his arms and began to explain the significance of the ceremony. Kit rested his head on Drew's shoulder and listened until the last staff of office had been broken and the last words had been spoken over the fifteenth marquess of Templeston.

When it was over, Mr. Smalley, the undertaker, herded the crowd of mourners toward Swanslea Park and the funeral feast that awaited them.

Drew and Wren and Kit, along with Martin, Ally, and

the archbishop, remained at the cemetery waiting as Mary Claire O'Brien's coffin was lowered into a grave directly above George's. The hired mutes and several other mourners—mostly women from the opera company—waited with them. There was another funeral to attend.

Her funeral service was much shorter than George's, not because her life was any less important, but because they knew so little about her. She was a stranger surrounded by Ramseys and Munnerlyns, but her right to be there was unquestionable. George Ramsey had loved her and that, Drew decided, was reason enough to welcome her into the family plot.

As the service ended, the mourners said their last good-byes to George and Mary Claire and made their way to the waiting carriages. The undertaker signaled the gravediggers, who had retreated to a respectful distance, to move forward and begin the sad task of shoveling the earth back into place.

Drew escorted Wren and Ally into a carriage, then leaned forward and deposited Kit onto Wren's lap.

"I want to ride with you," Kit grumbled.

"I'm riding in the coach with His Grace the archbishop and Mr. Smalley," Drew told him.

Kit wrinkled his face.

"Exactly," Drew said. "Boring company for a little boy, especially since we've business to conclude. You go with Mama and Ally and I'll come up and see you before you go to sleep."

Kit nodded. "Can we go to the barn and see Lancelot and Jem when I wake up?" The barn and carriage house had been extremely busy during the past few days and Drew had had to declare them off limits to Kit for fear that the boy would get hurt during the hustle and bustle of moving carriages and horses around.

Drew glanced at Wren and Ally, awaiting their nods of approval before answering, "I don't see why not."

"Can I ride Lancelot?"

Drew ruffled Kit's blond hair and smiled. "We'll see."

"Capital!" Kit exclaimed, using Jem's favorite expression, copying it right down to the lad's Cockney inflection.

"Yes," Drew agreed. "Capital!" He leaned close to Wren and said, "I have to make an appearance at the funeral feast."

"I know."

Drew sighed. "After hearing the whispered speculation, I've no doubt that attending the feast will be an ordeal for you. I want nothing more than for you to stand beside me, Kathryn, but I'll understand if you change your mind about attending."

"It's no more of an ordeal for me than for you," she said. "And my place is beside you." She favored him with a dazzling smile. "I'll join you as soon as Ally and I get Kit fed and settled into the nursery for his nap. The plan is for Ally to prepare a luncheon plate while I get him out of his formal clothes and into bed."

"All right," Drew said. "I'll see you when you're done." He brushed his lips against the silk of her veil.

❦

The buffet tables set up in the ballroom were loaded with food. The crush of people surrounding them appreciated the largesse of the new marquess of Templeston and the talents of his Swanslea Park kitchen staff and the army of caterers hired to provide the delicacies for the mourners.

Wren made her way down the stairs from the nursery after tucking Kit into bed and reading him a story. She paused on the staircase and scanned the crush of black-garbed mourners, looking for Drew. He looked up, spotted her, and smiled. Wren returned his smile and started toward him.

She was passing the open door of the study when someone reached out, grabbed her by the arm, and pulled her inside.

"You!"

Wren recognized the voice and the venom in it and turned to face the person who had her by the arm. "Lady St. Jacque." She stared down at the gloved hand on her arm. "Please take your hand off my arm."

"I cannot believe you have the nerve to show your face at Lord Templeston's funeral after what you did to his son. And I cannot believe that the new Lord Templeston would allow you to set foot on Swanslea Park, much less ask you to stand up with him at the funeral."

Wren stared at the older woman. "What did I ever do to you to earn your enmity?"

"You've kept our grandson away from his father and his grandparents."

The air left Wren's lungs in a rush. Her palms grew clammy and she became so light-headed she was sure she'd faint. "You are mistaken."

"No, we're not." Lord St. Jacque stepped from behind the door. "We saw the boy at the funeral. With his blond hair and brown eyes, he's made in Julian's image. There's no doubt that he's a St. Jacque and we want him. We heard the rumors about your condition shortly after you left young Templeston standing at the altar, and your hasty marriage to a man old enough to be your father only served to confirm them. Our only son is dying. We want our grandson."

"You cannot have him," Wren said, "because Kit is not your grandson."

"Of course he is," Lady St. Jacque insisted. "We know the truth. Julian told us all about it and about you."

Wren swallowed the bile forming in her throat and prayed she wouldn't disgrace herself by vomiting at their feet. "I barely knew your son. What could he possibly tell you about me?"

"He told us that you weren't the proper innocent miss you appeared to be." Lady St. Jacque spat the words as if they were poison arrows. "He told us how you teased and tormented him, how you pitted Julian and Drew— two best friends—against one another. He told us that he fell in love with you and you with him and that the two of you carried on an intimate affair beneath Drew's nose."

Lord St. Jacque took up the tale where his wife left off. "Julian told us that he begged you to marry him, but you chose Drew because he possessed an older, more exalted title and a much larger fortune. He said you laughed at him and proclaimed that you'd rather be the countess of Ramsey and the future marchioness of Templeston than the Viscountess St. Jacque."

"I'm very sorry, Lord St. Jacque, but everything that your son told you was a lie," Wren said, forcing her voice to remain steady.

"Before he left with Wellington, Julian came to us and told us that if we should hear that you were with child, that child would be our grandchild and if anything happened to him, we should lay claim to it as his heir." Lord St. Jacque stared at Wren. "Our son is dying. You've had our grandson for four years; it's time you gave him to us."

"I can't do that," Wren said, "because the little boy you saw is not your grandchild. He's the son of the late Lord Templeston."

"I don't believe you," Lady St. Jacque announced.

"He has to be our grandson. Why else would Julian tell us that he was? Why else would you fail to appear at your own wedding? If what Julian told us wasn't true, then why didn't you marry Drew Ramsey four years ago?"

"Tell them, Kathryn. Because I've asked myself that question for the last four years and I think it's time I learn the answer."

Wren whirled around at the sound of Drew's voice. He stood in the open door of the study and she had no idea how long he'd been standing there or how much of the conversation he'd overheard.

Drew crossed the threshold into the study and closed the door behind him. The color had left Kathryn's face. She was trembling and white as a sheet. Drew could tell from the expression on her face that the St. Jacques knew some of the truth, if not all of it. And he knew, in his heart, that whatever the rest of the truth was, he wasn't going to want to hear her answer. Or have anyone else hear it. "Why didn't you marry me four years ago, Kathryn? Why didn't you come to the church? Why wouldn't you see me when I came to your house?"

"I-I c-couldn't." Although she struggled mightily to control it, her voice shook as badly as her hands. "I-I j-just couldn't."

"So, you changed your mind about marrying me," he said softly. "Why didn't you tell me face-to-face?"

"Oh, Drew, I didn't change my mind about marrying you," Wren cried. "I wanted to marry you more than anything in the world. But if I had gone to the church you would have found out and I never wanted you to know."

"That you had a love affair with my best friend?"

"That he raped me."

Chapter 31

The web of our life is of mingled yarn, good and ill together.
—WILLIAM SHAKESPEARE, 1564–1616

*D*rew recoiled from the force of her words as if she'd physically struck him. He went weak in the knees and all the air seemed to leave the room. He gasped. "What?"

Wren sank onto the leather ottoman at the foot of Drew's favorite chair. "He raped me."

Drew looked stunned. "I don't believe it," he breathed. "Julian's my friend. We were at school together. We stood shoulder to shoulder against the French. He's a man of honor. An officer and a gentleman and I wouldn't hesitate to trust him with my life." He knelt beside the ottoman.

Wren looked Drew in the eye. "And you didn't hesitate to trust him with my life," she said. "Your mistake was in trusting him with my virtue."

"I never . . ."

"That last night at Vauxhall," Wren reminded him.

"I didn't see Julian or speak to him, so I couldn't have asked him to escort you and your aunt home." Drew reached for her hand, but Wren pulled it back out of his reach. "I asked my father to escort you."

Wren read the look in his eyes. "And all this time you've believed that George was responsible for what happened to me. . . ."

Drew focused his gaze on the Turkey carpet and raked his fingers through his hair. "I believed I could depend on my father to accompany you to your home. I asked him to escort you and your aunt home from the concert that night and I didn't see you for four years. When I do see you again, you're living on my father's estate and proclaiming yourself to be the mother of his son. It wasn't so hard to understand. Not when I knew my father had a weakness for younger women and that he kept several mistresses." He shook his head. "But Julian? Never in a thousand years would I have believed Julian capable of what you're accusing him of."

"Believe me," Wren said bitterly. "He's quite capable of grabbing a woman—even his best friend's fiancée— in a coach and forcing himself on her."

"Not Julian. Not my friend."

"Why is it that you were perfectly willing to believe I was your father's mistress, but unwilling to believe that a fellow officer and a gentleman is capable of rape? You went to war, Drew. You know the terrible crimes of which men are capable. Your friend is no different. He may be an officer and a gentleman, but he was quite willing to strike a woman across the face, grab her by the back of the neck, shove her face down into the dusty seat cushions of the marquess of Templeston's carriage, tear off her undergarments, and push his way inside her without regard for his friendship with the man she was about to marry or the fact that the wedding was two days away."

"You go too far, madam!" Lord St. Jacque shouted.

"You defame my son by accusing him of a heinous act."

"I haven't defamed your son. I haven't said anything about your son except the truth." She took a deep breath. "When he was done with me, he dropped me off at the front door of my aunt's town house and drove away." She turned to Drew. "The day we were to be married, my face was bruised and swollen and my eye was black. How could I face you without telling you what happened? And how could I tell you that your best friend had raped me?"

Drew buried his face in his hands. "That night at Vauxhall, I asked my father to escort you safely home because I knew I could count on him to do it."

"George didn't escort either of us home," Wren replied wearily. "Aunt Edwina begged a ride home from her friends and Lord and Lady St. Jacque's son came to the coach and told me that you'd asked him to see me home."

"I didn't speak to Julian that night . . . and I didn't tell anyone about the message except you and my father."

"He told me you sent him to escort me home," Wren said. "And I believed him because I knew that you would never send anyone who would do me harm. But the man who raped me was your closest friend. I trusted him because you did and my life changed beyond recognition."

"Ian?"

"Yes," she whispered. "Ian. He was the reason Bertrand Stafford agreed to marry me."

Drew shook his head once again. "I can't believe this of Julian."

Wren managed a grim laugh. "I know," she said. "That's the sad irony. I told him that you'd kill him if you ever found out what he'd done to me and he laughed at me. He laughed and said that he intended to live a very long life as the earl of Ramsey's best friend because you were an honorable man who could never conceive of dishonor in his friends." She stood up and walked to the door. "And it seems he was right." Wren reached for the doorknob, then turned back to Lord and Lady St. Jacque. "Kit is my son and if you ever attempt to do so much as speak to him, I'll make certain you live to regret it."

With those final angry words, Wren opened the door of the study and walked away.

"*Were you ever going to tell me?*" Drew demanded. "Or did you plan to keep me in the dark forever?"

Wren started at the fury in Drew's voice. He had followed her up the stairs, past the nursery, to the master suite, where he'd flung open the door and shouted her name. She met him in the doorway of her bedroom. Drew took hold of her arm and guided her back inside the room, slamming the door behind him with such force that it shook the frame.

"No." Her heart seemed to tighten in her chest. "Yes."

Drew stared at her. "Which is it?"

"Both," she answered. "I never planned to tell you because I never wanted the man I loved to know that his closest friend had betrayed him and because a part of me was afraid that *he* knew you better than I did. I was afraid that he was right—that you'd believe him and not me. And if I had to miss our wedding to keep you from finding out what he had done, I was willing to do it."

"Why?"

"What could you do, Drew?" She met his piercing gaze without flinching. "Change what happened? Kill the man you loved like a brother? Believe me? Believe him? Blame him? Blame me?"

"I don't know."

"How could you know what to do? When you don't know whom to believe."

"I didn't say I didn't believe you," he attempted to defend himself.

"You never said you did, either."

That stopped him in his tracks. "Kathryn, you're asking me to question everything I've ever believed about Julian St. Jacque and myself."

"No, Drew." Wren shook her head. "I've told you the truth. That's all I can do. You either believe me or you don't."

He didn't reply.

She was tempted to let go and walk away, but she loved him and she couldn't let go without one last fight to win his love. "I don't understand why he did what he did to me. I don't know why he used me to hurt you. I only know that he seemed to think it was a great joke—something he could do to get back at you or to get even with you—as if I were some sort of prize to be won. He wanted me to marry you. Bruising my face was a mistake. Even as he raped me, he apologized for hitting me. He told me he hoped he hadn't ruined my appearance because he wanted me to look my best on my wedding day." Tears rolled down her face, but she was unaware of them. "He seemed to think that you would know I wasn't a virgin and that that would be a great trick to play on you." She turned away from Drew and began to pace back and forth in front of the fireplace, occasionally stopping long enough to extend her hands toward the low-burning flames in an attempt to warm them. "And

I never understood why George was always so kind to me or why he felt compelled to help me after the embarrassment and humiliation I caused you," she said. "Until Martin remarked that I could always count on George to see to my future. You said almost the same thing when you said you knew you could count on your father to see me and my aunt safely home. You escorted me to your coach and left me alone there while you set out to ask your father to see me home."

"Yes," he said.

"But George didn't come to the coach; your friend came in his place," she continued, "and he told me that you'd been summoned to the War Office by your commanding officer. You say you didn't see your friend at Vauxhall that night or tell anyone except George and me about the urgent message."

"I didn't," Drew said. "It was confidential."

"*I* didn't tell anyone," Wren said. "So your friend could only have known about it if he delivered it to you or if he spoke to George."

Or unless he wrote it. The unbidden thought popped into Drew's mind and refused to leave. But he didn't give voice to it. It hurt too much to say the words aloud because saying those words aloud meant that Julian had planned to betray him, had planned Kathryn's rape.

She wanted him to say something—anything—to give her an idea of what he was thinking, what he felt. But Drew didn't say a word. He simply continued to watch her.

Unable to bear his silence a moment longer, Wren walked over to Drew and handed him the gold and sapphire wedding ring he'd placed on her finger three days before.

He shook his head.

"I believe I have something that belongs to you. I'm

giving it back because it's much too dear for me. I don't deserve it. After all, we aren't really married. We repeated words but they're only vows if you believe in them. And apparently, only one of us did." She stared at him as if she were memorizing his face. "You paid the archbishop for the special license to marry us, so you should be able to pay him to *un*marry us. There hasn't been an announcement of our marriage and the archbishop has the register we signed, so dissolving our union should be a simple matter of scratching through our signatures and pretending it never happened." Her words stuck in her throat along with the burning tears she had yet to shed.

He looked stricken.

"I wanted to marry you more than anything in the world. But marriage is nothing without trust and I don't want to share a bed or a life with a man who would rather believe his friend's vicious lies than admit that his wife might be telling the truth." Wren touched two fingers to her lips before pressing those fingers against Drew's mouth. "Good-bye, my love," she murmured.

"Kathryn . . ." He finally found his voice. "You're my wife and the mother of my adopted son and heir. You belong here with me."

"Did you happen to mention that fact to the St. Jacques? Or did you allow them to continue in their belief that I'm the faithless and mercenary whore who broke their son's heart and stole their grandchild?"

Drew sighed. His world was falling apart and he had no idea how to prevent it. "They're grieving parents, Kathryn. Parents who wanted to believe that the boy they saw here today was their grandson."

"The product of their son's romantic clandestine liaison with his best friend's betrothed. What a charming portrait they've painted of me. I'm sure they can't wait to tell all their friends how they rescued their grandson by snatching him from my clutches."

He frowned at her. "I've known them most of my life. The St. Jacques are good people. They were upset and angry this afternoon, but they would never try to take Kit away from here or do him any harm."

"I pray you're right," she told him. "But I don't trust them and I won't feel safe until they're gone."

"They're leaving tomorrow."

"Not a moment too soon." Wren walked past him.

He watched her leave. "Where are you going?"

"Home."

I cannot rest easy in my grave until you know that I never meant to fail you. You counted on me and my momentary thoughtlessness drastically altered your life's path in a manner neither of us could have foreseen. I hope that, one day, you'll forgive me. I bear a heavy guilt for my misplaced trust.

Drew nearly cried out as his father's confession returned to haunt him. But even more of an indictment were his own words, spoken the day he'd taken her riding in the rain: *You don't have to tell me anything until you're ready. And whenever you're ready to tell me, I'll be ready to listen.*

Spoken when his heart was full of love and forgotten when it filled with fear.

Drew knew in his heart that Kathryn had spoken the truth about Julian. And she'd been right about him as well. He didn't want to admit that the man he loved like a brother was capable of betraying his love and trust. It was easier to believe the worst of her than it was to face the fact that a lifelong friendship was based on a lie.

If he believed her, he would lose the one friend he trusted most in the world. If he chose not to believe her, he would lose Kathryn—for the second time in his life.

And Drew was just beginning to understand the magnitude of that loss and the fact that he wouldn't get another opportunity to win her love. He closed his eyes and pinched the bridge of his nose. That last night at Vauxhall Gardens sprang to mind as crisp and clear in detail as if it had happened yesterday.

The urgent message from Lieutenant Colonel Grant summoning him back to the War Office hadn't arrived by military messenger or in a military pouch. Drew hadn't noticed the irregularity at the time, but he remembered it now. That urgent message had been hand-delivered by a street urchin who told him that a dandy swell had pointed him out.

And although the message had been written on official stationery, it hadn't carried the seal or signature of his commanding officer and it hadn't been written in code.

Because Lieutenant Colonel Grant hadn't sent it.

Someone else had.

He had recognized familiar handwriting and accepted the message as authentic, but the note was a forgery. He hadn't noticed the irregularities in the way the message was written or in the way it had been delivered at the time because the handwriting had been as familiar to him as his own. An hour ago he would never have suspected Julian but now he knew that his best friend had forged the note because the familiar handwriting had been Julian's. And Drew had been too distracted by thoughts of his upcoming nuptials to notice.

He'd walked Kathryn to the coach and left her there while he set off in search of his father, never doubting for a moment that the coachmen and the driver would keep her safe until his father arrived to escort her home.

But his father hadn't arrived. Julian St. Jacque had arrived instead and he'd raped Kathryn before depositing her at her aunt's front door as if nothing had ever happened.

And on the day of their wedding, Julian St. Jacque had stood beside him at the altar watching and waiting for Kathryn's arrival. Thinking back on it now, Drew realized that Julian had fully expected Kathryn to appear at the church and go through with the wedding as scheduled. Julian had been as outraged as the groom because he had wanted Kathryn to marry him so that by the time Drew found out his bride wasn't a virgin, it would be too late.

When she failed to appear, Julian had been the first to condemn her. He had been the first to call her a heartless bitch for disappointing Drew and breaking his heart. And Julian had been the first to encourage Drew to forget her.

But forgetting her had proved impossible then and it would be just as impossible now. He couldn't forget the only woman he loved. He didn't want to forget the only woman he would ever love. Nor did he want to lose her. But he would lose her if he didn't make amends. If he didn't show her how much he loved her.

Drew sprang into action. There was much to be done and very little time in which to do it. He must dress carefully for the occasion and assemble the cast of characters.

Chapter 32

If I lose thy love, I lose my all.
—Alexander Pope, 1688–1744

A persistent tapping on the windowpane in the front door of the cottage woke her. Wren climbed out of bed and made her way to the main salon to answer the door. Her eyes were red and swollen and her throat raw from crying herself into a fitful sleep. Now, her head ached abominably and her temper was stretched to the breaking point at being awakened by the tapping that would not go away.

"I'm coming," she called, as she pushed her arms into the sleeves of her robe. She yanked the front door open as the clock on the mantel began the first of its four and a quarter chimes.

"I'm gratified to hear it, my love." Drew stood in the doorway holding Erin in his hand. "But I'm afraid it's a bit premature, for I've only just arrived."

"What are you doing here, Drew?" she snapped. "For I'm in no mood to spar with you tonight."

"I have something that belongs to you." He held the

hedgehog up so she could see that Erin was wearing a blue ribbon tied around her neck.

She reached for the animal, but Drew held Erin out of reach. "Aren't you going to invite me in?" he asked.

"Why should I?" she countered.

"Because I love you. Because I can't live without you. Because I want to marry you again and again and again—however many times it takes until you believe that I love you with all my heart. Until you forgive me for my momentary doubts. Until you learn to love me again."

Wren flung her arms around his neck.

Drew held her tightly.

Erin shrieked in protest and they both stepped back. "She brought you something." He nodded toward the blue ribbon and Wren saw that her gold and sapphire wedding band was hanging from it.

She slipped the ribbon over Erin's head, then carefully deposited the hedgehog in her nest and clasped the ring to her heart. "Oh, Drew, I do love you. I've always loved you. I will always love you."

"And I love you," he said simply. "Can you forgive me?"

"I already have."

"Thank God," he breathed. He pulled the blue ribbon out of Kathryn's fist, untied the bow, and gently pushed the ring onto the ring finger of her left hand. He smiled down at her. "With this ring, I thee wed."

"And I you," she whispered just before she pressed her lips against his. She unleashed a raw need in him as she used her tongue and teeth and mouth with a talent that shook him down to his boots, threatening to steal what remained of his breath along with his tenuous control.

"I missed you," he murmured against her lips. "More

than I ever thought possible. Promise you'll never leave me again."

"I promise."

"Even when I persist in behaving stupidly."

"Especially when you persist in behaving stupidly," she said.

"I intend to hold you to that." Drew kissed her again, suddenly as hard as rock behind the buttons of his skin-tight trousers. His taut muscles and his rigid, insistent member stretched his control almost to the breaking point. His blood pounded in his head and every nerve in his body cried out for release, urging him to seek the hollow in the vee of her thighs, and press himself against her.

Knowing that after another minute or two of kissing, he'd be unbuttoning his too-tight trousers and pressing into her instead of against her, Drew forced himself to regain some distance. He broke contact with her mouth and stepped away from her. "Kathryn." He pulled the ribbon from the end of her braid and raked his fingers through it, freeing her thick blond hair. "Please, stop."

"But I like kissing you," she murmured, burrowing inside the folds of his cape, seeking contact with his flesh. "It makes me feel safe and secure and wanted."

"I'm very pleased that you do, my love, but a man can only take so much and I'm seconds from tearing off our clothes and taking you on the floor."

"Then why don't I get you started?" She shrugged out of her robe, let her cotton nightgown fall to the floor, and began unbuttoning his breeches. She shoved his buff breeches over his slim hips and buttocks, down his thighs. Drew splayed his feet as far as he could to keep from crashing to the floor like a fallen oak tree.

"Boots!" Drew laughed. "Boots first, then trousers."

"Sit." Wren pressed her palms against his chest and gently pushed him onto the sofa.

He sat on the sofa and extended one booted foot.

Wren bent and tugged off his boots, then grasped the hem of his trousers and pulled them off.

Drew sat on the sofa wearing his coat, waistcoat, shirt, linen briefs and his white stockings. He leered at her and wiggled his toes. Wren burst out laughing.

Crudely embroidered on his stockings in black thread were the words: *My Kathryn has my love. To my heart she has the key. Never let there be a doubt, she's the only wife for me.* A heart, embroidered in red, punctuated each line of the poem.

"I married a poet." She giggled.

"You married a fool who's too bloody slow with the needle," he grumbled. "I'd have been here much sooner, but it took me most of the night to fashion the embroidery."

"Tell me, my lord, do you wish to discuss your talents or experience mine?" Wren knelt between his knees, freed his hard length and favored him with a suggestive smile.

"My talents are nothing compared to yours, milady."

"Then lie back and enjoy the experience."

Wren leaned forward and kissed him, using her tongue to tempt and tease him. Remembering the way he'd touched her, remembering the attention he'd lavished on her, Wren traced his velvety length with the tip of her tongue, then took him into her mouth and worked her own special brand of magic on him.

Drew writhed beneath her tender ministrations. He tangled his fingers in her hair, arched his back, and bucked his hips in an effort to get closer. He groaned her name. Wren glanced up at him, recognized the look of intense pleasure on his face and smiled—a wicked smile that promised greater pleasure, just moments before she delivered it, applying her mouth and tongue and teeth to him with tenderness and love and extraordinary finesse.

"Kathryn, please . . ." Balanced on the precipice between selfish desire and unselfish love, Drew's control was tenuous at best. His voice shook with emotion as he struggled to form coherent thoughts. "You must stop."

Her eyes sparkled with mischief. "Do you want me to stop?"

"No!" he breathed. "God, no!"

"Good." She swirled her tongue around his velvety-soft head and flicked it across the sensitive flesh beneath it. "Because I don't intend to stop."

"If . . . you . . . don't . . ." He forced each word. "I . . . won't . . . be . . . able . . . to . . ."

Wren felt a tingle of awareness as she stared at him—the heady thrill of power that came with the knowledge that she had brought the most powerful man she'd ever known to a state of intense, writhing pleasure—the knowledge that she could harness his strength and use it against him in a way that was meant not to harm, but to heal him. Because that was what she wanted. She wanted to heal the fragile bond of trust. To restore his faith in his judgment and in himself. To show him beyond all doubt that he was safe with her, that he could trust her not to hurt him or think less of him because he was a very human man with very human flaws.

Drew had asked for her forgiveness and in doing that, he had shown that he'd forgiven her for trying to protect him, for shouldering her burden alone when he was there to help lighten it, for not trusting, for not knowing, that if given a choice, he would have done the right thing—that he would have chosen her. And Ian.

All the love in her heart shone in her eyes as she looked at him.

"Kathryn . . ." Drew sounded her name as a frustrated groan and as a warning. He couldn't wait any longer. He'd reached the limit of his endurance. "I . . . can't . . . hold . . . on . . ."

"Then let go," she murmured. "I'll catch you." She swirled her tongue around him, surrounding him with love and warmth, catching him as he let go of his last ounce of pride.

When he recovered his strength, Drew pulled her into his arms and lifted her onto his lap. He kissed her and Wren returned his kiss, following his lead as they played the age-old game of advance and retreat, of give and take, of mutual surrender. She followed his lead until he relinquished control and followed hers and then they played the game again, leading each other on a sensual path marked by kisses that were so hungry and hot and wet and deep that they begged for consummation.

And Wren and Drew indulged that need, making love on the sofa throughout the long hours of night, making their way to the bed as dawn was breaking in the east.

"Kathryn?" Drew whispered, as he tucked the covers around them.

"Hmm?" She nuzzled the warm place beneath his right ear.

"Join me at Swanslea for breakfast this morning."

Wren groaned. "Can't we dine here?"

"No, milady." He brushed his lips against her brow. "I'd like to keep you to myself, but it's time I introduced the new marchioness of Templeston to her guests."

"Will the St. Jacques be there?"

"Most assuredly."

"What will you say to them?"

"I'm going to tell them that we're married and that

Kit is my legal son and heir and that they have no claim to him." Drew squeezed her. "I'm going to tell them everything I should have told them last night and I want you there to witness it."

And when I've done with the St. Jacques, he added silently, I'm going to make my feelings known to their son.

Drew and Wren entered the mansion later that morning to find it in an uproar. Half a dozen guests were crowded into the marble foyer along with Miss Allerton, Martin Bell, Lord Canterbury, Newberry, Mrs. Tanglewood, several housemaids, Mr. Isley, Riley, and Jem. The fact that Isley, Riley, and Jem were in the main house instead of the parkland and the stables immediately alerted Drew to the fact that the crisis involved Kit.

"What's happened here?" he demanded.

Ally rushed to meet them. "Lord Templeston! Wren! Please tell me Kit's with you!"

Wren paled. "He's not."

"Oh, God!" The governess sagged and would have fallen if Drew and Newberry hadn't taken hold of her arms to support her.

"Have you tried the stable?" Drew asked.

Ally looked up at Drew. "I took him to the stable to see Lancelot early this morning. He begged me for a ride and Mr. Riley and I gave him a lesson. I left him happily mucking the stalls with Jem, while I came back to arrange for his snack and a bath, but when I went back to get him, he was gone."

Drew turned to the stable boy. "Jem, did you see Kit leave the stable?"

"No, sir." Jem's voice quivered with emotion. "He was helpin' me clean stalls. I sent Kit for an armload of fresh straw while I emptied the pail 'cause he tries hard to help even though he's too little to carry the heavy stuff. But he di'n' come back. I thought Miss Ally had come and got him." Jem wiped his nose on his sleeve. "I di'n' mean to lose him, sir."

"You didn't lose him, Jem," Drew said. "Don't worry. It isn't your fault."

"But, sir, I shoulda watched him better. He's such a little mite," Jem protested.

"We'll find him," Wren tried to reassure the stable boy. "Please don't blame yourselves." She gave Drew a meaningful glance.

"Have you searched the house?"

"We were in the process of doing so when you and Lady Templeston arrived, milord," Newberry informed him.

"Ask the guests to assemble in the ballroom," Drew said. "Someone must have seen him."

"Yes, sir."

Three-quarters of an hour later, all of the guests remaining in residence at Swanslea Park were gathered in the ballroom. Wren was the first to notice that the two guests Drew had invited to breakfast were not in the ballroom.

She turned to Newberry. "Please send someone up to Lord and Lady St. Jacque's suite to ask them to join us in the ballroom."

"I went there, Miss—I mean, my lady—" the young housemaid Polly interjected as she bobbed a curtsey. "They weren't in their rooms."

Drew was busy questioning the guests and the rest of the staff. Wren had to raise her voice to be heard. "Drew!"

He turned to look at her.

"Lord and Lady St. Jacque aren't here."

Drew whirled around, searching the crowd until he caught sight of Riley. "Did any of our guests leave the estate this morning?"

"On horseback or carriage, my lord?"

"Both." Drew made his way through the crowd and enfolded Kathryn in his arms.

Riley scratched his head. "Three gentlemen and three ladies and two grooms rode out on horseback this morning, but they're all here." He pointed to the duke and duchess of Kerry, the archbishop of Canterbury, Lady Mumford and Martin Bell and Lady Seaborn. "The grooms are in the stable seeing to the horses. Miss Allerton thought that you and Lady Templeston might have ridden out as well, but I saw that Abelard and Felicity were in their stalls."

"Would that we had," Drew muttered, "but my wife and I overslept."

Though she was frantic with worry over Kit, Wren's heart felt as if it would overflow with love and tenderness for Drew. Most of the guests assembled in the ballroom were the cream of the London *ton* and he was taking every opportunity, making every effort to acknowledge her place in his heart and in his life.

"Anyone else?"

Riley nodded. "Lord and Lady St. Jacque ordered their coach brought around and readied just after dawn."

"Jem, was the coach there while you and Kit were cleaning stalls?" Wren asked.

"Yes, ma'am."

"Do you remember seeing it after Kit failed to return with the straw?" Drew asked.

Jem shook his head. "I thought Kit might have been playing in it," he said, "because he likes to climb up and down on the vehicles, but when I went to check, the carriage was gone."

"They've taken him," Wren whispered. "Oh, Drew, they've taken my baby."

He lifted her chin with the tip of his finger and looked her in the eye. "But, my love, we know where they've taken him," he reminded her. "We know who they've taken him to see."

Wren paled.

"Julian."

Chapter 33

Histories are more full of examples of the fidelity of dogs than of friends.

—ALEXANDER POPE, 1688–1744

The trip to London was the longest journey Drew had ever made. Lord and Lady St. Jacque had a three- or four-hour head start on him, but they were traveling in an older, heavier coach pulled by a team of older, heavier, and slower horses while he and Kathryn and their solicitor, Martin, were traveling in a lighter, well-sprung coach with a continuous relay of faster teams. Drew had sent Riley and two grooms to ride ahead of the coach and arrange for fresh horses at every stop on the Old Roman Road.

They arrived in London while the lamplighters were still at their appointed rounds, lighting the way on the city streets. They bypassed Drew's town house and went straight to the St. Jacques' home. Drew leaped from the coach and bounded up their front steps before the vehicle rolled to a stop. He pounded on the front door and kept pounding until the St. Jacques' butler admitted him.

"My lord, the household has retired for the evening." Porter tried to block the entrance.

Drew pushed his way past him and started up the stairs. "Then we'll just have to wake them, won't we? The doors of the St. Jacque home are always open to the hero who saved Master Julian's life and who continued to provide for his care, remember?"

"Of course, my lord," Porter replied, "but the master and mistress forbade me to open the doors to anyone this evening."

"Don't worry about it, Porter," Drew said. "I'll make certain Lord and Lady St. Jacque and the magistrate know you did your best to prevent me from collecting my son."

"Your son, my lord?" Porter was aghast. "I was given to understand that young Master Kit is the grandson of the house."

"Not unless my parentage is in question as well," Drew told him grimly. "His mother and our solicitor will be arriving any moment. Please show them inside." He stood on the landing of the first floor and shouted, "Now, where the bloody hell is my son?"

"In here, Drew."

Drew opened the door to Julian's room.

"If you've come to kill me, you're four years too late." Sitting propped up on a mound of pillows was the shell of the handsome, vibrant young man who had once been Julian St. Jacque.

Four years ago, he'd had chiseled features and sparkling brown eyes and thick, dark brown hair that curled on his forehead. He'd had expensive taste and a tendency toward dandyism, but Drew had never minded. Now, his face was hollowed and sunken, his complexion was gray, and a sheen of perspiration gave him a waxy cast. He was dying.

But not quite fast enough.

"Where is he?" Drew demanded.

"There." Julian pointed to the foot of the bed, where Kit was lying sound asleep.

Drew walked over to the bed and lifted Kit into his arms.

"I thought I was first," Julian remarked snidely. "But I see you were first after all. He's the mirror image of you."

"Yes, he is," Drew said. "And your parents could have spared us a great deal of terror and heartache if they hadn't been blind to the resemblance."

"They didn't want to see it," Julian said. "Or they were willing to overlook his parentage to claim him as theirs. I'm not. Take him and be damned."

"You be damned, you bastard." Drew was glad he was holding Kit or he would have choked the rest of whatever life remained in Julian out of him.

"I'm afraid not." Julian laughed. "He's your bastard, Drew, not mine. And I have no intention of claiming him. The whole point of my encounter with Wren was to produce a bastard you'd be forced to claim."

"Why?" Drew asked. "For God's sake, Julian, I loved you like a brother. Why would you rape the woman I was going to marry?"

Julian shrugged. "I wanted her."

Drew was stunned. This was a side of Julian he'd never seen and would never have guessed existed. "But you knew she was mine."

"That's why I wanted her," Julian said. "Because she was yours. Don't look so surprised, Drew. Or so shocked. You were always bigger, better, smarter. You had everything. A more prestigious title, more wealth, a better position in the War Office. You were always better than I was. I wanted to best you in something, just once. I wanted to be first where it counted."

"You raped a woman to get back at me for imagined faults?"

"I raped her because I could," Julian said, "because I knew she'd never tell you and that even if you found out she was raped, you'd never suspect me. You're too loyal, Drew. Too trusting. You take it for granted that everyone likes you and is like you. Some of us despise you for being so damned perfect."

Drew shook his head. "I was never perfect. Nor did I ever pretend to be."

"You didn't have to pretend," Julian sneered. "You've never made a wrong step in your life."

"And you've never made a right one."

"So nice of you to finally notice."

"I always noticed, but you were my friend and I did everything I could to help you—even going so far as to save your miserable life on the battlefield." Drew fought to keep from choking on his disgust. "We've been friends for five and twenty years and I never knew you at all."

"You knew me better than anyone," Julian said. "But like most noble men, you saw what you wanted to see. You saw the friend you wanted. So tell me, Drew, what do you intend to do now that you've seen Wren again and learned she had *your* child out of wedlock rather than mine?"

"I did what I always planned to do. I married her."

Julian began to laugh. "You married her? When?"

"Five days ago."

"You are a fool, Drew."

"I was when I was listening to you," he said, "but not anymore. I married Kathryn because I love her. Because I've always loved her and I always will. If I'm a fool it's because I trusted you so much I was willing to risk losing her. And let me tell you, Julian, nothing—not even a lifelong friendship with you—is worth losing her."

Julian snorted in contempt. "And what if she had presented you with my bastard nine months after you married? How noble would you have been then? I know you, Drew, and I know that you've plenty of pride in yourself and in the family name. You wouldn't have been as willing to accept another man's son as your own as you think."

"Yes, I would. Being a father is more about rearing a child than siring it. And any child born of Kathryn's body would be as much my child as hers because I'd want it." Drew smiled down at Kit.

"That's what you say now. Too bad I didn't leave a bastard on her four years ago, then we could have put your convictions to the test."

"You did. His name was Ian Wesley Stafford."

Julian looked up to find Kathryn standing in the door. "You're looking well, Wren," he said. "Exceptionally well."

The way he leered at her body made her skin crawl, but Wren refused to show it. "You look exceptionally evil," she said. "And all but dead."

Her comments stung. Julian had always taken his exceptional good looks for granted. He'd never had to develop inner strength and character because he had such a handsome exterior package. Julian liked to think he was sensitive, but the truth was that he was shallow. He turned to Drew and snapped, "Get her out of my house. She has no right to be here."

"As long as you have my son, I have every right to be here," Wren told him. "But now that I've seen what you've become, I think that facing my fear of you and learning to look evil in the eye without running and hiding would have been reason enough to come here—even if you hadn't held my son hostage." She looked Julian in the eye. "Kit is not your son, nor is he related to you in any way."

She turned to Drew and smiled at him. "He's ours."

Drew placed Kit in her arms and draped his arm over her shoulder and held her close. "Let's go home."

Julian ignored him. "You said something about a child."

"Yes, I did," Wren said. "But you don't deserve an explanation from me."

"What about us?"

Wren turned to find Lord and Lady St. Jacque standing in the doorway. "You don't deserve my consideration either," she said. "You stole my son and brought him to the man who raped me!"

"He didn't. . . ."

"He did. Two days before my wedding. He deceived Drew and tricked me. He attacked me in the coach on the way home, raped me, then dropped me off at the front door of my aunt's town house as if I were rubbish. I prayed I'd never have to set eyes on him as long as I lived. I prayed I could forget what had happened, but that was impossible because your son left me with a child." She stared at the older couple. "Ian Wesley Stafford was born nine months from the day of the rape and he died eight months later."

"How?" Lady St. Jacque demanded. "Tell me how he died."

"You're in no position to make demands of me," Wren reminded her. "And when this day is done, I will never speak to you or utter your name again." She turned away from Lady St. Jacque and Julian and fixed her gaze on Lord St. Jacque. "I didn't ask for him, but I loved him. Unfortunately, Ian was born with a bleeding disease. My father told me that that horrible affliction sometimes occurs in our family. Boy babies with Markinson blood in them don't always live very long. Ian was eight months old and attempting to crawl when he bumped his chin and bled to death."

Lady St. Jacque gasped. "The babies I bore before and after Julian suffered the same affliction." She looked at Julian. "My son's sin was visited upon his child."

Drew was shocked. He'd never known there had been other children. "No, madam. Julian's sin forced his conception, but it went no further than that. Ian was an innocent baby and had his mother been able to marry me, I would have claimed him as mine and given him a home and as comfortable a life as possible. I don't believe God punishes children for their fathers' sins."

He looked at Julian. "I can't pretend to understand why you did what you did to Kathryn or to me, but I want you to know that you have my undying contempt and my pity."

"I don't give a bloody damn for your contempt and I don't need your pity!"

"You have it nonetheless," Drew told him. "You earned it. You wasted your life envying me and coveting what I had instead of making a life of your own." He reached for Wren's hand and took hold of it. "My wife and son and I are going home."

"Wait!" Lady St. Jacque reached out and touched Wren on the sleeve. "Where is he buried?"

Wren didn't answer.

"He was our grandson. We have a right to know."

Wren faced the other woman, her voice cold and uncompromising. "You have no rights—to my memories of Ian. They belong to me."

"What of him?" She nodded toward Kit. "He has no grandparents. We could fill that void."

"Kit is a Ramsey. He doesn't need you to be his grandparents, he has us."

Kit opened his eyes at the sound of his name. "Mama?"

"I'm here, my darling."

"Can we go home now? I don't like it here. I want to see Lancelot and Jem and Ally." He yawned widely and stretched.

"We're on our way." Drew pressed his lips against Kit's forehead as they approached the bedroom door.

"There is one more thing." Drew turned his full attention on Lord St. Jacque. "You and your wife are guilty of kidnapping, my lord. And if either one of you or your miserable son attempts to come near my family or contact me in any way for any reason ever again, I'll see you prosecuted to the full extent of the law. Julian's crime has already cost us four years of our lives. That's long enough. I'll brook no more interference from you."

"What about me?" Julian shouted as Drew ushered Kathryn and Kit out of the bedroom. "What do you intend to do about me?"

"I'm going to wait for you to die your slow, painful death. And then I'll murmur a prayer for your immortal soul, because I can't bring myself to waste the effort of hating a man who's little more than a pitiful husk."

"You're a fool, Drew!" Julian called out to him. "You always were. Have you any idea what sort of woman you've married?"

"I have a very good idea. I married a lady, Julian. The finest lady in all the world." He leaned down and covered Kathryn's lips with his own.

"I'd like more children," Wren said, when she and Drew and Kit were settled in the carriage and heading home to Swanslea Park. She and Drew sat side by side in the carriage. Kit had fallen asleep. He lay sprawled across them, with his head in Drew's lap and his feet in hers. Wren retied his bootlace and traced the tip of her finger down his leg.

A rush of tenderness surged through Drew when Kathryn met his gaze and spoke those words. "So would I."

"I'd like very much to have your children."

"I'd like that too," he said. "But . . ." He frowned, unable to put his concerns into words.

"Drew, I know what could happen to our babies. I know there's a chance that they might suffer the same fate as Ian. But there's an equal chance that they won't and I'm willing to risk it." She smiled up at him. "I'm willing to trust that everything will be all right."

"And if it isn't?" he asked.

"We'll still have each other and Kit," she said. "And the love we share."

Drew nodded. "And we can always adopt." He reached over and covered Kathryn's hand with his own. "I've asked Martin to try to locate the other mistresses. My father charged me with their care," he reminded her. "And they may have need of us." He shrugged. "And there may be other children who have need of us."

She smiled. "We could fill the house with Ramsey children," she said. "Half-brothers and sisters and all of them miniatures of you."

"It's possible," he agreed. "But not very likely."

"We could fill the house with Ramsey children anyway."

"Kathryn?" He looked in her eyes and saw his dreams reflected in them.

She nodded. "We don't have to confine ourselves to George's offspring. There's a world of children in need of a home, a family, and parents who love them."

"Then we'll see that they get them," Drew told her, leaning down to plant a kiss on her brow. "Because no child could ever wish for a better mother than you."

Epilogue

If ever two were one, then surely we.
If ever man were lov'd by wife, then thee;
If ever wife was happy in a man,
Compare with me ye women if you can.

—Anne Bradstreet, 1612–1672

Three months later

Wren read *the society page of the* Times *of London* to Drew over breakfast:

" 'The sixteenth Marquess of Templeston presented his lovely marchioness at court on Friday last after a grand reception to celebrate their nuptials. The marquess and marchioness were married by special license by the archbishop of Canterbury at the marquess's county seat of Swanslea Park in Northamptonshire.

" 'The bride wore a gown of black velvet for her presentation at court as the family is mourning the death of the current marquess's father, the fifteenth Marquess of Templeston.

" 'The groom wore formal court dress, including brocade knee breeches, buckle shoes, and stockings embroidered with a love poem for his wife. Stockings patterned after the marquess's have become all the rage at court, with some men even going so far as to embroider their own.

" 'His Royal Highness the Prince Regent is said to be quite enamored of the style.

" 'As a wedding gift to his bride, the marquess has donated several thousand pounds to the Royal Society for the Preservation of Flora and Fauna Native to Britain and provided the funds to renovate and rename a wing of the British Museum to honor Lady Templeston's late father, renowned naturalist Sir Wesley Markinson, and her late husband, the preeminent animal anatomist, Bertrand Stafford. The renovated Markinson-Stafford wing of the museum will be opened to the public early next autumn in order to coincide with the publication of the complete works of *Flora and Fauna Native to Britain* begun by Lady Templeston's father and completed by Lady Templeston.' "

"Good morning, Mama!"

Wren set the paper aside. She waved as Kit rode past the terrace on Lancelot, followed close behind by Ally on a gelding named Porthos. Wren smiled at her husband. "I can't thank you enough for the museum wing honoring Papa and Bertrand."

"I'd do just about anything to get those damned butterfly and bird carcasses out of the cottage." He shuddered. "I don't mind the live menagerie, but facing the dead ones nearly every afternoon . . ."

"And I can't believe you wore your embroidered stockings to court."

"You dared me," he reminded her. "Besides, you were wearing painted ones."

"Mine weren't visible."

"Thank goodness."

Wren shook her head. "I still can't believe I agreed to such a ridiculous wager. Or that I lost."

Drew leered at her. "I wouldn't say lost. Think of the fun we'll have afterward."

"Think of all the scandal it will cause if someone else sees me."

He laughed. "What good is having a married mistress if I can't arrange a lusty spectacle on occasion?"

"Drew, I'm serious. If the new rector sees me, I'm sunk."

"If the new rector sees you, he's dead," Drew promised. "So we'll just have to arrange your Lady Godiva ride very early in the morning or bar everyone except me from the estate and the village."

"How do we accomplish that?"

"We give them all a Saturday off and coin to spend at the market fair in the next village."

"You would go to the trouble and expense of buying them off just to watch me ride naked across the estate?"

"My love, I would buy off the whole of England for the privilege of seeing my fantasies come to life."

"Let's hope that won't be necessary." She giggled. "I've an entire month of fantasies to fulfill." She leaned close enough to brush her chest against his arm. "We have a huge house with dozens of rooms. Surely you can find something for me to do indoors on occasion?"

Drew frowned, pretending to weigh the matter. "I'll try," he said. "But indoors seems entirely too tame for a marchioness who paints erotic scenes on her stockings to entice me and who likes to pretend she was once a notorious mistress."

She closed the distance between them in order to kiss him. "You, Lord Templeston, are a complete and utter rogue."

"And you, Lady Templeston, are the love of my life."

Turn the page for a preview of

EVER A PRINCESS

the next novel about the
Marquess of Templeston's heirs

Coming in spring 2002 from Jove!

Prologue

APRIL 18, 1874
Palace at Laken
Baltic Principality of Saxe-Wallerstein-Karolya

"You must wake up, Your Highness!"

Her Royal Highness Georgiana Victoria Elizabeth May heard the whisper, recognized the voice, and placed her hand against the soft fur at her side to quiet the low, menacing growl coming from the throat of Wagner, the huge wolfhound sharing her bed. She opened her eyes and found Lord Maximillian Gudrun, her father's private secretary, standing in the dim glow of the lamplight beside her bed.

"Thank the All Highest," he whispered reverently. "I've reached you in time."

Alarmed by the old man's reaction, Princess Giana pushed herself into sitting position and leaned against the mound of feather pillows propped against the headboard of the old-fashioned half-canopied tester.

"What is it, Max? What are you doing here? You're supposed to be in Christianberg with Father and Mother."

A sheen of tears sparkled in Lord Gudrun's eyes and ran unchecked down the weathered planes of his face. The old man clutched at his side, then dropped to his knees by the side of the bed and bowed his head. "Something terrible has happened at the palace, Your Highness."

A frisson of foreboding prickled the fine hairs at the back of Giana's neck and her voice echoed her terror. "Max?"

Lord Gudrun reached across the fine snowy white linen and across the thick eiderdown comforters to clasp Giana's right hand. His hand left a dark smear of blood on the covers and Giana drew in a sharp, horrified breath as he slipped a heavy gold signet ring onto her right thumb.

"His Serene Highness Prince Christian Frederick Randolph George of Saxe-Wallerstein-Karolya bid me bring this to you, Your Highness."

"No." Giana began to tremble as she stared down at the gold ring Max had slipped on her thumb. The royal seal. The seal of state worn by every ruler of Saxe-Wallerstein-Karolya since the principality's beginnings in 1448—a gold seal now stained with blood. "My father . . . Max?" She glanced up at him. "He can't be—"

Lord Gudrun bit down on his lip to stop its quivering, and then gave a sharp affirmative nod. "I'm afraid so, Your Highness."

Although she understood the meaning of the transfer of the royal signet ring, and had always known that one day this day would come, Giana couldn't bring herself to utter the words. To do so would be to confirm the thing her heart and her mind could not accept. Her beloved father was dead. She was now ruler of the principality.

A sudden rush of hot, salty tears stung her eyes as Giana pushed back the covers and scrambled to her feet. The wolfhound bounded to his feet beside her. "We must go to the palace at Christianberg at once. My mother will . . ." Her mother would know what to do. Her mother would put aside her own deep overflowing grief and help Giana get through the ordeal ahead; to do what must be done.

Lord Gudrun struggled to stand, then gripped Princess Giana's hand with his left one and squeezed it hard. "I'm sorry, Your Highness, but your mother . . ."

Giana wrenched her hand out of his and shook her head. "No, Max, please . . . Not my mother, too."

"I'm sorry, Your Highness."

"How?" she asked. Giana was willing to admit that a healthy, hearty man in his early fifties might meet an untimely death, but she could not concede that his wife might meet the same fate. Unless . . .

"Treachery, Your Highness. Your father and your mother were stabbed this evening by hired assassins."

Giana's breath left her body in a rush. "Why? Who?"

"Prince Victor has been inciting the young men of the ruling class, denouncing your father's support of a constitution and a Declaration of Rights for the masses. Victor has been promising estate grants, titles, and funds to the foolish younger sons of aristocratic families to gain their support and he has convinced these young traitors that your father's aim was to reward the poor with the landed estates of the rich."

"Victor?" Giana struggled to comprehend the meaning of Max's words. "My cousin assassinated my parents?"

"Yes, Your Highness," Max confirmed. "Your parents were murdered in their bedchamber after retiring from the State dinner celebrating the opening of Parliament. The palace has been overrun. Your father's loyal servants are being slaughtered and Victor's men are searching for you."

"How did you escape?" She asked the question, though she dreaded hearing the answer.

"I was delivering the nightly dispatch box to your father's bedchamber. I heard Prince Christian cry out a warning as your mother entered the room. I entered your mother's chamber from the south door through the dressing room and hid the dispatch box under a bonnet in one of the Princess's hat boxes, then I drew my dress sword and entered your father's bedchamber." Lord Gudrun took a breath. "Your father lay on the floor, bleeding from several wounds. Your mother lay dead beside him. One of the traitors was attempting to remove the seal from the Prince's hand. He turned and discharged his pistol as I entered the room."

Giana suddenly realized Max was bleeding—that the blood from the seal hadn't belonged only to her father. "How badly are you injured?"

Max shrugged. "A minor wound, Your Highness. The ball glanced off my rib." He uncovered the wound in his side so Giana could assess the damage.

Giana's face whitened at the sight of the spreading red stain. *Please, don't let me faint*, she begged, *please; let me do what must be done.* Her stomach muscles clenched and her head began to spin, but she refused to give in to the weakness. Stiffening her resolve, Giana reached across the bed for the nearest pillow, stripped off the pillowcase, and pressed the white linen into Max's hand to help staunch the flow of blood. She found, to her amazement, that the task was what she needed to help dispel her light-headedness. "It may require stitching." She bit her bottom lip. "But for now, I think it best if we wrap it."

"Yes, Your Royal Highness."

Giana met Max's gaze. His eyes were dark and shadowed with pain as she withdrew her hand from the makeshift bandage at his side. Giana wiped her bloody hands on the sheets, then took a deep breath to steady herself. She reached for another pillow, removed its case and bit a hole in the seam, tearing the fine linen into strips of bandage. She repeated the procedure with another pillowcase, then helped Max remove his waistcoat and jacket. He lifted the bandage as Giana unbuttoned his shirt, then placed it back over the wound as she wrapped the strips of linen around his chest. She talked as she worked, speaking in the clipped and precise, regal tone that was as much of an imitation of her father as she could manage, hoping her questions would keep the old man's mind off his pain. "The traitor who shot you?"

"I ran him through, Your Highness."

Giana tightened the last strip of linen, knotted it into place and stepped back to view the results. "And Papa? Did he suffer?" She knew the answer, but she had to ask.

"No, Princess," Max answered, softening his tone and reverting to the familiar form of address. "Nor your mother. She died instantly. Your father tried to save her and when he could not, he bid me to deliver his seal to you, to get you to safety, and to guard you with my life. Those were his final orders to me." Max's voice broke on a sob and his rounded shoulders shook from the force of his grief. "And I shall, Your Highness, I will not fail you again."

Max buttoned his shirt over the bandage and struggled into his brocade waistcoat and wool jacket. He stared at the princess. To him, she was still a girl—barefooted and dressed in a demure white lawn nightgown with her long blond hair plaited into a single braid. She was too young to be the ruler of a wealthy principality. Too young to bear the crushing burdens of the state. Her blue eyes were dark with sorrow and red-rimmed from the sting of tears she refused to let flow. She stood tall and looked him in the eye, her gaze unflinching as she accepted responsibility for her country and for her people. She was a girl on the brink of womanhood, a princess and rightful heir to the throne, filled with strength and courage and compassion.

Her Serene Highness Princess Georgiana Victoria Elizabeth May of the house of Saxe-Wallerstein-Karolya.

Max knelt before her, kissed the ring that had belonged to her father, and swore to serve her as he had served her father and as his father and grandfathers had served the rulers of Saxe-Wallerstein-Karolya for four hundred years.

Giana reached down and buried her fingers in the soft brindle-colored fur just above her wolfhound's shoulders. She held on to Wagner, bracing herself against the tide of anguish that threatened to overtake her. She was the sovereign ruler of her country and she was alone and terribly afraid. She wanted to throw herself into Max's arms and weep as she had done many times as a child, but she stayed the impulse. The ruler of Saxe-Wallerstein-Karolya could not succumb to emotions. She couldn't behave like a grief-stricken daughter. She had to behave like a princess—like the ruler of her country. She had to behave as her father would have behaved, so she accepted her due, nodding regally as she helped Max to his feet. "Wake the others," she ordered. "We must prepare for the journey to Christianberg."

"Your Highness, you cannot return to the capitol,"

Max told her. "Your cousin will kill you if he finds you."

"Finds me?" Giana asked. "The fact that I'm on holiday here is common knowledge. My program is published each month. Victor knows I'm at Laken."

"No, Your Highness, he does not. Your schedule was altered before it was made public."

"By whom?" Giana demanded.

"Your father."

"But why?"

"Prince Christian knew of the unrest among the young aristocrats in the capitol and suspected your cousin might be behind it. Prince Christian received word of your cousin's traitorous activities shortly after he refused to consider Victor's request for your hand in marriage."

"Victor offered for me?"

Max nodded. "Your father knew Victor was plotting to overthrow him. He refused his offer for your hand because he feared Victor would use you to gain the throne. But Victor was incensed by Prince Christian's refusal, so your father suggested this trip to Laken in order to get you out of the capitol and away from possible danger."

Giana's eyes widened at the revelation. "Papa sent me away? On purpose?"

"Yes," Max confirmed. "He suspected Victor might try to use the opening of Parliament to incite rebellion."

"He sent me away. But he allowed Mother . . ." Giana couldn't finish the thought.

"You were the heir-apparent," Max reminded her.

"But . . ."

"Prince Christian tried to send your mother away. He begged her to accompany you, but Princess May refused to leave him. She refused to allow him to face the traitors alone."

"Oh, Mama." Giana tried mightily to keep her sorrow

in check, tried to keep the tears at bay, but one solitary droplet slipped through her lashes and rolled down her cheek. While her father had ruled the principality, her mother had been the glue that held everything together. Prince Christian was the hereditary leader of Saxe-Wallerstein-Karolya, the embodiment of goodness, justice, and might, but Princess May was the heart and soul of the country—the mother of its heir, the champion of the common people, keeper of centuries-old traditions, and social arbiter. Without her mother to guide her, Giana was lost. Overwhelmed. Terrified. Unequipped to rule. She didn't understand government; she didn't understand the nuances of negotiating treaties, or foreign trade rights. Giana had always known that the continued beating of her father's heart was all that kept her from assuming the throne, but somehow the knowledge hadn't seemed real. She had never seen herself ascending the throne, had always assumed her role as heir-apparent was temporary—until a brother came along. She didn't know how to do her father's job. She wasn't prepared to be a ruler. She only knew how to be a princess. She glanced at Max. He had been her father's confidant and advisor for over twenty years. Surely he would know what to do. Surely he would have all the answers.

"How many people do we have, Max?"

"Only myself, Your Highness, and those serving you here at Laken."

Giana frowned. The permanent staff at Laken was kept to a minimum. Those presently serving at Laken were Langstrom, the butler; Isobel, his wife, who served as housekeeper; Josef, the stable master; and Brenna, Giana's personal maid. Everyone else lived in the village and came to work on a daily basis. "That gives us four," Giana said. "Six counting you and me. Seven with Wagner." She glanced down at her beloved wolfhound. "Seven against Victor's traitors."

"There are many landowners and men in the government and the army who will remain loyal to your father," Max assured her.

"Then we must return to Christianberg to rally them."

"You cannot, Your Highness. I swore a solemn oath to your father that I would see you to safety. The palace isn't safe and neither is the capitol."

"But we can't let Victor win," Giana protested. "We can't stand idly by and allow Victor to ascend my father's throne. To get away with murder—with regicide."

"We must for now," Max told her. "The tide of rebellion is running high. Victor will not risk losing his chance to gain the throne—however briefly. We cannot risk your life. We cannot risk the life of the rightful heir to the crown."

"The crown," Giana breathed, slowly, reverently, as understanding dawned. "The crown. If Victor wishes to wear the crown of Saxe-Wallerstein-Karolya, he must abide by the Law of Succession. He must endure the wait. He cannot marry until the traditional period of mourning for the late ruler is over. And he cannot be crowned until he is married. Until that year is over, Victor can govern the principality, but he cannot be recognized as its rightful ruler."

Max managed a slight smile. "And because you are recognized as your father's successor, not Victor, the Peoples' Parliament of Karolya will require him to marry a princess of Karolyan blood."

"There are no princesses of Karolyan blood left to marry. I am the only one." She looked at Max. "Unless he marries one of his sisters."

"An act none of the other European ruling families could or would condone." Max shook his head. "No, Your Highness, in order to be crowned His Serene Highness, Prince Victor IV of Saxe-Wallerstein-Karolya, your cousin must marry you."

"Or produce my body," Giana reminded him. "And my father's seal of state."

"Then we have no more time to waste. We only have one year."

"We must leave the country before Victor closes the borders. For the time being, we must bide our time, go to ground like the fox, and endure the wait."

Max studied his princess, marveling at the strength and sense of determination he heard in her voice. He knew, even if she did not, that until the year was up there was no safe haven left to them, knew Princess Giana's life was forfeit if her cousin found her, knew she would never agree to marry her parents' murderer, and also knew that Victor would search the countryside for the princess and post spies in every remaining monarchy in Europe in an effort to find her. "Where shall we go?" he asked. "What is to be our destination?"

Giana's mouth thinned into a firm hard line. "I don't know. But it must be a place where no one would ever think to look for a princess."